SOMETHING DIFFERENT
A NEW ADULT EROTIC ROMANCE
BELLA CHAL

Published by Cotton Nightie Press, 2014.

This is a work of fiction. Similarities to real people, places, or events are entirely coincidental.

SOMETHING DIFFERENT: A NEW ADULT EROTIC ROMANCE

First edition. December 25, 2014.

Copyright © 2014 Bella Chal.

Written by Bella Chal.

10 9 8 7 6 5 4 3 2 1

I'd like to thank my friend Annie for her help turning my idea into a story. Any mistakes belong to me, but I'm happy to credit any success to her able assistance editing. I'd also like to thank my early beta readers Leona and Frances.

No book is the work of a single person, and once released all books belong to the readers. Thank you all for helping me prepare this book to fly.

Bella

Chapter 1: Charlotte

"Christopher?" Charlotte whispered in shock. She could hardly believe her eyes. He had just gotten out of her brother's car wearing jeans and a t-shirt that was stretched tight across his chest and shoulders. The Morgan City Mardi Gras parade would be starting any minute, but she suddenly didn't care.

Her brother, Kurt, was wearing the black pants and loose white pirate shirt he'd worn at Halloween. She'd made the green coat he was wearing for his parade costume out of the same fabric from both her and his girlfriend Polly's dress. Glancing at Polly, she saw a loving hunger in her expression as her eyes followed Kurt's approach.

"You rat!" Charlotte said to her brother in mock outrage, then turned to smile at Christopher. "When did you get here?"

Instead of answering, Christopher grinned back up at her and said, "Wow, you look amazing!"

Their dresses widened around the hips, but stopped just above the knees to show off their shapely legs. The flared sleeves had gold piping and lace, and the bust was cut low and tight. Polly's was predominantly green to match the feathered mask Kurt had given her at Christmas. Charlotte's dress was its mirror image in a deep purple.

She glanced at Pawpaw Garson and saw that he was still talking to one of the parade organizers, so she raced down the steps to get off the float and jumped into Christopher's arms.

"Oh, what a great surprise," she said, thinking to herself that he smelled as good as he looked, that rough scent of leather and lavender he exuded like a fine cologne.

Christopher lifted her feet off the ground as he hugged her, then sat her back with a big grin. "I'm glad you think so. I was a little worried you might not like it so much."

"Why?" she asked, already suspecting the answer. She had been doing her best to keep him at arms length, much to his frustration. In the previous few weeks, he'd made it clear in dozens of little ways that he wanted something more from their relationship.

Studying her face with squinted eyes he said it out loud for the first time. "You know I want to be with you."

"And here you are," she replied with a nervous laugh, pretending she didn't understand.

"I get you want to take things slow. You're still in college out here for a few more months, and maybe you've even got someone here you like. I'm just here to let you know that I like you, too."

Luckily the sound of Pawpaw's truck starting kept her from being forced to speak. "We'll talk later. I gotta get on the float."

"You really do look amazing," he said to her back as she skipped back up the stairs into the float.

"Thanks!" she said as she tossed him a plastic jewel necklace and gold doubloon. "I'll see you at the fais do-do after the parade."

As Pawpaw Garson pulled the truck away slowly, Christopher smiled and waved at Charlotte, making her stomach twist into knots.

* * *

It's not that I don't like him, she thought as she threw handfuls of the fake jewelry and coins to the crowds of people lining the main street of Morgan City. *I like him too much.* And that would inevitably lead to him finding out she was still a virgin at twenty-four and irrationally terrified of having sex. Then he'd drift away like all the others had, slowly breaking her heart in the process.

She had tried to overcome her fear before. Her high school boyfriend, Peter, loved her hand jobs and she'd even enjoyed using her mouth on him when they'd gotten time alone. The fact that he had never seemed interested in returning the favor actually made her feel safer, but the reason became clear when they were in the hotel room after prom.

Peter loved hunting and sports as much as the next guy. He just happened to love the next guy as well. When they were in bed together, he couldn't stay hard, and that was when he broke down and shared the secret that he was attracted to men. She put his obvious pain before her own, but deep inside she was also relieved. After agreeing to keep his secret, she told no one except her brother why they'd really broken up. In the seven years since it happened, her panic had grown worse whenever someone started to get close.

After they got to the end of the parade route, Kurt leaned in close to whisper, "Did I fuck up? Christopher really wanted to come see you. I know you like him."

"It's fine," she sighed as she threw a final handful of beads and coins. "How's Christopher getting to Meemee and Pawpaw's house?"

"He's got my keys and the address for his GPS," Kurt said as he sat down next to Polly on the wooden bench. "I saw him hanging out with Uncle Jack, so he can always follow them."

Charlotte sat down on the other side of him and leaned in out of the wind. "Thank you for arranging that," she grumbled half-heartedly.

Polly shook her head and laughed, "He's crazy about you, girl! What are you waiting for, an engraved invitation?"

Charlotte looked at Kurt with a silent plea for him not to say anything. "It's complicated," she sighed, before the lie burned its way out. "I'm not so sure I want to get involved with him yet. I'd rather just stay friends."

"Has he got kids or a crazy ex?" Polly asked, but Charlotte dropped her eyes and kept shaking her head hoping Polly would change the subject. After a long silence, Polly asked, "Did you see little Jackson? He actually caught one of the necklaces I threw! I bet Julie won't be able to pry his fat fingers away from it all night."

"I know, right?" Charlotte said, hoping her relief wasn't too obvious.

"So, I've never eaten crawfish before," Polly offered, looking at them both. "How do I do it?"

"It's easy," Kurt replied. "You just break the tail off and split it open to get the meat. I'll show you the trick, but you'll need to wear something you don't mind getting dirty."

"They taste like a cross between shrimp and lobster," Charlotte added as she glanced behind to look for Kurt's car. She sighed in relief when she saw it peek out from behind Uncle Jack's van as they turned into the yard.

Pawpaw and Meemee's house was a sprawling two-story farmhouse that had been built over a hundred years before. There was a large yard with a red wooden barn sitting on an elevated rise in the back. The yard was filled with picnic tables and benches for the meal. Meemee was overseeing the crawfish boiling in large steel pots, the steam rising in the cool evening bringing the aroma of spices that made Charlotte's stomach grumble.

The float stopped on a flat spot between the house and the barn to serve as the bandstand at the fais do-do later in the evening. Kurt and her cousin Michael helped the three ladies out of the float, then Kurt and Polly led the way to a table.

"Want a beer?" Kurt asked his girlfriend.

Polly nodded, "Definitely, and something to nibble on. Crackers, chips, anything."

When Kurt left, Polly and Charlotte sat down at one of the tables across from each other. As Charlotte leaned in to rest her elbows on the table, she whispered, "You and Kurt will be all everyone can talk about tonight."

It was envy, pure and simple, she told herself. Polly was a striking beauty with the blended complexion of her African father and American mother. Watching Kurt fall in love with her was so sweet, but it stung as well. They may not have had an easy start, but fighting off her own irrational fear of being with Christopher had made watching them fall in love pure torture.

When Kurt had given Polly a Mardi Gras mask as a Christmas present, he claimed he'd forgotten it was a family tradition one step below announcing their engagement. While he may have forgotten, the fact that Polly wore it at the Mardi Gras parade made it a clear sign she returned his feelings. Everyone was buzzing about it now, and Charlotte found herself uncomfortably jealous.

"Are you okay?" Polly asked with a concerned frown.

Mustering a thin smile, she answered, "I'm fine."

Something caught Polly's attention and she stood with a smile. "What a great surprise, Christopher! Good job keeping that secret." They hugged briefly as he chuckled.

Kurt came up in time to hear their exchange and sat two beers in red plastic cups down on the table. "When we all went to Uncle Jack's to watch the Superbowl, Christopher said he'd always wanted to see a real Mardi Gras. So I arranged for him to hide out at the house until the parade tonight."

The words made her sit up straight as chills ran up her back. "Wait, he's been hanging out with Mom and Dad all day?"

"He and Dad really hit it off, too. They were talkin' about racing when I went there to change for the parade." Her heart pounded in her chest and she started feeling light-headed.

Christopher put a beer down in front of Charlotte as he sat. "Your dad's a great guy. Hell, everyone has been great so far." He looked around the yard at all the activity. People were still coming in from the parade and elsewhere, but there had to be forty people already milling around. "I've never seen a family party this big in my life before."

"I know how you feel, but you'll get used to it," Polly said before taking a big swallow of beer. "Where are my crackers?" she asked Kurt.

"Damn, knew I forgot somethin'. Be right back." He got up and ran back over to the kitchen.

Shutting her eyes, Charlotte tuned out for a moment to gather her thoughts. It felt like everyone was making decisions for her, prompting fear and frustration. She hadn't brought a date home since Peter back in high school, so she could only imagine the kinds of questions her mother would ask. *It isn't fair*, she complained silently. *I don't want this right now!*

When Christopher leaned in to kiss her, Charlotte turned her face so he had to kiss her cheek instead of her lips. Fighting back tears, she drove her sharp thumbnails into her fingers to keep control of herself.

"Here you go," Kurt said, putting a plate of crackers on the table between them all. "The first batch of crawfish are comin' out of the pots now, so we should be eating soon."

"Charlotte, why don't we go change before we ruin our dresses?" Polly said with an odd tone in her voice. Despite their growing friendship, Charlotte didn't want to discuss intimate things with Polly yet, but they did need to change clothes. When she nodded at last, Polly said, "Be right back boys. Hold our seats!"

Polly was staying in a small upstairs guest room in Pawpaw and Meemee's house. The protective bags Charlotte brought the dresses over in were still on her bed. After getting her dress and slip off, Charlotte flopped across the end of the bed with a sigh as Polly bagged the dresses. There was a headache building behind her eyes and a sick feeling in her stomach.

"Want to talk about it?" Polly asked.

And say what? she thought to herself. *I'm a virgin and scared to death of letting Christopher get close to me?* "Not really," she sighed. "Let's get back out there. I need a beer."

"That may not help," Polly said.

"It sure as hell can't hurt at this point," Charlotte grumbled.

Unwilling to ignore Christopher, Charlotte kept him busy dancing and drinking. Without letting him stop to talk, she could live in the moment for a while. But as the beer eased her fear and the music slowed down, she found herself swaying with her head against his broad chest while he kissed her hair and hugged her tight.

As she knew would happen, Kurt and Polly were all anyone could talk about. Many of the party goers sought Charlotte out for juicy details about her twin brother. When she couldn't take it anymore, she and Christopher hid out on the trunk of Kurt's car, sipping beer from their red plastic cups as they waited for him to finish saying goodbye to Polly and take them home.

"So," Christopher said low and quiet. "I had a great time today."

She'd had entirely too much to drink and her head was spinning. The temptation to kiss him was intense, but she forced herself to take another sip of beer instead. Sighing deeply, she said, "I'm glad."

"You don't sound glad."

"I can't keep stringing you along," she said in a rush. "This is never going to work out." The alcohol numbed the pain as the barbed lie ripped her throat.

She didn't look to see his expression, but she did feel him slide off the trunk. Squeezing her eyes shut, she pinched her lips tight and waited for his reaction. He took the cup of beer from her hands and pulled her to sit at the edge of the trunk.

"Stop," she begged, but didn't push him away.

He tilted her chin up and kissed her softly, melting her anxiety along with her will. She kissed him back then, her arms moving by themselves to reach around his shoulders. He pulled her closer, moving her knees apart to press himself against her body. The tingling sensations made her shiver as his fingers moved up her back and into her hair.

The beer freed her desire as an intoxicating rush. Before she could think about what she was doing, her hands trailed down his body and pulled his hips close to rub him against the crotch of her tight jeans. As she panted into his mouth, he ground his erection against her until the panic returned to blot out her desire, turning it off like a switch.

"Stop," she commanded.

"You can't tell me you didn't feel anything," he whispered against her ear.

"I can't," she whimpered. "You don't understand."

"Then explain it to me."

She opened her eyes to look at him, seeing nothing but affection in his expression. "Why can't you jus' leave me alone?"

She was surprised when he chuckled. "You obviously don't understand. Playing hard to get is the surest way to keep me interested."

He was so cute and his patience with her went beyond anyone else she'd dated, but he still didn't know the truth. "Why me? You prolly have women throwin' themselves at you."

"Sometimes that makes you more careful who you pick," he said, still refusing to step back from their embrace. "You're funny and cute. I love your Cajun accent. I like your brother and parents, which counts more to me than you probably think. You've told me why you want to be a nurse and I totally get it."

"No," she closed her eyes again and leaned her forehead against his chest. "You can't do this to me."

"I want to be with you," he said. "Why are you so afraid?"

When she couldn't formulate an answer, Christopher leaned in with his eyes darting between her eyes and lips. She let him kiss her, shutting her eyes when the chills raced up her arms. The kiss warmed them again until they were breathless. Panting with their foreheads together, she reached up to touch his rough cheeks with her palms.

"Tell me, I swear I'll just listen. I won't judge."

"I can't," she whispered.

He sighed deeply and tucked her head under his chin. "Then I'll just keep waiting."

Kurt came up whistling *À la Claire Fontaine* as he fished out his keys. "You two ready to go home?"

Christopher said, "I'm beat. I hope your couch doesn't suck."

* * *

Charlotte wasn't able to sleep with Christopher in the house. When he got up to go to the bathroom at night, she was paralyzed with the fear he'd stop by her room. When he slowed by her door then continued back to the couch, she told herself the feeling that brought tears to her eyes wasn't disappointment.

In the cold light of morning, Charlotte convinced herself of what she needed to do. He was too perfect, too dangerous. She couldn't stand the temptation of being around him any longer. She had to end it.

After an early shower, she dressed in jeans and a red Ragin' Cajun sweatshirt to help her mother, Noëlle, make breakfast. While the sausage sizzled and the coffee percolated, Charlotte set the dining room table with biscuits, orange juice, and the other necessities.

Noëlle was standing at the stove when she returned. "You want some coffee, sha?" she asked, using the familiar Cajun term of endearment.

"If it's ready, sure," Charlotte said as she sat at the small chrome accented table in the kitchen. After bringing two mugs of coffee, Noëlle joined her at the table to spoon in the powdered creamer and sugar.

"I really like him," she said with a small smile.

"Don't get too attached, Mama," Charlotte warned.

Noëlle looked up with a sad expression. "Sha, why you always run 'em off?"

"I don't want to be with someone right now. I need to stay focused on school."

The skeptical look on her mother's face made the heat rise in her own. "It ain't none of my business, but if you keep runnin' these good ones away, you may not like what you end up with."

"I'll worry about that day when it comes." Her abrupt tone ended that discussion, but her mother had to complete the whole circuit of topics before she would stop.

"Are you sure about movin' to Houston?" The question was asked without eye contact. "I know Polly better now and am glad you won't be livin' alone, but it's so far away."

"It's only five hours, Mama," she sighed. "Besides, I still got school until May. I don't come home every weekend now anyway and I'm just in Lafayette."

"It feels different though. I wish you'd take a job at Lafayette General instead of goin' all the way to Southwest Hospital in Houston. It's bad enough your brother moved out so fast."

There it is, she thought. "I been at school for almost four years, Mama. Kurt moves out for two months and *now* you miss me?"

The embarrassed look on her mother's face told her she'd hit close to the mark.

"Boys are supposed to move away," she whispered. "That's how things are supposed to work."

"Well, you got to enjoy yours for seven years longer than most," Charlotte said as she took a sip of coffee. "Hey, at least *your* daughter actually made it through college."

Noëlle got up to turn the sausage without a word.

Noëlle's best friend was Mandy Arsenault, and her daughter, Kendall, had been talking big about being a lawyer for years. She had dated Kurt for a while and Mama heard wedding bells after their first date. When they broke up in July, Mama kept trying to get them back together until Kendall recently ended up pregnant by someone she still refused to name.

The comment made Noëlle look over her shoulder with a raised eyebrow. "You leave poor Kendall out of this."

"Poor Kendall?" Charlotte laughed. "Hell, Mama, don't you know she's probably carrying your great niece or nephew?"

That turned Mama around with her mouth agape. "What?" she asked with a rising tone of disbelief.

"You didn't hear it was Trey's baby she's been carrying?"

"No," she gasped. "When was they together?"

"Thanksgiving weekend. Remember, he was the one who called Kendall and told her we was going to the Carillon Tower? He was chasin' after Polly and used Kendall to trip up Kurt. We never saw him after Polly left that Saturday afternoon, but I found out he didn't leave for Houston 'til Monday."

"So *that's* what happened?" she asked. "And Kurt blamed me for weeks thinkin' I told her where you was."

"You prolly thought about doin' it," Charlotte said with a chuckle.

"Maybe, but I didn't do it," Noëlle said with red cheeks. After putting the sausage on a plate covered with paper towels, she muttered, "Trey Tibideaux. No wonder Laurie didn't show her face yesterday."

"I only feel sorry for Claire. This would have been her first Mardi Gras in the parade." The family had a tradition that the unmarried adult children rode in their parade float. Aunt Laurie's four children should have all been in the float this year since Claire turned eighteen. Knowing the rumors about Trey had probably reached Kendall's father, if Trey had dared show his face, he would have been marched to the church at gunpoint.

"Claire's the only nice one in the bunch, but don't you tell anyone I said so," Noëlle said with a sly grin. "Go wake up the boys and tell'em breakfast is ready."

* * *

Walking into the living room, she stopped to look at Christopher sleeping on the couch. His sandy hair was tousled, but if anything that made him more attractive. He was sleeping in blue shorts and a plain white undershirt with the sheet kicked down around his feet. She could see a colorful tattoo peeking out from under one sleeve, but it was his thick, braided muscles that stole her attention and made it hard to think.

Just as she bent to wake him gently, his pale blue eyes snapped open. "Hey," he whispered and patted the couch to indicate she could sit.

"Breakfast is ready. I gotta go wake up Dad and Kurt."

His expression was unreadable when he whispered, "What if I'd come to you last night?"

She felt her chin quiver until she clamped her teeth together. "Then Dad would have hidden your body out in the swamps this mornin'." When her smile wouldn't stay away any longer she sat down next to him with a sigh. "I know you don't understand, but will you please stop trying so hard? Why can't we just stay friends?"

He frowned and took her hand in his. "Tell me you don't feel anything for me."

"I don't feel anything for you," she said, but the tears welling in her eyes betrayed her words as lies.

"It's driving me crazy not knowing why."

"Just drop it," she pulled her hand away and stood up to go wake up Kurt.

"Charlotte," he called out, and she found herself looking back against her will. "This is really hurting me." His eyes were clear, his face hard, but something in his expression spoke to the pain he clearly felt.

She couldn't apologize because she wasn't sorry enough to stop. She couldn't stop because it was better to end it now on her terms than later when she loved him. Nodding once to acknowledge the truth, she turned her back on him and went into her brother's room.

Kurt was already awake, laying with his hands behind his head and grinning as she stopped in the doorway. "Mornin', Sis."

"Breakfast is ready," she said and turned to leave.

"You okay?"

"Nope." Not wanting to talk about it, she left to wake her dad. He was already in the shower, so she went back to the dining room and sat at the table next to her mother. Kurt and Christopher ate quickly, hardly speaking a word except to answer Noëlle. After they left to start moving Kurt's bedroom furniture, Charlotte washed the dishes, then retreated to her room.

By some miracle she fell back asleep, but in her dreams she was locked in a dark room and Christopher was begging her to let him in. She kept explaining that the door was locked from the outside and that he had the key, but he couldn't understand. When she finally woke up, she heard him tapping quietly and calling her name. "Charlotte?"

She got up and tried to open the door, but realized she must have locked it without thinking when she came in. "Hey," she whispered. His hair was still damp from the shower.

"We're leaving." He was searching her face, but she wouldn't meet his eyes.

"I'll walk you out," Charlotte said. Polly had shown up at some point, and she was walking with Kurt towards the rental truck. Charlotte faced Christopher before putting in the final nail. "Thanks for helping Kurt. He needs good friends in Houston."

"Yeah," he said, glancing over as Kurt helped Polly into the large truck. "He's a good guy, but I'm more worried about you."

"I'll have plenty of friends there. You know about the girls' night out with Polly and Aunt Julie. And once I start working at the hospital…" She trailed off as she remembered he was already working there. He'd started after they'd met in the Human Resources department just before Christmas. "Shit."

"I'm willing to take things as slow as you want—"

"I don't want to see you anymore." The words hung there like a bleeding wound between them.

"I see." He nodded. The truck started and Kurt honked the horn as he pulled into the street. "That's it then."

Charlotte crossed her arms and squeezed herself tight, trying to force the lie to be real. "Goodbye."

Christopher clearly wanted to say something else, but his expression hardened as he turned away. Charlotte watched him put his overnight bag in Kurt's car, climb inside, then drive away. She stood there until Noëlle came out and pulled her into a soft embrace, letting Charlotte sob it out while her mother stroked her hair.

Chapter 2: Christopher

One nice thing about Kurt's car was the amazing engine and transmission. Christopher floored it when he got on Highway 90, blowing past the slow moving rental truck Kurt and Polly were in. His pulse pounded in his temples as he shrieked his war-face out the front window.

"Argh! Fucking fucking fuck!" he shouted as he pounded the steering wheel. After his outburst, he slowed down and sat back into the drivers seat with a growl.

He'd never met anyone so utterly infuriating in his twenty-seven years on the planet. He'd suffered through bad teachers, tough drill sergeants, stupid second lieutenants, and crazy insurgents, but no one had managed to get under his skin like Charlotte did. She was like a chigger and the itch was driving him crazy.

Playing hard to get was his one major weak spot. She was that perfect mix of sexy and smart that caught his eye, but she had an innocence that made him feel protective of her as well. She couldn't even explain why she ended their brief relationship, and it had utterly wrecked him.

He'd stopped dating other people for the last month, even Ashley, and she was in a class by herself. After unlocking his cell phone, he pressed Ashley's picture then put the call on speaker so he could drive and talk.

"I didn't expect to hear from you today," her voice purred. "So I take it there are congratulations in order?"

"No," he said, then clenched his teeth until he could get control of his voice. "She dumped me."

"What?" she exclaimed. "What the hell did you do?"

"Nothing!" he screamed. "God damned nothing! She was so fucking... gorgeous yesterday in that purple dress. We danced to crazy Cajun music, then when I kissed her at the end of the night it was like... I don't know. She shut down or something." He ended his tirade confused and sad. "Shit, Ash, I don't know what the hell happened."

"When was the last time you struck out?" she asked, sounding genuinely curious.

"With someone I liked as much as her?" he chuckled. "Never."

"You've never swung and missed with a girl." Her incredulous tone made him feel guilty, like he was bragging.

"I've only liked one other person like this. And it's not like I picked Charlotte off the street or anything. We really hit it off. I could feel her responding, but she shut me down and I can't figure out why."

"What did she say?" Ashley asked.

"Nothing. She wouldn't explain it. She just kept telling me she couldn't be with me."

"So what are you going to do now?" Ashley asked with a hint of invitation in her voice.

"I know I said I wanted to stop the benefits part of our friendship, but I really need a friend tonight, Ash." He felt raw even asking, but he had to get Charlotte out of his system somehow.

"Come on over when you get back in town," she said. "I'm just reading case law for an exam next week and I'm gonna need a break later anyway."

"Thanks," Christopher said.

"What are friends for?" she laughed, then dropped the call.

The drive back to Houston was torture. Every mile he traveled left Charlotte further behind, but he couldn't stop thinking about her. Her eyes were so brown they almost looked black, but were so expressive he couldn't stop staring at them when she spoke. Her laugh came from deep inside, a real laugh, not the brainless college girl giggle he'd gotten so sick of hearing at Rice for the last four years.

She had strong relationships with her brother and parents that showed how deeply she cared for them. Meeting her extended family reminded him of his own wide- flung clan, though his Scottish relatives were not as tight as her Cajun brood was. It was that strong sense of family that moved her from someone he was merely interested in to someone he wanted to be with.

And she wanted to be a nurse to help people. It wasn't just a job for her, it was her vocation. She had the same kind of undiluted idealism about nursing that he did about working with kids. She *cared* about people, but for some reason she didn't seem to care about hurting him. It made no sense.

Sniffing hard, he blinked to clear his eyes as he drove through Lafayette. She went to school there, he knew, the University of Louisiana at Lafayette. As he pushed the pedal down to get on I-10, he focused on the road in front but he couldn't stop glancing in the rear view mirror with thoughts of turning around and going back for her.

* * *

Christopher left Kurt's keys under the drivers seat and locked the car door before shutting it. After getting in his truck, he drove to Ashley's apartment in the West University area near where she went to law school at Rice University. They had met in their junior years, she was twenty, and he was two years out of the service at twenty-five. Ashley was in pre-law at the time while Christopher was studying clinical social work. Her first question over coffee was, "What is a big, strapping Marine like you studying social work with a bunch of bleeding heart liberals?"

It didn't take long before the two of them fell into bed where they both decided they could never be more than friends. She was laser-focused on her law degree and had no time or interest in pursuing a relationship. Christopher was older than the average college student and, because of his time spent serving overseas, didn't have much in common with most of his rich, spoiled classmates.

So while Christopher occasionally dated someone and stopped having sex with Ashley, she remained a fixture in his life regardless. He valued her opinions, enjoyed her company, and grew to depend on her advice. Needing that advice, amongst other things, he found himself standing at her door late on Wednesday afternoon after arriving back in town.

She was still wearing the long t-shirt she must have slept in. "I lost track of time," she said as she pulled her long, straight hair out of her face. "I meant to put on some clothes." After taking a look at his face, her demeanor changed and she took his hand to pull him inside. "Come on in and tell me everything."

After seating him on the couch, she went to make tea in the kitchen. He had turned her on to the strong, dark tea he'd gotten a taste for in Afghanistan. After taking a deep breath, he said, "You know most of it already."

"You're not telling me, you're getting it off your chest. Go on and rant, you know you need to."

"I've been talking to myself the whole way back. As stupid as it sounds, I found myself arguing with her ghost, trying to convince her to give me a chance." He laughed sadly and rubbed his face.

"Tell me everything, start at the beginning." She came back in while the kettle pinged and clicked as it heated.

"She was waiting for an interview with HR when I came out of the restroom in Southwest Hospital right after mine. The sight of her sitting there stopped me. And after I made her laugh that first time, I was addicted and had to do it again."

"Nice laugh?" she asked.

"Warm and deep. Genuine." He had to stop for a minute to breathe. "So we went out a couple of times. Lunch at the mall, then dinner one night. It just clicked with her. I kissed her the first time on New Years Eve."

Ashley nodded with a grin. "That explains it."

"I didn't plan to stop seeing you then, it just happened." For some reason it embarrassed him to admit it to her. "After New Years, I saw her when she came up on the weekends. I even started hanging out with her brother, Kurt, and her Uncle Jack when she wasn't around. She has a great family."

The whistling tea kettle drew Ashley back into the kitchen. "I'm still listening. Keep going."

"Things never got physical between us. I mean, we'd kiss, but she turned down going back to my place and she never invited me over unless her brother or roommate was around."

"How old is she?" Ashley asked from the kitchen.

"Twenty-four."

"Is her family religious?"

"She's Catholic, but not crazy or anything. I know her brother is banging his girlfriend despite going to church every Sunday with their Uncle Jack."

She came back in with two steaming mugs of tea. "Okay, then maybe she's got something wrong down there."

He took the cup of tea with a serious expression. "I hadn't thought about that."

"It happens," she said as she sat again. "A friend of mine in high school had no internal sex organs or sex drive, but looked like a normal girl otherwise."

"Damn, that sucks," he muttered as he sat back. "But Charlotte definitely has a sex drive. There was a moment last night when I thought I'd finally reached her, but she shut down again."

"So what are you going to do?"

Christopher shrugged and took another sip of the malty tea. "Nothing I can do."

"So like the old song says, *If that chick don't wanna know, forget her.*"

He nodded with a sad smile. "Thanks for letting me come by."

"You're not leaving yet," she said as she sat her mug on the coffee table. Then she took his mug away and moved to sit closer to him. She sang again quietly, "*If that chick don't wanna know, forget her...* but I do."

When she kissed him, his heart fought for a second. But Charlotte didn't want him. He kissed Ashley back then, letting her rest against his chest. As he pulled her closer, she kissed him harder and pushed back the pain in his heart. After a few moments, he had to shift to allow his expanding cock room to grow. She reached down to tug open his snap and lower his zipper.

"*The boys are back in town,*" she sang as she reached inside his boxers with a grin.

Leaning back, he lifted slightly to allow her to pull his jeans and boxers down. After taking them down to his feet, she pulled off his shoes and socks to get his jeans off. While he pulled his own t-shirt off, she did the same.

"You don't have panties on?" he asked as he scanned her neatly trimmed bush.

"It just slows things down."

When they came back together on the couch she wasted no time drawing his head and shaft into her mouth. "I'm a little pent up," he said in a strained whisper.

"I'll fix that, then we'll finish our tea and talk some more." Returning to her task, he sat back and opened himself to her ministrations. She knew his cheat codes and had him on the edge in moments as she pressed firmly against the base of his shaft.

"Now, Ash," he whispered while he caressed her hair. She hummed deep in her throat and took his seed on her tongue, sucking gently throughout his orgasm as he groaned, "Oh, God, I needed that."

"So did I," she said after popping him out of her mouth. She got their mugs of tea and scooted close against him. "Here."

Kissing the top of her head, he put one arm around to cup her breast as he drank some of the cooling tea. "I hope I didn't screw up your plans today."

"Nope, I was just studying. Between you and my friend Tara, you know I don't do that much during the week."

"What did you get on that paper I proofed for you?"

"A ninety-eight. The professor docked me for some formatting issues. I wish they'd let me submit PDFs instead of docs. I swear he has a virus or weird fonts installed on his laptop that always screws up my papers."

"I didn't really understand all the legal jargon, but you explained it well enough for me to get your point."

"That's because you're smart." He squeezed her breast as he smiled at the compliment. "Do that some more," she commanded as she put her tea down.

He put his down as well, then placed both his hands on her chest, squeezing gently and rolling her nipples between his fingertips. Her breasts were small, but she had relatively large areolas and protruding nipples. One time when he'd teased her for a long afternoon, she swore she came just from him playing with them.

Leaning her head back against his shoulder, he began to nibble along the edges of her ear. Flicking the lobe with his tongue, he continued to work her breasts with his hands. She didn't make a sound, but her body tensed as she squeezed the muscles in her hips and thighs.

While one hand moved down her stomach, he began to suck where her neck and shoulder met. He could feel her skin prickle as she opened herself to his fingers. In moments she was gasping as he traced through her wet folds. "Don't stop," she whispered.

Keeping the same tempo and motion, he sucked harder on her shoulder, biting down gently on her tense muscles. The response was immediate as she sucked air through her teeth and whimpered. The wet handful of flesh began to pulse as she held her breath until it passed. He relaxed when she did.

"You know just what to do," she whispered as she lounged against his chest.

"Years of practice," he muttered and kissed the marks he'd left on her shoulder.

"It feels like you might be recovering back there." He pressed his awakening shaft against her back. "Yup, definitely something going on."

"Getting you off always gets me back faster," he whispered as she crawled away, raising her hips to him. "Is that how you want it?"

"Yes," she purred as she hugged the couch pillow.

Keeping one knee on the couch to match her height, Christopher brought his head against her soft, wet skin. "Bow your back a little," he said, prompting her to change the angle of her hips. Sliding in was like being wrapped in a velvet heaven.

"Stop once you're all the way in," she murmured. "I like feeling you there."

He pressed all the way in, then flexed his shaft to make her gasp. "I like it when you try to push me out." She tensed around him then, and he moved out to slide back in again. "Oh, so nice."

"Now pound me," she commanded with a grin over her shoulder.

He didn't jump right into it because he knew what she wanted. Starting slow, he worked up to a faster pace with her matching his motions. Once they got to a certain pace, she stopped moving and let him drive her along while she concentrated on getting herself off again.

"Oh, damn," she hissed. He could tell when her orgasms rippled through because her muscles went crazy, squeezing and releasing in rapid pulses. He kept the pace steady and enjoyed watching her pleasure. She could go for a long time, but each subsequent orgasm would drive her deeper until she collapsed and lay twitching for minutes at the end.

With his first one out of the way, maintaining his stamina was a simple act of will. He ran miles in the mornings and was still in fighting shape, so sex with Ashley was an easy workout by comparison. As she began to sweat, her hair first fell in disarray, then began sticking to her face. Her final release was a frenzy, clawing the couch as she pulled away from his relentless stimulation.

"Oh, fuck," she panted as she shook. "Fuck yes."

Letting her rest where she fell on the couch, he took their tea mugs back to the kitchen for refill. By the time he got back to the couch, she was still shivering from the impact of the last orgasm.

They didn't need to say anything. Once he was back on the couch, she curled up in his lap with a contented sigh. "Thanks," she whispered against his chest before picking up her tea.

"And thanks for letting me come over and vent." Despite the physical relief he felt, Charlotte's rejection still ached like a bullet in his chest.

"If you want to finish with a slow one…" she started to say, but he was already shaking his head.

"No, I'm fine. I got work in the morning… What?" he asked as she gave him a sad smile.

"You're so tough." Her expression was unreadable as she searched his face, but her tone was playfully mocking.

"What's that supposed to mean?"

"You never want to go slow with me when your heart is with someone else."

That stung him enough that he had to examine how true it was. He knew that every time he started getting serious with someone, he'd backed things off with Ashley. But now Charlotte had gotten in his head somehow and left him feeling broken and conflicted. "You're right."

"Look, I'm not gonna play armchair psychologist, but it looks like she really hurt you. Give yourself some time. You know we'll always be friends."

Her words seemed to finally lance his swollen wound and let out the pain. He didn't do more than stare at the floor, but inside his stomach was quivering as he realized he had to let Charlotte go. It just wasn't meant to be.

"Thanks, Ash."

* * *

Walking into the hospital the next morning felt different for some reason. As he thought about it, he realized that knowing Charlotte would be joining him there someday soon had colored his work experience. Now that she had rejected him, the taint had soured his mood as he took the elevator to his floor. He shook off the feeling to focus on his job.

Checking in with the nurses station, he grabbed the charts for the kids on the floor. His routine after orientation had been to note when a physician or nurse flagged a patient having difficulties. Most kids would come in for a few days with a broken bone or for minor surgery. He would assess their demeanor and behavior during their treatment, but most didn't really need his assistance.

Some patients had chronic problems, such as birth defects, cancer, or other diseases. These kids often struggled with adult-sized issues like mortality or debilitating pain. It was hard to see them and their families struggling, but it was rewarding when he could help in a small way, even for a little while.

But the ones he always looked out for were the kids who suffered from loss, injury, or abuse. Back in Afghanistan, he'd seen so many kids he couldn't help that when he got back he knew exactly what he wanted to do. So instead of going into law enforcement or becoming a government contractor, Christopher had gone to school to help kids.

He spotted a new kid in the unit in the pile of folders. Noah Vasquez was seven with a congenital heart condition. The insurance coding indicated he was covered by the Veterans Administration, so one or both of his parents were vets. Looking back, Christopher saw a history of surgeries to insert pacemakers and leads going back to birth.

After putting the charts back, Deborah, the nurse on duty said, "Hey, you see the new kid with the pacemaker?"

"I saw the chart, what's the story?"

"He was admitted by Dr. Jenks for a pacemaker upgrade and isn't doing very well. I only saw his mother a couple of hours yesterday, but she seems nice." That was Deborah Code for a mother who wasn't obviously neglectful. Some parents hardly ever stayed with their kids and it made caring for them more difficult. But sometimes parents had to work or balance time caring for their other kids, so they didn't get to stay as long as they might like to.

"I was going to see him first. I'll let you know what I can find out."

As he walked into the little boy's room, Christopher was reminded of how small kids appeared in the big hospital beds. He had wires and tubes running off to monitors, a tree full of IV bags, and a bored expression on his face.

"What's up?" Christopher said as he plopped down in the chair next to the bed. As Deborah noted, there was no parent present in the room. "I'm Christopher."

"Noah," he croaked.

"You sound like you need a drink of water." Christopher poured some water out of the styrofoam pitcher into a cup with a straw. "Here you go."

Holding the straw next to his mouth, the boy obediently sipped then relaxed with a sigh as if it had taken an enormous amount of energy to drink. "You the water boy?" the kid asked.

"Naw, I'm just helping out the nurses 'cause they're cute. What do you think of Nurse Debbie?" The conspiratorial tone and wink brought a weak smile to Noah's face.

"I think she's too old for me," he said, then coughed with a wince. "Sorry, can't laugh yet."

"That's cool, I'll save the jokes 'till you're feeling better." Watching the boy carefully, he noted that he kept eye contact and had good color in his face. "So when do you think you'll be ready to toss a ball around?"

"Dunno. Doctor Jenks says I've got to be here a few days until things heal up inside." He shifted uncomfortably. "It hurts like shit."

"Isn't that language a little salty for someone your age?" Christopher already liked the boy just for being willing to curse in front of a new adult.

"You get your chest cracked open and see what *you* say," he muttered as he closed his eyes. "So really, what do you do around here?"

"Well, I'm a clinical social worker. I try to figure out how to help kids feel better."

"Is it fun?" he asked.

"Rewarding is probably a better word, but yeah, it's fun sometimes." The kid was watching him through his eyelashes. "What?"

"I was afraid you were a physical therapist."

"Why?" Christopher asked.

Noah whispered, "I hate physical therapists." Then he opened his eyes and broke into a wide grin.

"I hear ya. So what do you do for fun?"

"Minecraft. Xbox. Books."

Christopher looked around the room for personal items and didn't see anything. "What kind of books? Maybe I can find something to keep you busy."

"Mom says I'm too young for Harry Potter, but I read the first one before she found where I'd hid it. I read the Hobbit three times because she wouldn't let me go to see the movies."

That's an impressive feat for a seven year old, Christopher thought. "I guess you have a lot of time to read."

"Aw, it ain't so bad between surgeries. I'm a Wolf Scout and play soccer, it's just every time I hit a big growth spurt, I have to come back here and get a different pacemaker. This time they had to do the leads, too, so it was worse."

"Maybe I'll bring you the second Harry Potter book if you promise not to tell your parents where you got it." Christopher watched for his reaction to the comment.

Shaking his head, Noah said, "It's just me and Mom. Dad died in Afghanistan. He was a Marine."

That brought back the memory of the stench and hot wind over there like it was yesterday for Christopher. "Me, too. I served there for a while."

"My dad was Emilio Vasquez. Did you know him?" It hurt Christopher to see the hope in the boy's face.

"No, but there were thousands of us over there. What about your Mom?"

"She works in an insurance office and has to help take care of Nanna because she has Parkinson's Disease."

"I'm sorry to hear that."

"It's okay. Nanna can still get around and do most things. She lives in a special place that helps take care of her, but it's expensive."

"I bet." Christopher watched as Noah shut his eyes again. After a few minutes, he appeared to have drifted off to sleep.

As Christopher stood up to leave, Noah whispered, "It's *Chamber of Secrets*... Don't forget."

"I won't, buddy." His eyes burned by the time he left the boy to sleep.

Chapter 3: Charlotte

"The acute phase of many illnesses is often followed by a prolonged chronic phase, which may last from days to years and may involve the delivery of a number of health care services..."

The words swam together in a wash forcing Charlotte to close her textbook with a sigh. Taking another sip of coffee, she sat back and closed her eyes against the headache she felt building.

"You're up early," Tiffany said as she padded into the kitchen wearing a long t-shirt and fluffy pink slippers. She poured herself a mug of coffee from the half-empty pot on the counter.

"Couldn't sleep," Charlotte said as she gave her roommate a rueful half-smile.

"So how was Mardi Gras back in Morgan City?"

Has it only been a day since he drove away? she thought. "Christopher came," she said, getting right to the point and making Tiffany spin around like she'd heard a shot.

"No way! How'd he get there?"

"Kurt brought him in from Houston and hid him at our parents house until the parade to surprise me."

Tiffany brought her coffee over and sat at their small dining room table. "Ok, spill. I want details."

Charlotte shook her head sadly. "I broke it off with him before he went back to Houston."

"What! Why?"

Continuing to shake her head, Charlotte leaned over her cooling cup of coffee to avoid her friend's eyes.

Tiffany finally put the pieces together and said, "I'm so sorry."

"Yeah." Charlotte pinched her lips and let out a slow breath. "It wasn't fair to keep stringing him along."

"I still don't understand what the big deal is. It's not like you're super religious or anything."

"So why don't you jump off the high dive at the pool?" Charlotte asked with a sideways glance.

"That's not fair. I panic when I get—" Stopping with her mouth still open, she said, "Wow, I never thought of it like that."

"Exactly. If I could stop feeling this way about sex, I would. Trust me. It's no fun being alone all the time."

"Maybe you should see a shrink or something?" Tiffany suggested quietly.

"Maybe I should." It wasn't the first time she'd considered the idea, it was just so embarrassing to discuss, even with her closest friends. "Well, it's over and done with now, and I've got to get ready for my shift."

* * *

The last semester of the nursing program was the most interesting to Charlotte. She had to write papers and take exams on the categories of treatments for chronic illnesses. The shifts that were part of her residency at Lafayette General were a good introduction to the kinds of things she expected to do at Southwest Hospital in Houston. Plus staying focused on school work kept her mind off other things.

She volunteered for all the shifts she could take to keep herself busy over the weekend. Mardi Gras has worn out all the girls that she usually shared girls' night with, so the cancellation meant she could pick up that shift as well.

The next week crept by more slowly as her willpower began to crack. She almost called Christopher on Wednesday night, but threw her phone on the bed at the last second. To keep her head together, she made herself study ahead and write papers that weren't due for weeks yet.

For lunch on Friday, she had a bowl of soup and grilled cheese sandwich. After washing and putting her dishes in the rack to dry, she went into her room and closed the door. Trying not to think about Christopher had created an itchy feeling of frustration she had to take care of or she'd never be able to concentrate on her next paper.

After making sure the door was locked, she took off her sweats and t-shirt. Her underwear didn't matter, but she didn't want sweat on her clothes. When she was on the bed, she lay on her stomach and placed a folded pillow under her hips so it pressed against her mons. Clearing her mind, she took a few deep breaths and tried to let herself go. This didn't always work for her, but it was worth trying to get her focus back.

As she pushed her hips against the firm pillow, she found herself remembering Christopher pushing himself between her thighs as she sat on the trunk of Kurt's car. She'd been wearing tight jeans over a lavender pair of satin panties. There had only been four thin layers of fabric between them, she realized with a shiver.

His hard erection had pressed into her, just like the pillow was doing. Rocking herself more rhythmically, she got lost in her memories of that night. He had pulled her closer to the edge of the trunk to grind himself into her dampening crotch.

Later that night when she'd taken off her panties, the evidence of her arousal had glistened on the lining. He had made her so wet it had soaked through to darken the satin on the outside. Some madness had taken hold of her then, standing in her bedroom with Christopher only steps away sleeping in the living room. She had lifted the damp panties to her mouth and kissed the wet spot in the middle of the cotton panel.

She'd tasted her own arousal for the first time that night and wondered what he would think if he'd known. As she approached her release, the compulsion to taste herself returned, so she reached into her panties to gather some moisture on her fingertips. She was so close to cumming that simply touching herself there made her groan. As she lifted her fingers to her lips, she returned to grinding hard against the pillow.

Sucking her slick fingers, the orgasm she'd been working towards crested, forcing her to drive herself against the pillow in a final frenzy before the pulses stopped. Panting with her mouth full of her own slick flavor she whispered, "That's it, I'm going insane."

Breaking up with Christopher clearly hadn't ended her obsession. He had dominated her thoughts for the last week no matter what she had done and he obviously still ruled her fantasies as well. Rolling off the pillow, she stared at the ceiling as tears fell along her cheeks. She hated herself for being a coward and hated him for making her feel the way she did.

Mentally shaking herself, she grabbed her workout clothes and sports bra. Ignoring her slick panties, she changed quickly and headed toward the gym. Maybe it would help if she could exhaust herself enough. Jogging to warm up her muscles on the way there, she got on one of the free elliptical machines, put on the headphones connected to her phone, and tuned out the world for a little while as she listened to her favorite workout jams.

With every step she breathed in and out, concentrating on the repetitive motion to keep from thinking about anything else. Yet every guy that walked by prompted her to mentally compare them to her sandy-haired obsession. That one was shorter, another one too fat, a litany of characteristics that failed to reach her new standard of male perfection; Christopher Dunlop, Scots-American, Marine, social worker. *But never lover.*

Just as she finished her workout, her phone beeped. Polly had texted to find out when she was arriving. There had been a change of plans and the girls were meeting up for dinner instead of going drinking at Dave and Buster's. Hopping off the machine, she texted back her ETA and jogged towards her room feeling refreshed by the thought of spending the evening with her friends in Houston.

On her way through the campus she passed a group of guys in one of the common areas and recognized her last boyfriend before Christmas among them. Brian was a little shorter than she was, but she'd thought he was nice at the time. He avoided her eyes as she jogged by, but when she passed she heard him say, "Yeah, that's her."

It enraged her because she knew what he was telling them, but she didn't dare confront him in front of his friends. Back when they were still dating, she'd hoped he might be willing to help her try to overcome her fear and told him her secret shame. Instead of helping, he'd dumped her, claiming that inexperienced virgins were *too much trouble*. Her wet cheeks were cold by the time she got back to her room to shower and change.

* * *

Charlotte made it to her and Polly's apartment in Houston before dark. She lined up the boxes she'd packed back in Lafayette before opening the front door. As she struggled to get them in, her brother opened the door of his apartment across the way.

"Hey sis! I thought I heard you out here," he said as he lifted the largest box to carry it in for her.

"Thanks, Kurt," she put down her box and hugged him. "How's work?"

"Not bad this week, but I've got to head out next week on *Cinnamon Wind* for a run off the coast near Padre Island. Should be back by the weekend, though." Kurt had been working with Uncle Jack and Great Uncle Charlie to start a transport company. According to everyone, he was doing really well, but her proud smile faltered when Christopher poked his head in her door.

"You ready?" he asked Kurt without even glancing her way.

"I'll be down in a sec," he replied, then Christopher nodded and left. When she looked back at Kurt, he was uncomfortably red-faced. "Look, I know things didn't work out between you two, but he and I are friends now. It's not like *he* hurt *you* or anything."

"No," she admitted. No matter how irrational she knew she was being, his friendship with Christopher still felt like a betrayal. Before she could stop herself she asked, "Is he seein' anyone?"

Kurt's first reaction was an expression of pity, but he quickly schooled his face. "I ain't gonna torture you by answerin' that. Let it go and move on. I know he has."

It cut her to hear him say that, but she deserved it and worse. Nodding, she pinched her lips and said, "Go have fun."

Before he closed the front door, he looked back with a sad smile. "We're just playing video games with his friends Joe and Ryan. Don't worry." She tried not to show the relief she felt, but Kurt winked at her just before he left to let her know he'd seen it.

Polly was working until right before dinner, so Charlotte spent the time unpacking the boxes in her room. Aunt Julie had been such a huge help getting furniture. Since she remodeled rich people's houses, sometimes they got rid of perfectly good furniture just because it was the wrong style.

One family had a daughter moving back home after college and wanted to update her room. So now Charlotte had an amazing queen-sized bedroom set that looked like something out of a magazine for free. She'd been bringing over clothes and little knick-knacks to remind her of home every time she came to Houston.

By the time Polly came flying through the front door, Charlotte had finished unpacking, changed into a little black dress, and was putting on eyeliner as she looked in her bathroom mirror.

"Hey sis!" Polly yelled as she ran by to change. "I'll be ready to go in five minutes."

True to her word, she came walking out of her bedroom putting on a necklace with a huge grin on her face. "Help me with this, would ya?" she asked as she turned to show the clasp to Charlotte. It only took a second, then Polly turned to give her a big hug. "I missed you! I wish you would hurry up and graduate."

"Me too," Charlotte said as she straightened the straps on her friends black dress. "You look great!"

"You, too," she said as she stuffed her phone into her slim evening purse. "Is that L'Air Du Temps I smell?"

"Yeah, Mom gave it to me for Christmas and I hardly ever have a reason to wear it in Lafayette, so I brought it over here."

Polly's phone gave a muffled beep. "I bet that's Julie in the van. Let's go!"

"Julie never drives!" Charlotte said as she locked the door behind them.

Polly had a secretive smile on her face as she danced towards the parking lot. The van door was open and Cathy was leaning out with a big grin.

"I started without you," she said with a twinkle in her eye. "But I brought a flask, so you can catch up."

There were five girls going out this time, though Julie's boss, Bonnie, who was well into middle age hardly qualified as a girl. Julie and Polly had been life-long best friends and had welcomed Charlotte into their group over Christmas. Cathy was a bit younger than Charlotte and a former coworker of Julie's. Being a bit of a wild child, Cathy had had a threesome with Kurt and her former roommate before he and Polly had started dating.

Julie pulled out of the parking lot while Bonnie turned around and asked, "So how was Mardi Gras?"

Letting Polly gush, Charlotte listened to her description of the events and Kurt's reaction to her wearing the mask during the parade. They'd all helped Polly plan it out during a previous girls' night out, so hearing it had gone off without a hitch was heralded by hoots and applause from the others.

Polly ended by saying, "And y'all have no idea how great Charlotte is at making dresses. I hope you bring them next time you come up so we can wear them out for fun!"

With the attention on herself, Charlotte blushed and said, "I just did what Meemee taught me. It was really easy, I swear."

There was a lull in the conversation as Julie pulled into the parking lot of the steak house she'd picked. Charlotte didn't think anything of it until she caught Cathy and Polly having a conversation composed largely of nods, head shakes, and significant looks. "You can just say it, Polly."

"It's none of our business," Polly said quietly as she opened the van door.

Cathy followed Charlotte out of the van and put her arm around her shoulders. "But I'm sorry to hear it."

"It's fine," she said, feeling anything but fine. "It just wasn't working out for me." The lie hardly stung at all anymore.

"Well, let's get some booze and meat. I propose that men are off the table as a topic of conversation!" Cathy zoomed ahead to lead the group inside.

After being seated, a hunky young waiter came by to take their drink orders. Cathy went for a tequila shot, Bonnie had wine, Polly and Charlotte had beer. Then when Julie ordered an unsweet iced tea the whole table stopped talking.

As the waiter walked away, Cathy whispered, "Oh my God, you're pregnant."

Charlotte noticed Polly smiling down at the table as she played with her napkin while Julie protested. "No, I'm just the designated driver. I've made everyone else drive, even poor Kurt, so it's my turn this time. That's *all*!"

Charlotte looked more closely at her aunt as she tried to recall if she drank anything over Mardi Gras, but couldn't say for certain. Knowing how risky the first trimester was, it was probably prudent to delay making an official announcement if she really was pregnant. Charlotte decided to help cover for her just in case.

"Yeah, Aunt Julie was shit-faced at Mardi Gras. Poor Uncle Jack had to carry her to bed," Charlotte said with a straight face. When Julie looked up, masking surprise, Charlotte gave her a quick wink. "Thanks again for drivin' tonight!"

"My pleasure! Sorry for the change of venues, but I've been craving steak all week and Jack's been too busy to grill." Julie scanned the menu to hide her thin smile.

Gotcha, Charlotte thought, pleased she'd figured it out. Polly patted her leg under the table, confirming it with a brief nod.

"So what's everyone having?" Bonnie said with her reading glasses down at the end of her nose. "I'm thinking shrimp or maybe the surf and turf."

"Steak for me," Cathy said. "Probably a ribeye."

"Me too," Julie echoed. "Rare and bloody."

"I can't decide," Polly said. "Maybe I'll have dessert first."

"What?" Cathy said with a laugh. "You can't do that!"

"Why not? I can always take my meal home for lunch tomorrow, but an ice cream chocolate lava cake… you can't just box that up to go."

"I never thought of it that way," Cathy said. "It still feels wrong."

"This coming from a bisexual, threesome having, freewheeling sex machine," Polly said with a good natured laugh. She and Cathy had long since resolved whatever issues may have lingered over Kurt sleeping with Cathy and Camden. The group laughed, even Bonnie who Charlotte hadn't quite figured out yet.

"You got me," Cathy answered, shooting Polly with a finger gun. "What can I say? I'm only traditional when it comes to meals."

They got their drinks and placed their orders, relaxing around the table to chat about jobs, school, and sex. Even though the rule about men was still in force, no one considered talking about sex breaking the rules. The jokes were funny, the detailed tips hilariously embarrassing, but all the frank discussions made Charlotte extremely uncomfortable. By the time they had finished their meal, the conversation still hadn't ended.

"I'm just saying that beyond a certain minimum, size matters less than enthusiasm," Cathy said and tossed back the rest of her shot.

"What about toys?" Bonnie asked with the calm assurance of middle age. "You *have* to have a preferred size when it comes to those, surely?"

"Not really," Cathy said, leaning into speak. "My favorite vibrator is a little bullet sized thing that gets right to the point. I have a medium-sized glass dildo that I *love*, with little colored bumps all up and down the shaft. But I still love the rubber cock I can stick to the wall of my shower with a suction cup that's seriously a foot long."

Julie was fanning herself. "Is it hot in here?"

"Glass dildo?" Polly asked as she leaned in too. "Isn't that dangerous?"

"No, it's not like window glass. It's more like that stuff they make kitchen cookware out of. It's super hard, but doesn't break like regular glass. You can heat it with hot water and it stays warm for hours. Plus it's super easy to clean."

"I guess I'd have to see it," Polly said, shaking her head. "I just can't imagine it at all."

"So let's go to Erotic Boutique," Bonnie suggested. "It's on this side of town and I know they'll have one or two we can look at."

"I'm in," Julie said. "All this talk is making me want to do unspeakable things to Jack when I get home."

When they all piled into the van again, Polly got in the back seat with Charlotte. "This is just what you need," Polly whispered with a conspiratorial nod.

"What?" Charlotte asked, her mouth suddenly dry. *What if Kurt had told her?*

"Nothing gets a man out of your system like a nice, long session with a toy. I'm serious, I swear by mine." Her smile was so open and warm that Charlotte hoped maybe she didn't know.

"What kind do you have?"

"A little wand and my old faithful Hitachi massager," Polly grinned. "Although I think after being with Kurt I need an... upgrade."

"Uhh..." Charlotte felt her skin crawl from the embarrassment.

"Sorry! Oh my God, he's your brother! Forget I said anything." Polly covered her face. "Jeez, like you want to hear how your brother is hung."

"Actually, I thought there was something wrong with my first boyfriend, Peter, because of Kurt." Charlotte couldn't believe she said it, but that last round of shots was making her bold. "I mean, you share a bathroom long enough, you're gonna see something eventually. And let's just say Peter didn't exactly measure up."

Polly laughed so hard she snorted, which made everyone look back at the two of them. Cathy demanded, "Share!"

"Tell them," Polly said, waving her on as she tried to stifle her giggles.

Given the floor like that, Charlotte mustered her courage and said, "My brother is pretty well-endowed. We shared a bathroom the whole time we grew up, so I occasionally saw him naked. No big deal. But the first time I saw a... normal- sized guy, I thought there was... something... wrong with him."

They all howled laughing, so bad in fact that Julie had to pull over in a parking lot to blow her nose. "Oh my God, let me tell you, that trait runs in the family," Julie said as she wiped her eyes. "I'm not sure I could ever go back to normal-sized now, even if I wanted to."

Cathy, who also knew Kurt's dimensions first hand, sat fanning herself like Julie had at the restaurant. "Is it hot in here?" she repeated in Julie's soft southern accent.

Bonnie just shook her head. "You're all nuts."

"So what's the gay equivalent of well endowed male?" Julie asked Bonnie. Charlotte nearly smacked her forehead when the light went on. *Of course Bonnie is gay*, she thought, *how could I have missed it?*

"Well, toys are always an option, but I had one friend who liked me to use my whole hand and forearm."

"Holy shit!" Polly exclaimed. "Ouch!" She crossed her hands over her crotch.

The idea of sex was tough enough for her, but that description made Charlotte shiver and close her eyes.

"You work up to it," Bonnie explained. "It's not like you just jam it in there."

"Well that explains those funny arm dildos I saw online," Cathy said with a thoughtful expression.

"Ok, now we *have* to go to Erotic Boutique," Polly said. "But if they have one of those, I'm going to die laughing when I see it."

Parked in front of the blue building, Charlotte felt trapped. She was insanely curious, but even after spending the whole evening drinking and discussing sex, it still wasn't enough to overcome her fearful hesitation.

She stuck next to Polly as they went inside and was immediately overpowered by the exotic scents of incense and spices. The showroom was mostly clothing racks full of sexy costumes, negligée, and lingerie. Along the walls were outrageous shoes and boots with platform soles, along with kinky accessories like leather whips and restraints. Along the back walls were all the toys.

As they browsed, one of them would hold up something to gauge the interest of the others. Despite being nervous, Charlotte was fascinated by all the options available to enhance the sexual experience. She had occasionally seen things like these in porn, but nothing up close. And here were four other women casually discussing how to satisfy themselves or their lovers. It was eye opening and actually calmed her down enough to enjoy herself.

She made her way to the back where the toys were while Polly trailed along nearby. No one was paying attention to her at all, so she picked up a rubber dildo from the counter that was shaped like a well-endowed cock and balls. It was heavier than she anticipated, and the texture was close enough to skin for fantasy. She imagined this going inside her and was surprised when it didn't immediately make her feel afraid.

Putting it down, she looked at the colorful and less anatomical wand vibrators that were arrayed on the counter by height and thickness. She touched each one on the tip as if to verify it was real, suddenly curious if the experience would be as exciting for her as it seemed to be for everyone else. She felt the familiar itch building and realized she wanted to find out.

Next were the glass dildos that Cathy had mentioned over dinner. Polly was already there turning one over in her hands. It was mostly transparent, but there were ridges of glass along the sides to give it texture and color.

"What do you think?" Charlotte asked, nodding to what she was holding.

"I think I need to buy this one," Polly said as she licked her lips. "What about you?"

"I don't know," she said and glanced back to the colorful vibrators. "Maybe. How much is that one?"

"Fifteen. I'll let you know if it's worth it later."

"I think I want one of those," she said and reached over for a smaller vibrator. Her face was hot and her hand shook, but she picked it up anyway.

"Good choice." Polly said, confirming her selection. "Basic, small enough to hide in your purse, and it gets the job done."

"Hide in your purse?" Charlotte said with a gasp. "You take yours around with you?"

"Sure," Polly shrugged. "Sometimes work gets *so* boring."

Charlotte covered her mouth to laugh and shook her head. "I don't know you at all."

"You're my roomie now, so you get to know all my secrets. Besides, you know what your brother and I are doing on the other side of the wall. What's the big deal?"

Charlotte kept silent about the big deal as she turned to get the clerk's attention. "I can't believe I'm doing this," she whispered to herself.

In the end she bought the slim wand vibrator, extra batteries, a bottle of lube, a small box of condoms, and some massage oil the clerk recommended. The others had gotten a number of things as well, so she didn't feel like a complete freak when she carried her heavy bag out to the van.

The ride home was a riot as Julie dropped off Cathy first, then Bonnie. As each one left they were forced to share what their plans for their purchases were in broad terms. Cathy intended to try out the jewel-tipped chrome butt plug she'd picked up. Bonnie had gotten a leather mask and feathered whip and had already called a friend to come over to her place from the store.

After Julie pulled up into their apartment complex, she waited for Polly and Charlotte to get out and close the sliding side door. She was smiling at them through the open drivers window when they turned to say goodbye.

"Thanks for helping me keep my secret at dinner," she said quietly.

"I didn't know for sure, but if you're still in the first trimester I understand why you didn't want to make a big announcement yet," Charlotte said as she clutched her bag.

"Yeah, I never expected Cathy to buy it, but Charlotte looks so innocent no one would believe she was lying," Polly added and bumped her friend with her hip.

"So how far along are you?" Charlotte asked.

"Twelve weeks, finally! Jack and I still want to wait until Easter to say anything. The girls will be the first we tell officially, of course."

"I'm so happy for you guys. You're such great parents." Charlotte could see the happy glow in Julie's face now.

Julie sighed, "We try."

"Have a good night," Charlotte said as she turned to go.

"Oh, no, don't you have something to say to us?" Polly asked as she pulled her back around.

"What?" she asked, then remembered the bag she was holding. "Shit. I'm… uh… gonna do stuff?" She felt her face heat up and shrugged hoping it was enough to get her off the hook.

"Oh my God, look at that blush, Polly," Julie said. "If she wasn't twenty-four I'd swear she was a virgin!"

The words hit her like a slap in the face. Backing away, Charlotte intended to run and lock herself in her room, but Polly and Julie both reacted instantly.

"Shh, stop, it's okay," Polly said as she took Charlotte's arm to stop her. "Wait, we didn't know."

"I'm so sorry, Charlotte," Julie said as she dashed up from the van. "I never would have said something like that if I knew it was going to hurt you."

There were tears on her face and she was panting, clutching the bag to her chest as the panic overran her totally. "I… can't…" she gasped but the words were stuck because she couldn't catch her breath.

"Let's get her inside," Polly said. "I'll make us some tea."

When Charlotte finally got herself under control, the shame over her reaction made it impossible to talk. While Polly made tea, Julie sat with her on the couch and tried to get her to say something.

"You can trust us, Charlotte," Julie whispered. "I'm trusting you with my biggest secret already and Polly loves you like a sister. I swear I never meant to hurt you. Please forgive me."

Charlotte kept nodding, but her mouth refused to work. Polly brought in a small bamboo tray with three mugs of her family's favorite bush tea.

"When I was in high school," Polly started. "My boyfriend, Bobby, and I thought we were in love. I was determined to have sex with him, but I was scared out of my mind. I didn't know it at the time, but Julie had been a teen volunteer at the local free clinic for a while."

She handed mugs to Charlotte and Julie before taking her own, then she continued. "One of the nurses there called Julie the *Fearless Fornicator* because she gave out more condoms and advice about sex than their own employees. You don't need to feel embarrassed about anything. We're both here to listen if you want to talk."

And with that the long wait began. Charlotte sipped her tea wishing she had never come to Houston. The boys on campus were probably still laughing after her ex-boyfriend had told them everything. And now her aunt and friend knew as well. She didn't want to talk about it; she *hated* it.

"I want to go to bed," Charlotte whispered at last.

"Okay," Julie said and patted her leg. "You can call me anytime if you want to talk."

When the two of them went outside, Charlotte took her bag into her bedroom. After locking the door, she took off her clothes and pulled out a long nightshirt to sleep in. But sleep was still a far off dream.

She turned off the overhead light in favor of the dim lamp on her night stand. Putting her phone down in its charging base, she brought up a Pandora stream of trance music and club remixes. After climbing on the bed to sit cross-legged, she glared at the bag in the middle of the bed for a long time before she leaned over to drag it into her lap.

She took out each item and examined it carefully. Getting the vibrator out of its box, she opened the battery compartment and carefully put the batteries inside. It buzzed when she put the cover back on, which startled her. The dial at the bottom adjusted the rate of vibration, she noted, then she turned it off and put it aside.

The lube was in a bottle with a pushdown dispenser. She broke the seal and squeezed a drop on her finger, then rubbed it with her thumb. When she brought it to her nose, the slick gel had no strong scent at all.

The massage oil smelled like rosemary of all things, but it felt good when she rubbed some on her legs and feet. The scent that filled the room helped her relax.

She pulled the condoms out and looked at the box. They were a different brand than the ones she'd bought for prom night seven years ago. Looking at them, she pinched her lips, then leaned over to put them in the night stand drawer with the massage oil.

After throwing away the all the empty containers and bits of trash, she took off her panties and climbed back into bed. Pushing the pillows up against the headboard, she leaned against them, raising her knees as she picked up the vibrator and the lube.

Without turning it on, she covered the tip with a few squeezes of the lube and spread it around with her fingers. Then steeling herself, she reached down to open her lower lips, sliding her lubed fingers in to spread it around. Taking the still silent vibrator, she pressed its cool tip where she imagined it went in by feel alone and began to press it inside her.

She was so angry about her status and so embarrassed by her friends finding out, that her determination forced her fear away completely. Finally feeling something more substantial than a tampon penetrate her made her gasp as it went in. It wasn't bad at all, no pain to speak of, just a bit of cool tightness at first, then the slick vibrator slid all the way in.

"That's it?" she whispered to herself. It felt interesting in a way, but hardly worth the loud groans she'd heard her friends make through the walls. She twisted the bottom of the handle to start it vibrating. It tickled more than anything, an intense sensation that left her covering her mouth to hold in her laughter.

The sense of relief she felt with these initial explorations was enough to make her giddy. Moving the device out and in created a more interesting feeling, but when the tip slipped out and accidentally went up her slit, she squeaked out loud.

"Are you okay?" Polly called from the living room.

"Uh, not a good time," she answered as she tried not to laugh.

"Okay. I'll be up for a while watching TV. Loud."

It wasn't long before her arousal overrode the need for lube entirely. She found the tip was especially buzzy, so she pressed it above her slit for long minutes while her eyes shut from the pleasure it gave her. Moving it down and around gave her waves of pleasure with each pass. And when she began to fill herself after becoming fully aroused, she felt the first urges to make noises at last.

She kept at it for minutes, trying to find the mental trick she'd always had to use when she rode a pillow to orgasm. The stimulation was so different that she found it hard to get into the right frame of mind to let go. Eventually, she just left the tip sitting above her swollen nub, focusing on the pleasure until she felt the pulses begin at last. The stimulation quickly became too much and she had to turn off the toy.

Panting on her bed, she tried to find a place in her mind for this experience. It wasn't sex, but it was a close enough proxy for her to argue with herself. There was nothing to fear about it, she told herself. It hadn't hurt, it wasn't wrong or bad or even weird.

But how would it feel with a man? She tried to imagine Christopher filling her up the same way her toy had but it just made her stomach tight. She knew someone as old as him and as good looking as him had been with lots of women. When she thought of him having sex with other women, it made her stomach feel even worse. Pushing those uncomfortable thoughts away, she focused instead on how good it had felt to use the toy.

After she recovered her breath and put on her panties again, she put away the lube and carried her new favorite toy to the door. She had to clean it, the store clerk had been very careful to explain how to do that.

Opening the door, the television in the living room was still on very loud. Polly had to know what she was doing and wanted to afford her a little privacy. The thought made Charlotte feel embarrassed as she went into the bathroom, but she refused to be ashamed.

Running the water hot, she cleaned off the toy with soap and then dried it with her bath towel. After putting it in her night stand drawer, she went out into the living room to see what Polly was watching.

Plopping down on the couch next to her friend, she stared at the show without recognizing it. When the commercial came on, she looked over at Polly and said, "Thanks."

Polly chuckled as she lowered the volume and said, "I didn't do anything."

"Yeah, you did and you know it." After taking a deep breath she said. "I'm a virgin. I don't want to be, but sex scares me like some people are scared of heights or snakes. Now I'm not so afraid." She said it with a degree of pride and Polly smiled.

"It certainly explains a few things for me. Your brother must know because he's been worried like crazy about you and I couldn't get him to explain why."

Charlotte nodded. "He and my two roommates at school were the only ones who knew, other than my last boyfriend. Who dumped me. Because dating a virgin makes things *too complicated*." She wiped her eyes. "Fucker."

"In a way he's right, though." Polly had a serious expression when Charlotte glared over at her.

"What do you mean?"

"It's different for different people, but sex bonds me to the person I'm with. Before she married your Uncle Jack, Julie could fall in and out of bed with people and it never seemed to touch her. I couldn't do that in a million years. Kurt is the fifth person I've been with. My first three were all special and I was close to all of them before we had sex. And my fourth was Trey, a mistake I'll regret for the rest of my life."

Charlotte nodded as she considered Polly's words. "I don't want to be a virgin anymore. I'm sick of being scared but I don't want to regret it either."

"I don't suppose this had anything to do with your decision to break up with Christopher?"

Thinking of him now, Charlotte lost it completely. *He's probably having sex with someone else right now*, she thought. *It could have been me!* "Oh, God, I'm such an idiot." When the tears came, Polly rubbed her back until they passed. "I was so afraid. It was easier to push him away."

"So pull him back," Polly said with a shrug. "It hasn't been that long."

"I don't know." Charlotte dried her eyes and looked at her friend. "Do you think he would listen?"

"It can't hurt to give him a chance," she said, then looked serious again. "But if you don't you'll live to regret it. I can promise you that from personal experience."

Chapter 4: Christopher

Running through the neighborhood surrounding his apartment complex gave Christopher time to think. Spending a weekend blowing stuff up was just what the doctor ordered. Kurt was a natural and picked up their favorite video game like he was born to play it. He claimed to have never played war games that much, being more of a racing gamer, but all those years hunting in the swamps must have honed his instincts.

Joe and Ryan had both given Kurt an unqualified thumbs up. Christopher's two buddies had been overseas with him in the Marines and they all stayed close after coming back to the states. Outside of his brothers and Ashley, those two were his closest friends and their approval was an important milestone.

When he'd gone to pick up Kurt on Friday night he hadn't expected to run into Charlotte as well. Seeing her again had tested his will, but he was happy to say he passed the test with flying colors. She still looked gorgeous, but he managed to keep his eyes off of her and his damn mouth shut. Another week or two and he was sure he'd be able to get her completely out of his system.

Rounding the last corner heading back to his apartment, Christopher stepped up the pace to a sprint. Two steps, breathe in, two steps, breathe out, he forced his burning legs to move faster until he was back in the parking lot of his complex. Walking to cool down, he panted hard most of the way back to his apartment. *Fuck her*, he thought. *Who needs her anyway?*

After a quick shower, Christopher headed into work. When he got to his floor, he grabbed the stack of patient charts to see what had happened over the weekend with his kids. He was happy Shelly had been released on Sunday as planned, Franklin was leaving later in the day, but Noah had gotten an infection and a fever. *Damn it.*

The protocol for infections meant that Christopher would have to go in to see Noah basically wearing a hazmat suit to avoid cross-contamination with other patients. Deciding to get that hassle out of the way first, he put on the bright yellow jumper, elastic shoe coverings, and mask before going in.

"Holy crap, it's an alien," Noah muttered from the bed.

He looks better, infection or not, but still way too thin, Christopher thought. "Take me to your leader," he intoned in a robotic voice.

"Did you bring me *Prisoner of Azkaban*?" he asked with a hopeful grin.

"Affirmative," Christopher said as be brought the book out from behind his back.

"You rock, dude," Noah said as he took the paperback and examined it. "Mom finally agreed to let me read them after I showed her I finished the last one in a week."

"Good," Christopher said, returning to his normal voice. "I didn't like you having to hide it from her. What did you think about the story?"

"I liked the polyjuice potion. I could have some fun with it around here."

"Who would you want to turn into?" Christopher asked.

"You, dude, and I'd ask Nurse Debbie out," Noah laughed. This time his laugh didn't make him cough or wince, which Christopher counted as a win. His eyes were bright with mischief and he seemed to have more energy.

"I don't think Nurse Debbie is my type," Christopher said as he sat down in the chair next to the bed. "I like brunettes, myself, with dark eyes." Realizing he was thinking of Charlotte, he let out a sad chuckle.

"What?" Noah asked as he turned in the bed.

"Nothin'. So you think Nurse Debbie is hot?"

"Naw," he answered with an embarrassed grin. "She's just nice is all. You both are."

"She is that, and she's worried about you not eating enough." The comment was accompanied by a piercing frown. "I don't want to hear about you leavin' stuff on your tray anymore."

"Jeez, it was just lima beans. I freakin' *hate* lima beans."

"Yeah, but they have the protein you need to get healed up, so you eat them and stop giving the nurses hell, ya' hear me soldier?"

"Yes, sir," he said with a beaten moan.

"Alright." Christopher stood up and stretched his back. "I'm heading out now, but I'll be back this afternoon to check on you."

"Hey, Christopher?" he asked just before Christopher got to the door.

"Yeah, kid?"

"Thanks." His stoic expression made Christopher smile.

Such a tough little dude. "Tell your mom I said I'm looking forward to meeting her."

Chapter 5: Charlotte

When Charlotte discovered her pillow trick at eleven years old, she tried masturbating every morning and evening for months with varied success. Using her fingers had always been like trying to tickle herself and never worked for her, so the pillow trick had been like finding a magic spell. She had started rubbing against a stuffed animal, but that hadn't lasted a month before the accumulating evidence forced her to secretly dispose of it. Her mother seemed pleased when she offered to start doing her own laundry and never seemed to suspect the real reason was that she wanted to wash her own pillow cases to keep her secret.

So after spending the weekend with her new toy, she didn't think twice about bringing her vibrator back to school for the week. Since she was scared someone would accidentally see it in her purse, she wrapped it in tissue and hid it at the bottom under everything else. It still made her blush when she carried it past her roommates when she returned on Sunday. Knowing it was irrational didn't stop her from worrying that they could tell she had it somehow.

Utterly addicted to the new experience, she found any excuse to lock her door and explore herself with it. In the mornings she gave herself a nice start on the day with a fast warm up. At lunch she'd spend a quick ten minutes with some direct stimulation. In the evenings she put on music to tease herself along until she couldn't stand it anymore.

In the evenings especially, she imagined Christopher taking her in different ways, using her vibrator in those positions to stimulate herself more fully. Sometimes she fantasized him being on top, or taking her from behind, or when she was feeling bold, with her on top riding slowly. In her dreams he would be as gentle or rough as her mood demanded, but no matter how it happened, she loved how reliably she could orgasm with her toy.

It changed the way she thought about everything. Walking to class, she would look at couples without the envy she used to feel at their apparent happiness and closeness. The cloud of fear she'd lived under for years that something was wrong with her began to clear and she loved that the sunlight was starting to filter through day by day.

Unfortunately, the clouds came back on Friday morning. After her workout on the elliptical machine, she was drying off when a guy she didn't recognize approached her.

"Hey," he said, raising his chin and smiling at her. The good mood she'd been in all week masked her normal reluctance to speak to strange men on campus. "I'm Curtis."

"Hi," she said, oddly flattered by the unsolicited attention. "I'm Charlotte."

"I heard you might be looking for a workout partner," he said with a straight face.

"What? Where did you hear that?"

"Brian," he said as his cruel humor showed through at last. "He may not be interested in doing it with you, but I've never had any complaints."

A cold rage boiled up as she scanned the room for her ex-boyfriend Brian or his friends. "Do you think that's funny, you asshole?"

"Hey," he said with a chuckle, stepping back and holding up his open hands. "I was just making the offer. There's no need to go mental."

If she'd had a scalpel right then, he'd have needed a trip to the emergency room and a surgical urologist. Seeing her expression, he turned and jogged away, laughing as he made his escape to give a few other guys high fives.

Blowing off her afternoon classes, she packed up a load of her things and left for Houston in a rage. Her temper was burning hot until she got to Lake Charles, and it softened into a dark depression as she crossed the Calcasieu River Bridge on I-10. By the time she made it to her apartment and got her things into her room, her mood had soured even further.

She considered her situation as she sat on her bed. The asshole in the gym was only a symptom of the real problem she faced. Christopher was the first guy she'd met in a long time who seemed to value the same kinds of things she did. He was masculine and strong, but had a soft heart that had won her over, at least until her fear had driven him away.

Maybe it isn't over, she told herself, recalling her conversation with Polly. Maybe he would forgive her if she could explain it somehow.

Pulling out her phone from her back pocket, she stared at his contact for a long time before finally pressing it to place the call. It rang so long she thought it would end up going to voicemail until he answered.

Chapter 6: Christopher

The week rolled along in a comfortable routine until he got a call late Friday afternoon. He was returning to his floor from an early dinner in the cafeteria when his phone started playing a familiar tune. He realized he'd never deleted Charlotte's entry, so it played the song *Jambalaya* until he accidentally flicked the icon the wrong way and answered the call.

"What?" he asked abruptly, irritated with himself for not letting it go to voicemail.

"Christopher?" she asked in a trembling tone. "Don't hang up."

He had to admit the idea was tempting, but instead he said, "I'm at work. What do you want?"

"Sorry, I didn't know," she said. "Look, I think I've made a terrible mistake."

"Really." His tone sounded flat and unsurprised.

"Are you free this weekend? I'd like to take you out to dinner and try to explain—"

"I'm busy," he interrupted.

"I... I see. Would you call me then? When you have some time?"

He sighed as his blood pressure increased. "I don't think so, Charlotte."

After a long pause, she whispered, "I'm sorry, I won't bother you again."

"I'd appreciate that." When he dropped the call, his heart was racing and his temper was as hot as the day he'd left Morgan City. Pushing open the door to a nearby supply closet, he grabbed a folded towel, pressed it to his face into it and screamed.

In one moment, everything had come back like it had happened yesterday. He could recall her scent perfectly, the feel of her lips, the texture of her hair. All his careful work to pry her out of his life was undone in a thirty second phone call.

With the phone still in his hand, he pressed Kurt's contact. His first reaction was to yell at her brother about the call, but by the time Kurt answered he realized that was a bad idea.

"Hey man," Kurt answered after a few rings. "I'm still on the ship, but we finally made it back to Houston a little while ago. You need something?"

"A beer. You doing anything tonight?"

"Actually Uncle Jack invited me over for scotch and cigars while the girls are out tonight. You wanna come hang out with us?"

The idea had definite appeal. "Yeah, that sounds great. Can I bring anything?"

"Meat for the grill?" Kurt suggested.

"Burgers okay?

"Perfect. I'll bring buns."

"Text me the address again so I can find my way when I get off work."

* * *

Christopher carried the box of frozen burgers up to the door and rang the bell. Jack answered with a grin and swung the door open wide.

"Come on in! It's good to see you again," he said as Christopher passed him.

"Thanks for having me."

"There he is!" Kurt said as he came out of the kitchen. "The girls are out, the kids are asleep, and there's nothing for us to do but drink and smoke stogies. What could be better than this?"

"Nothin'," Christopher answered as he followed the men out the patio door to dim backyard. Jack had a nice setup, with a fire pit surrounded by padded outdoor furniture, a large glass-top dining table, and a stainless steel grill. "Want me to do the honors?" he asked, nodding at the grill.

"Help yourself," Jack said as he grabbed the triangular shaped bottle off the table. "I'm out of Jameson tonight, so we have to drink the good stuff." After pouring a dram in a crystal glass, he held it out to Christopher.

Holding the glass near his nose, he swirled the amber liquid until it showed it's legs. "Glenfiddich?" he asked, detecting the sweet notes of the fine single malt scotch.

"Good nose. It's the fifteen year," Jack confirmed he sat down next to the dead fire pit. "I wish it was cool enough for a fire."

Christopher figured out the grill and got the burners going, then dropped the frozen burger patties on to cook. He noted the time, then he sat the padded chair next to the grill. "Thanks, I needed this," he said and raised his glass to Jack and Kurt.

The men didn't speak for a while as the gas hissed and the burgers sizzled, each one lost in their own thoughts for a while. Then Jack asked Kurt, "How'd the run go this week?"

"No problems. The new first mate is a real go-getter and basically ran the whole trip for me. It may be time to promote him if he can pass his OSV Master exam."

"So are you ready for a full-time desk job?" Jack asked with a wide grin that seemed to say he knew the answer already.

"Maybe I'm ready to buy some more ships," Kurt answered with his own grin, making his uncle slap his leg and laugh.

"So old Evan Johnson is finally speaking to you again?"

"He sort of had to. I started going to the Port Authority meetings and playing the political game a little. Great Uncle Charlie's name opened a few doors and got me invitations to some parties. Next thing you know, Evan and I are bumping into each other all over the place, so I asked him if he knows of any supply ships that might be coming on the market." Kurt took a drink and raised his eyebrows.

Jack chuckled and shook his head. "If you pull that off, I'll buy you a *case* of scotch." He turned to Christopher and asked, "So how's your job going at the hospital?"

"Really well," he said, leaning forward to put his elbows on the table. "After I got back from the service I knew I wanted to go into clinical social work. Dad always gave me shit about it, though, because he thinks it's a job for women. Now that I'm actually doing it, you couldn't pay me to stop."

"Pardon my ignorance, but no one ever explained what a clinical social worker actually does," Jack said.

"Help people learn how to help themselves and get along in life. My treatment area is kids with emotional or physical trauma. Basically, I help kids come to terms with what's wrong with them and come up with a plan to help them get better."

"I guess you're not talking about physically, then," Jack asked, his eyes narrowing a little.

"No, it's the physical side, too, it's just not *only* that, like a physical therapist. I'm working with kids in the hospital, so clearly there are some health issues, but I'm also keeping an eye on their parents, how they interact with staff, whether they're showing signs of depression or aggression. We want these kids to get better, but sometimes they have other issues that can get in the way. I help them see what's going on, then work with them to fix it when I can or recommend treatment plans they can continue with an outside therapist or social worker."

Nodding at last, Jack asked, "So what made you want to do that?"

Christopher got up to flip the burgers, allowing himself some time to think. "I served overseas in Afghanistan and one of our jobs was improving relations with the locals. There are so many kids over there…" He stopped to consider how to present it so Jack would understand. He'd always dodged the question before, but it seemed important to try this time. "One village had a single soccer ball that all the kids had to share, but it had a slow leak. So after every play, one kid had to pump it back up with this cracked hand pump. Language barriers aside, they were no different than the little kids I coached back when I was in high school. So my first Christmas over there I asked my dad to send me a few soccer balls."

"That's really cool," Kurt said with a surprised smile.

"Dad went crazy. He called our church, the high school I'd gone to, the local sporting goods store, begging everyone for soccer balls and field equipment. I can't image what it cost to send all that crap over there, but it transformed those kids' lives. Our platoon began to distribute balls and gear all over the place, and I had every second of my free time booked up coaching those kids to play for real. We set up teams, had games between villages, the works."

"That's incredible," Jack said as he poured himself another dram.

"What was amazing to me was how much it did for the families. You had these old poppy farmers who hated us and never smiled at anything, but they'd cheer on their grandkids playing soccer. One guy I knew said it reminded him of the way a vine only grows if there's a structure to grow on. We made the structure, and those kids *thrived* after that. There were improvements in the new schools, less reports of abuse from the hospitals, it made such a huge difference all around."

"You sound like Charlotte," Kurt said. "She gets on these rants about prenatal care for the poor or how early dental care can head off health problems later on, and..." He trailed off when Christopher slowly turned to face him. "Sorry, man, I forgot."

"It's cool," he said and returned to flipping burgers with a sigh. "She called me today."

"I didn't know," Kurt said as he poured himself another dram of Jack's scotch.

"What happened between you two?" Jack asked.

"You'd have to ask her. I thought things were going great, but she up and dumped me the day after Mardi Gras."

"That's a shame," Jack said.

"So what did she want when she called?" Kurt asked.

Christopher turned and raised an eyebrow at him. "She said she made a mistake." With the hamburgers turned, Christopher sat back down and picked up his scotch. "I decided not to let her make another one."

Kurt looked like he was dying to say something, but just pinched his lips and stared into his glass of scotch.

Chapter 7: Charlotte

When Polly got home from work, Charlotte was already dressed for their night out and sitting on the couch drinking a glass of wine. Looking up from the romance novel she was reading on her phone, Charlotte plastered on a fake smile and said, "Hey."

"You're already ready? Let me have a quick shower and change. I think it's just you, me, Julie, and Cathy tonight. Bonnie has some big pitch she's working on and can't get away."

Charlotte nodded and took another sip of her wine. "Hope you don't mind I opened that bottle of wine in the back of the fridge."

"That's what it's there for! Pour me a glass too," Polly said as she danced back to her room, then Charlotte heard the door shut. She got a second glass and poured some more of the chilled white wine for them both.

Sitting back on the couch, Charlotte let the wine carry away her sense of shame and failure. She had nothing to lose anymore. Her secret was out at school and apparently burning through the campus like a wildfire. Aunt Julie and Polly knew as well, so it was just a matter of time before everyone else found out. Maybe she'd just get drunk and let someone take her home. That would certainly solve part of the problem.

Wiping away the angry tears she downed her glass of wine and went back for another. By the time Polly came out dressed for the night, Charlotte's head was warm and spinning.

"Ready to go?" Polly asked. "I'm driving tonight since it's just the four of us."

"Aunt Julie can't drink."

"She's gonna tip the waiter to bring her a coke with a lime in it no matter what she orders. Cathy won't be able to tell unless she sneaks a sip."

With Polly driving and Julie in the front seat, Cathy and Charlotte sat in the back passing her flask of vanilla vodka back and forth.

"You're in a mood," Cathy noted with a grin as Charlotte took another large nip from the flask.

"I'm a woman on a mission," she whispered.

"Looking to get laid?" she asked with a grin.

"Why the hell not?" There was a bitterness in her tone that must have signaled Cathy that it wasn't all fun and games.

"You don't strike me as the kind of girl who picks up guys at the bar."

"There's a first time for everything," she smiled at her private joke.

"Well, if you're serious, let me be your wing-woman and I'll help you pick a winner."

"You're a good friend." Putting her head down on Cathy's shoulder, she sighed heavily as the alcohol blunted her fears.

"I'm glad you think so." After a quick kiss on her forehead, Cathy leaned against her as well.

Polly pulled up to the valet parking at the club entrance. "We're here!"

Climbing out of the car, Polly took the valet ticket as the four of them made their way to the line going into the club. Charlotte had never been to a club like this before. There were plenty of bars in Lafayette, but this one looked like it belonged in Las Vegas, with erotic statuary, colorful lights, and loud music playing before they even got inside.

After paying the cover, Cathy and Charlotte went to find a table while Julie and Polly went to get some drinks. The walls were lined with booths that had rounded benches behind knee-high tables. Cathy pulled her toward one where the people were leaving and plopped down with a laugh. It was nearly impossible to have a normal conversation with the dance music blasting.

Leaning close, Cathy asked, "What kind of guy are you looking for?"

She was feeling woozy when she put her mouth near Cathy's ear. "No macho jock types and no one who says *dude* or *brah*. Other than that, I don't give a shit."

Cathy grinned and nodded, then scanned the room while Charlotte clung to her arm. She pointed at a couple of guys standing near the wall. "What about one of them?"

They were dressed nicely, hair in artful disarray, and had genuine looking smiles. "They seem nice," she said just before one leaned over and kissed the other on the cheek near his ear. "Whoops!"

That made Cathy dissolve into a fit of giggles, putting her arm around Charlotte to say, "Sometimes it's still worth a try. I had a great one night stand with a couple of bi guys once."

"What's it like?" she asked, forgetting for a moment Cathy didn't know her secret. Cathy must have assumed she meant being with two guys at once.

"Well, at first we just kissed and played around, getting each other naked a little at a time. Then we both gave one guy head for a while. I'd done that with another girl before, but I have to admit guys know how to suck a dick."

"How did you *both* do it? Take turns or something?"

"Yeah, and kissing each other around it, lots of tongue and spit. The guy was getting off watching us more than anything. Guys are really visual."

"Then what happened?"

"Well, we switched up before he came and I got on my knees. One guy got in front and the other guy in back."

"How could you concentrate on two things at once?"

"I didn't. I just focused on the guy in front and let the guy in back take care of his end." She laughed and squeezed Charlotte's shoulders. "The whole night was about give and take, and we all left satisfied."

"You're so lucky," Charlotte said with a sigh.

"Not really." There was a sadness in Cathy's voice, even with the loud music pounding. "Don't get me wrong, I have fun, but when I see Julie's life now…"

Charlotte looked at her face then and saw an echo of her own longing there. "You get lonely, don't you?"

"When the party is hoppin' it's all fun and games, but most of the people I hook up with are just poor screw-ups like me."

"There you are!" Polly shouted as she scooted into the booth. "Here's your tequila shots." She put down four shots and a little plate of salt and lime slices.

Julie scooted in on the other side sipping her coke and lime. Winking at Charlotte, she said, "What'd we miss?"

"We've been scanning the place for suitable candidates for Charlotte to take home tonight," Cathy said. When both Polly and Julie frowned, Cathy asked, "What?"

Bending over to pick up a shot glass, Charlotte licked her hand, pressed it in the rock salt, then picked up a lime. "Here's to you and here's to me, and if we ever disagree, then fuck you and here's to me," she said to the girls, then licked the salt, downed the shot, and bit the lime.

"Are you sure?" Polly asked in Charlotte's ear.

"I called Christopher today," she said quietly. "He hates me. I don't care anymore, I just want this over with." The lip-quiver stilled when she picked up her second shot. Once more the salt, tequila, and lime brought her closer to the oblivion she sought. "Let's dance!"

The night got hazy after that as Charlotte was driven by a manic impulse. Her normal careful and shy demeanor was blasted away by a mix of rage and alcohol while her friends danced a fence around her to keep the wolves at bay.

The spinning lights and throbbing beat made her light headed, and the liberal application of tequila fed the fire inside her. She danced, flirted, and even kissed through the bars of the protective cage her friends wove around her. And by the end of the night, after a good cry alone in a bathroom stall, they guided her out the door to Polly's car.

Drowsing in the back seat on Cathy's shoulder, she hummed along with the songs on the radio. Her friends were all chatting about the night, recalling desperate men with amusement, and telling catty stories of other women dressed in outrageous clothes or wearing ugly shoes.

"Thank you," she whispered at last.

Cathy brushed her hair out of her face and said, "What for?"

"Keeping me from being stupid tonight."

"That's what friends are for. You rest, we'll get you to bed."

Chapter 8: Christopher

Christopher stayed until Julie came home, but the night lost its spark after the topic of Charlotte came up. Julie seemed surprised to see him there, but hugged him just the same as always. He and Kurt left together, but headed different directions after promising to get together over the weekend if they could.

Christopher found two texts from Ashley on his phone before he got home. The first was an invitation to dinner, which he'd clearly missed, and the second one suggested he could stop by if it wasn't too late.

Standing outside her door, Christopher knocked quietly in case she was already asleep. He heard the chain just before she opened the door to stand naked in the doorway. "Hi," she said as she leaned against the jam.

Heart fluttering in his chest, he said, "Wow."

The comment made her grin as she stepped back inside to let him in. "I love having that effect on you."

"My effect is going to love having you."

She locked the door again and took his hand to lead him upstairs to her loft bedroom. "Thanks for coming by."

Her ass wiggled in his face, so he leaned forward to kiss one cheek. "My pleasure."

Upstairs she undressed him with kisses, then pulled him into bed. "What are you in the mood for?"

"How about something soft and slow?" he asked. She grinned and nodded, pulling him down on top of her.

Her mouth tasted like mint, her skin smelled like watermelon, but it was her slick heat he needed to satisfy his craving. He pushed her thighs up to open her and buried his face in her creamy center. She kept herself trimmed, but he still had to lick through a few hairs to open her thin lips inside.

Ashley responded by arching her back and running her fingers through his hair. "Right there, oh my God, you are so fucking good with your tongue," she murmured.

Bringing her to the edge, he stopped to kiss along her thighs so she would cool down for a moment. "Yummy," he whispered as he nibbled along the creases of her legs. "I don't think I'm gonna let you cum for a while."

"No," she whined as she tried to force his lips back to her center. "Mama wants to cum now."

"Nope," he said as he trailed his fingertips down her leg. Sitting for a moment he took her foot in his hands and began to work up her arch. She purred like a cat and stretched out so he could do her whole leg.

"There's lotion over there," she said and flung her hand towards the night stand.

Getting a handful, he warmed it in his palms before running them along one leg, then the other. While he was working in the lotion, she tried to reach her own hand down between her legs. When he slapped it, she jerked it back with a hiss. "No cheating," he warned.

Working his way back to her thighs, he spread her wide and laid back down to breathe along her mons and stomach.

"If you don't make me cum soon, I'm going to kill you." Her face was playful, but her tone was serious.

By the time his tongue returned, she was leaking a puddle on the sheets. He lapped it up, then brought his hand up to penetrate her with two fingers.

"Are you ready?" he asked as he curled them to press against her sensitive spot deep inside.

"Oh, yes," she gasped.

His lips circled her large nub as he carefully sucked it into his mouth. She froze then, holding her breath and not moving at all. Sucking it deeper inside, he began to circle her nub with the tip of his tongue, barely touching it at all. At first she bore down hard against his face, then she made a wet gasp as her muscles began to pulse against his fingers.

Ashley was silent for a long moment as he kept his tongue circling and fingers flexing inside. Then she grabbed his hair and groaned out a long, low sound until the pulses slowed and finally stopped.

"I'm going to fuck you so good for that," she whispered as her legs twitched.

Christopher chuckled as he crawled up next to her to lie on his back.

She rolled over to put her hand on his stomach, tracing her fingers through the fine hairs around his navel. "I want to be on top, okay?"

"Sure," he said as his hard cock twitched. Running her fingers down his shaft, Ashley cupped his balls and rolled them around her palm. "That feels good."

"Are you ready?" When he nodded, she slipped one leg over and slid her warmth down his shaft, then up again. Tilting her hips to catch his head, she moved back to slowly slide him inside.

Christopher shut his eyes and enjoyed the rotating motion of her hips. There was no pressing need to hold himself back, but the pleasure was so intense and relaxing that he didn't want it to end too soon either.

Ashley began to hold her breath and make little sounds as she pressed her hands against his chest. She came quietly, but didn't stop that perfect pace she'd found. He flexed and moved with her, allowing her to lead their dance.

Late Wednesday night when he couldn't sleep, he used his last Tenga cup to edge for a long time, imagining Charlotte riding him slowly like Ashley was. In his mind, he could see her dark hair hanging down nearly to his chest, her soft Cajun accent describing her pleasure. Her breasts swaying slowly, casting shadows on his chest. First bringing herself pleasure, then finally bringing his.

"Oh, Charlotte," he whispered as he slipped over the edge. Ashley's chuckle was perfectly timed with his orgasm to make him squirm in more ways than one. He felt embarrassed beyond words and dragged a pillow over to hide his face.

"Charlotte?" Ashley asked with an amused tone. "What the hell?"

"Sorry," he whispered. The post-orgasmic glow was gone in an instant as his rage returned in a rush. "God damn it!" Ashley slid off to one side and let him get up to stalk around the room. "I'm so sorry. That was a jackass thing to do."

When he began picking up his clothes, Ashley stood up and touched his arm. "It's okay," she said gently. "It happened, it's over, it's no big deal."

"It *is* a big deal," he said, tears of frustration spilling over. "I can't stop thinking about her. It's driving me fucking mad! I swear I think there's something wrong with me!"

"Maybe you're in love with her?" Ashley suggested quietly.

"I do not love that cruel, selfish bitch! Fuck, I need a drink."

"If I get you a drink, will you calm down?" Ashley had kept touching him and taking his clothes back out of his hands until he finally gave up to sit on the edge of the bed.

Bending over, he put his face in his hands. "What the hell do I do, Ash?"

"Go see her. Work it out somehow or at least get closure. That's the only way."

He let out a manic laugh and said, "She called me today asking if we could have dinner. She said she made a mistake!"

"Maybe she did," Ashley said as she sat down beside him. "You'll never know unless you talk to her."

"I don't know if I want to." He fell back on the sheets. "She hurt me."

"I know," Ashley said as she examined her fingertips.

After a few moments, he uttered a long ragged sigh. "Tonight I was hanging out with Kurt over at his Uncle Jack's house. When I got excited talking about why I got into social work, Kurt said it reminded him of how excited she got about nursing."

"Wait," Ashley said as she turned to face him. "You were hanging out with the brother and uncle of the girl you never want to see again?"

"Well, sure, it sounds weird when you put it that way..." he trailed off. "Kurt's a great guy. It's not his fault his sister is a basket case. And I've liked Jack and Julie ever since I went over to their place for New Years."

Shaking her head and laughing, she asked, "Have you talked about things with Kurt?"

Christopher shook his head. "We've both been stepping around the topic. It's just too weird talking about it with him."

"But he brought up that you sounded like her when you got excited, didn't he?"

"Fine, maybe I'm the only one stepping around the topic. I just wish she would have told me why."

"She offered to explain it."

"Why are you so interested?" he asked, suddenly angry again.

She wouldn't look him in the eye. "Being your friend is all I want from you, you know that. And as your friend I can tell she is different from the other girls you've dated." She looked up looking a little embarrassed. "I just want you to be happy again, like you were after Christmas."

"I was happy before Christmas, too."

"Sometimes, yeah, but you've had a hard few years after you got back from overseas. I mean, I don't think you're some kinda head case or anything, but I know it was tough for you."

Christopher nodded and looked away. She was right. He hadn't been wounded or anything, but the sense of helplessness over there in the face of so much poverty, screwy politics, and open hostility had changed him. And when he came back, everything felt so different.

"You asked me when we first met why a big strapping Marine like me decided to get into social work."

"Yeah, and you gave me some half-assed answer if I remember correctly. But I eventually figured it out for myself. You hate feeling helpless. You hate being out of control. You couldn't save all those kids over there, but you could teach them soccer. And that ended up making a bigger difference than all the missions they sent you on."

He looked up with tears in his eyes. "I never told you all that."

"Yes you did," she said and scooted closer on the bed. "A piece here and a piece there, and I put them together like a legal brief over the last couple of years. I bet her brother's right. I bet she's just like you that way."

"She is," he nodded with a sad smile.

"So, go find out what she wants to say. You're miserable already, so there's nowhere to go from here but up."

Chapter 9: Charlotte

When she awoke the next afternoon, Charlotte couldn't recall getting home. There was a hazy memory of her lying down on her bed, surrounded by her friends as they dressed her in the long t-shirt she was wearing, but it had the quality of a dream.

Sitting up as her head pounded with each heartbeat, she smacked her lips in an effort to get her saliva working again. After toddling to the bathroom to empty her painfully full bladder, she padded into the kitchen for a drink of water.

"You survived," Polly noted with amusement as she passed the living room couch.

"Barely," she croaked as she got out a large glass and filled it with ice and water. "How bad did I embarrass myself?"

"Not too bad, actually," she said as she came into the kitchen. "But I never knew you could dance so well."

"I'm not sure I did either." Her body drank up the water like a dry sponge, so she got herself another full glass. A disturbing memory flashed in her mind and she decided she had to know the truth. "Did I kiss someone with a moustache?"

Polly chuckled as she leaned against the counter. "That would have been the aptly named Randy. He was harder to get rid of than most."

Shivering from disgust, she ran her hands through her tangled brown locks. "Never again," she said.

"I've said that at least three times in my life and it hasn't stuck yet." After watching her with a sad expression for a moment, Polly said, "Everyone needs to go crazy once in a while."

"Thanks for keeping me out of trouble."

"So what happened yesterday?" Polly asked with a genuine expression of concern.

Taking a deep breath, Charlotte described being confronted in the gym and being rejected by Christopher on the phone. As she made breakfast for Charlotte, Polly listened without interrupting, then nodded at the end.

"Kurt mentioned Christopher hung out over at Jack and Julie's last night until Julie got home," Polly said without much hope in her tone. "He said Christopher wasn't very open to the idea of seeing you again."

"I know it's over. I've given up hope he'll ever forgive me, let alone understand. Besides, it's not like we were exclusive or anything. He probably has a dozen other girls chasing him around." The thought made her stomach churn and twist.

"I'm sorry. I hate seeing you so torn up." Polly's concern made Charlotte smile.

"I'll be fine. After breakfast and a nap, I'm gonna eat ice cream out of the carton and watch old movies all day."

"Kurt and I are going to the beach for the weekend, so you've got the place to yourself."

"Isn't it a little chilly to get in the water?"

"Hell, we'll be lucky if we make it out of the hotel room," Polly said with a laugh as she walked away. "I'm gonna go pack. Why don't you take a shower?"

"Are you trying to say I stink?" Charlotte asked, but Polly's ringing laughter was all she got in reply.

* * *

After a hot shower, Charlotte put on her soft terrycloth robe and planted herself in front of the television on the couch. The classic movie channel was playing old love stories, so Charlotte drowsed away the afternoon, waking when the loud commercial breaks blared.

It was very late when she heard a quiet tap at the door. Pulling the robe tight around her naked body, she stood on tip toes to look out the peep hole in the door.

It was Christopher.

Her first reaction was shock, but she refused to allow herself to hope. Leaving the chain on, she opened the door a crack.

"What do you want?"

Christopher was staring at his shoes and shaking his head. "Can we talk?"

"I already tried that. Didn't work out so well for me." The bitterness turned to anger as she recalled the phone call the day before.

"I was angry. I'm sorry."

"Well, now I'm angry," she said and shut the door. Leaning her forehead against the cold steel frame, she listened for him to walk away.

"This is killing me," he whispered through the door. "I have to talk to you."

There was no way he could have known she was close enough to hear. It was almost like he was talking to himself. She unchained the door and opened it wide to find him still standing there, looking surprised. "Fine. You have five minutes."

Christopher came in and Charlotte locked the door again behind him. Glancing at the clock significantly, she glared at him until he spoke.

"I don't understand why you ended things after Mardi Gras, but I can't stop thinking about you. If you don't want to be with me, fine, I'll find a way to live with that. I miss you though, and I'd like to still be your friend."

He looked so worn. His face was thinner as well. There were dark circles under his eyes like he hadn't slept, and he still he wouldn't look her in the eyes. "That's not what you said last night at Uncle Jack's."

He looked up in her face for the first time, blushing a bright red. "I was still angry then."

"So what happened between then and now?"

"I was hanging out with my friend Ashley last night and she helped me find a little perspective."

"Ashley?" Charlotte asked as an electric spark shot up her back. "You left Uncle Jack's at two in the morning and stopped by to see *Ashley*?"

Now he frowned hard and growled, "You don't want me, so why the fuck do you even care?"

"I don't know, did you fuck her before you found your new *perspective*?" she asked, her own temper rising to match his.

"As a matter of fact, I did," he shouted. "And when I called her Charlotte at the end, things got a little weird. Is that what you wanted to hear? Are you happy now?"

"No," she cried. "No, I'm not fucking happy! I haven't been happy in weeks. Get out! Get out, just leave me alone!"

The pain inside felt like broken bits of glass and every breath seemed to cut her deeper. Christopher stood still for a moment, then grabbed her robe to pull her close, kissing her roughly while holding her hair.

In seconds, she felt a raw, sexual surge in her guts that took her breath away and left her panting for him. Her arms were around his neck, pulling him closer while he ate her lips, her cheek, her neck.

"I want you so bad it's killing me," he whispered in her ear. "I just want to be with you, only you, why can't you understand?"

"Then take me," she said. The words left her lips as she finally gave up her fight. *I need to get this over with.* Leading him to her room terrified her, but the panic was nothing compared to her desire to rid herself of her curse.

As nervous as she was, her hands trembled as she walked to her nightstand and pulled out the condoms and lube. When she turned to Christopher, he had a confused frown on his face, so she tore one of the packets open and handed it to him.

"Use these," she commanded.

He stared at the items for a moment, then put them on the messy bed. "Charlotte…"

He probably doesn't think I'm serious. Steeling herself for his judgment, she opened the robe she was wearing and allowed it to fall off her shoulders. When she laid her robe across the foot of her messy bed, he smiled and touched her shoulder.

"You're beautiful," he whispered and stepped in to kiss her. There was a twisting in her stomach, but she couldn't decide if it was from desire or embarrassment. She tugged at his belt to encourage him to to hurry up before she lost her nerve.

He stripped quickly, smiling at her as she sat back on the bed. As she laid back against the pillows, she resisted the urge to cover her breasts with her arms. His body was lean, with broad muscular shoulders.

He picked up the condom and rolled it on his erect shaft with a practiced hand while she watched, then smeared it with the lube. His hard cock was a little larger than Peter's had been, but his balls were heavy and swung freely. She was fascinated for a moment until he joined her on the bed, settling between her legs to kiss her again.

Riding the panic down, she forced herself to relax. Running her fingers along his back, she returned his kisses with a growing passion. When he began to rub his shaft against her mons she gasped, but it must not have sounded like passion because he raised back to look at her face with concern in his eyes. She tried to smile but wasn't sure it looked genuine.

"I've wanted you for so long," he whispered. He looked like he was going to say something else, but she was already losing her nerve.

"I need you inside me," she whispered. It was the truest thing she could say, but she had to clench her teeth to keep her chin from quivering afterward.

Using his hand, he guided himself inside her, filling her wider and deeper than her little vibrator had. There was some small discomfort as he slipped inside, just a feeling of fullness. *We're doing it! Oh God, I feel like I need to pee.*

Kissing her more with more insistence, he began to move his shaft in and out slowly. Trying to match his motions was impossible and she kept throwing him off. The battle between her fear and willpower kept her from doing more in the end than offering resistance against his thrusts.

Watching her between kisses, Christopher raised up on his elbows to see her face. Trying to smile, she was worried she wasn't doing it right because he seemed to expect something of her. Not knowing what else to do and bothered by the awkward silence, she finally said, "You feel good."

"You feel amazing," he whispered. "Tell me what you like."

"Okay," she whispered. Feeling him inside her body was so strange. *He must be somewhere behind my stomach*, she thought. The human sexuality and anatomy textbooks hadn't described what it would feel like to be full of him or what she should do during sex. After trying to adjust her hips and legs, the only thing that changed was the intensity of her need to pee. Feeling bolder at last she asked, "Can we try it a different way?"

"Sure, what do you like?" he asked, smiling at her with enthusiasm for the first time.

"I don't know," she admitted, but she forced herself to say what she'd been wanting to do all week. "Can I try being on top?"

"Yeah," he said, holding onto the condom when he pulled out. He rolled over to lay next to her on the bed. She straddled his stomach and then reached down between them to lift his shaft.

"Can you help me a little?" she asked feeling embarrassed. He adjusted his hips and lifted his knees, then reached down between the two of them to help slide himself in.

"Is that better?" he asked. She pushed back with a low sigh, making him strain. "Oh God, I've fantasized about being with you like this."

"Okay, wow." Now that she controlled the depth, angle, and pace, she began to get the familiar tingles that told her this position might work better for her. He held her hips at first, helping her establish a kind of undulating motion before reaching up to play with her breasts.

From the way he looked at her, she could tell he liked her body. Cupping her breasts, he rolled his thumbs over her nipples with a hungry expression on his face. She leaned forward to try a different angle and he took her sensitive nipples between his lips to suckle gently one at a time. The feeling added to her tingling, making her movements faster and more assured.

Just when the tingles finally became a warm pleasure, she felt Christopher stiffen suddenly. He tried to stop her hips and hold her still, but Charlotte was too fascinated by the expression on his face. His eyes were shut and his mouth was open. There was sweat beaded along his wrinkled brow when he let out a low groan. Inside her, she could feel him pulsing fast, then slower, but she didn't stop moving until he collapsed against the bed.

"Oh, damn," he whispered. "Sorry, I couldn't hold it back any more."

Her pent up orgasm was still there, but she felt a deep sense of satisfaction regardless.

"It's fine," she whispered as she kissed him lightly on his lips. "I'm happy."

Having sex felt so interesting, but despite how new it was, she'd figured out how to get him off her first time. It had taken forever before Peter had finally shot off in her hands and mouth. That had felt like an accomplishment, but Christopher's relaxed smile made her feel a thousand times better.

Reaching down to hold the condom, she climbed off to lay down next to him while her mind raced in a thousand different directions. He seemed content to snuggle, so she took the time to examine his body with slow caresses. He was heavily muscled in his chest and shoulders, but his legs were thicker than she'd assumed. His stomach was flat and he had less hair than most men she'd seen shirtless.

The tattoo on his upper arm was some kind of military design, but it felt no different than the skin anywhere else. As she touched him gently, he sighed at her attention.

His shaft had shrunk and was wet from their emissions with some leaking out of the condom into the short hairs around the base. Charlotte pulled off the condom and got up to throw it away, then cleaned him off with a tissue.

He cracked an eye open to see what she was doing. "Hey."

"Hey." She grabbed the robe that was laying across the foot of the bed and put it over her shoulders to cover her body.

Now that the moment had passed, she felt a growing sense of unease. It was killing her that he'd been with Ashley the night before. She didn't understand the rules for hooking up or dating or whatever they were doing now, but didn't want to make a mistake by showing her true ignorance. "Are you working tomorrow?" she asked standing beside the bed.

"Uh..." He looked confused and a little hurt as he sat up. "Yeah. I'm covering the seven to three shift for a co-worker."

"I've got to leave around noon to get back to Lafayette. There's a paper I need to finish before class on Monday."

"Can I call you?" he asked with a worried expression as she picked up his clothes from the floor.

"I'd like that." *Please call me.*

"Are you coming in to Houston next week?"

She nodded and tied her robe more tightly.

"Look, Charlotte, I..."

Something foolish was coming, so she put her fingers on his lips to stop it. "I'll see you next week. Call me this week and we'll plan to do something."

He dressed in silence, glancing at her as if trying to read her expression. She wished him luck, because she had no idea what she felt at that moment. Her thoughts were a wreckage, her heart a jumble. But there was a glimmer of hope for all that, even if it was just the oxytocin her body made during sex.

After he was dressed, she walked him to the door. "Thanks for coming by."

He chuckled to himself and shook his head as he looked her in the eyes. "Thanks for letting me in."

She stood on her tip toes and kissed him gently. "Be careful not to break anything, okay?" She hoped the significant look that followed got the message across.

The half-smile on his face seemed to say he understood as he nodded. "I'll talk to you tomorrow night."

She watched him walk away, glancing twice to smile at her before he disappeared from view. Then she closed and locked the door, went to lay in bed, and stared at the ceiling.

It wasn't such a big deal after all, she thought to herself. It wasn't the mindblowing experience she wanted or the painful ordeal she feared. He had been gentle with her, but she had been so focused on the act itself it felt like she had missed out on other, more intimate things.

What are we now? she wondered. *What am I now?*

It was a long time before she fell asleep.

Chapter 10: Christopher

Making his way inside in the hospital, Christopher couldn't get his mind off the odd evening he'd spent with Charlotte the night before. Just when he thought he'd blown it completely, she suddenly kissed him back and dragged him into her bed. The biggest regret of the night was his less than stellar performance in the sack. After being thrown off balance by her sudden reversal, having her fulfill his fantasy of riding on top had made him cum after a few short minutes.

She quickly shifted from this worldly woman who was naked under her robe and kept condoms in her night stand, to an innocent girl who hardly seemed to know what to do in bed. Despite a long, early run in the morning to clear his head, he was no closer to figuring out the mystery. But by the time he got on the elevator at work and pressed the button for his floor, he realized he didn't care. He liked mysteries and Charlotte had become a wonderful, sexy puzzle.

Her body was as gorgeous as in his dreams. She had tan skin and dark hair, with eyes so brown they were almost black. The soft curves of her breasts and hips were made to be touched, and her perfect brown nipples were made for his lips. She had the softest bush he'd ever felt and he couldn't wait to bury his face in it when he got the chance. Despite wanting to stay and redeem his initial disappointing finish, she'd cooled down so fast he was afraid she'd changed her mind again.

Then at the door she'd kissed him one last time and hinted that he was welcome back in her heart. *Please be careful not to break anything*, she'd said with that innocence he could never resist. As he took a deep breath and got off the elevator, he realized was already looking forward to their planned evening phone call.

"You've got a spring in your step today," Deborah said as he joined her in the nurses station for his morning patient review. Doctor Rebecca Jenks, one of the pediatric surgeons with patients on the floor, was writing in a chart so he toned down his normal jackass reply.

"I worked out something that's been bugging me," he said with a wink.

"What's her name?" Deborah asked with a smirk. She was older and married, but it didn't stop her from teasing him about the single nurses and volunteers who bugged her for information about him.

After hesitating a second he said, "Charlotte Guidry."

"A Cajun girl? Why didn't you tell me you liked 'em spicy?" Deborah laughed.

"I didn't know I did," he muttered, feeling his face heat as he sat down to review the charts. After scanning through the names, he looked around on the counter. "Do you have Noah's chart?"

"I've got it," Doctor Jenks said. "Are you the Christopher I've heard so much about from Noah?"

"Guilty as charged. You must be Noah's doctor."

"That's me. I've been impressed with your insight and comments in his chart."

"Thanks. Was he released on Saturday as planned?"

"Yup, we finally got him out, but I got a call at home last night. He was complaining about feeling shocks from his pacemaker. That's why I'm here at this ungodly hour on a Sunday." Doctor Jenks took off her reading glasses and looked his direction. "I'm pretty sure he's faking it, though. He was irritated when you didn't come by to meet his Mom on Saturday, and someone mentioned in front of him that you were picking up an extra shift today."

"I told him goodbye when I stayed late on Friday night," Christopher said with a shrug. The boy had really grown on him over the last couple of weeks, but it hadn't stopped Christopher from calling bullshit on the excuses he fed to his nurses and physical therapists. He'd noted the attempts to motivate Noah and improve his stamina in the chart.

"Look, I know it's unorthodox to ask you this and you're under no professional obligation, but I hoped you might be willing to continue helping Noah outside of the hospital."

Deborah was behind Doctor Jenks and gave Christopher a wide-eyed look of surprise. He knew the boy still needed some external motivation to take care of himself, but the chance to score points with an influential surgeon was too good to pass up. "What are you thinking?"

"Well, he's too bright for his own good, charming as hell, and can lie like a rug. But I don't need to tell you he's been fighting depression and has trouble making friends with kids his age. What he needs is exercise and emotional support, but that requires someone he looks up to pushing him to do it."

"And I guess I fit that description?" he asked with a grin.

"Judging from the way you played him last week to actually *do* his physical therapy for a change, yeah, I think you'll do fine."

"Let me think about it." It was an interesting offer, but this wasn't going to be a paying gig. Doctor Jenks was still giving him a probing look when they were interrupted.

"There he is, Mom, I told you he'd be here," Noah's excited voice called from the hallway near the elevators. "Hey, Christopher!"

Christopher turned and saw Noah tugging at the hand of an attractive Hispanic woman. She appeared to be in her early thirties, but could have been younger and simply exhausted from worrying all night about her son. She gave Noah a tired smile, then extended her free hand to Christopher.

"Nice to meet you at last," she said with a soft Spanish accent. "I'm Emily Vasquez."

"Christopher Dunlop," he said, then gave Noah a piercing look. "So, about those *shocks* you were having last night." The tone he used conveyed his skepticism.

"It's true, I swear! Every time I fell asleep, it would shock me awake." The wounded expression at being questioned appeared genuine, but Christopher held his gaze steady. Noah's eyes shifted at last, glancing to Doctor Jenks, then to his Mom before dropping to his shoes.

Christopher went on one knee to get down to Noah's level. "How about I give your mom my cell phone number so you can give me a call next time instead of scaring her to death?"

"Noah!" Emily narrowed her eyes at her son. "You were lying?" When he nodded his head slowly, she sighed and looked up to mutter something like a prayer in Spanish at the ceiling. Turning to the staff she said, "I am so sorry about this."

"Let me give him a check up while we're all here just in case," Doctor Jenks said as she reached to take Noah's hand.

When Noah followed the doctor, he glanced back and whispered, "Sorry, Mom."

After they were out of sight, Emily was still steaming over what he'd done. "I swear that boy is going to kill me from worry."

"He's a handful all right," Christopher said, noting Deborah nodding in agreement behind Emily's back.

"Listen, Christopher, I'd like to thank you for all you've done for Noah. Coming in every evening to hear you'd spent time with him and helped him with his reading…" She pinched her lips and took a deep breath. "I haven't been able to be here for him because of my job and taking care of Mama. You have no idea what it means to me knowing you cared so much."

Christopher was uncomfortable with her praise, but was glad she wasn't resentful of his intrusion into their lives. "It's a team effort. I know Deborah here and the rest of the staff have done way more than I have. All I did was hand him a couple of used paperbacks and give him a hard time for slacking on his physical therapy."

"I know all about Nurse Debbie," Emily said with a smile and nod in her direction. "I hear your name almost as much as Christopher's. I think he has a crush on you."

Debbie grinned and said, "He's a sweetheart."

"I appreciate you saying that," Emily said, gripping her purse tight in her hands.

"Hey, Doctor Jenks asked me to do her a favor. She's worried about keeping Noah motivated without someone pushing him to stay active. I don't know how you'd feel about it, but I'd be happy to make some time in the afternoons or weekends if you think it would help for me to work with him."

It was like he'd offered her a million dollars. She gasped, then tears formed in her eyes as she covered her mouth. "Oh my God, you'd do that?"

"Sure," he said with a chuckle at her reaction. "This isn't just my job. I actually like helping people." He grabbed a pad and wrote down his email and phone number, then handed it to her. "I get off at three most days I work, but I pull doubles or pick up extra shifts like this one sometimes. Do you guys have a neighborhood park or soccer field nearby?"

"I don't think so. We live in an apartment complex on the west side near the assisted living center my Mom is in. There's a field at his school, but he's missed so much I'm probably going to have to hire a tutor. He's been wanting to play baseball, but I'm scared the ball will hit him in the chest."

"Ask Doctor Jenks about it when they come back. I don't know how much time I'll have, but we can probably work something out."

When Noah came back out with the doctor, he was still looking guilty and unsure of his reception. Doctor Jenks said, "Noah, why don't you go sit over there for a bit while your Mom and I have a talk."

"Can I play on your phone?" he asked his mother with a hopeful grin.

"After you lied to me? I don't think so, young man," Emily said and pointed to the chair she intended him to sit in.

While he shuffled over to sit by himself, Doctor Jenks motioned for Emily and Christopher to follow her far enough away he wouldn't overhear. "He's fine," she said. "The pacemaker is working perfectly and the leads were still in place. What he needs at this point is regular exercise and emotional support."

"I offered to help with that," Christopher said to Doctor Jenks, with a nod in Emily's direction.

That made Doctor Jenks smile warmly and wink at him. "Good. He's cleared for any kind of physical activity at this point, so don't let him tell you otherwise."

"He wants to play baseball, but I'm afraid of the ball hitting his chest," Emily said.

Doctor Jenks gave her a reassuring smile. "When we replaced his old leads and pacemaker this time, it was all done through a small incision near his shoulder. I just checked the wound and he's healing fine. Getting hit might bruise him, but it won't affect his condition."

"How about we start with some batting practice then?" Christopher suggested. "There is a place down I-10 with batting cages and a putt-putt golf course if you're free this afternoon."

"I don't have much money right now," Emily said with an embarrassed frown.

Doctor Jenks took her hands and said, "Don't worry about that. There is a discretionary fund for things like this and I'm sure there is more than enough to cover an afternoon of fun if it gets him out and active."

Christopher had pulled the place up on his phone. "What's your number? I'll text you the address."

* * *

Later that afternoon while Christopher drove out to the batting cages, he was reminded of the feeling he'd had going to coach the village kids in Afghanistan. Making a difference to someone who needed help was addictive in a way. He didn't care if anyone knew. That wasn't the point at all. He felt blessed with good health and a strong family to support him, so sharing his time had always brought him a sense of peace like nothing else in life.

Pulling into the parking lot, he saw Noah and Emily were already waiting. The car they were leaning against was an old, rusty sedan that had red tape over a broken tail light. The joy on their faces when they saw him get out of his truck made it impossible not to smile back.

"Hey," he said as he approached. "You ready to practice that swing?"

"I'm gonna hit fifty home runs!" His enthusiasm was infectious as Emily roughed his hair.

"You just do your best," she said as Christopher joined them.

Doctor Jenks had invited him for coffee after Emily and Noah had gone. She had explained that the discretionary fund was actually a trust left by her late grandmother to help people in need. It had already helped pay for the treatment of a number of her patients when insurance wasn't adequate or available. Sliding him five $20 dollar bills, she asked him to give her the receipts later with a report on how things went.

"Let's see what size bat you're gonna need."

They walked over to the booth where a teenaged employee was reading a textbook behind the counter. "Can I help y'all?" he asked as he pushed the book to the side.

"Noah here wants to try out the batting cages for a bit."

They got him fitted out with a helmet and a wooden youth bat, then the employee loaded up a large bucket of yellow rubber balls in the hopper and set the pitching speed to its lowest setting.

Trying to show Noah how to hold the bat and swing was a trial. He already knew everything, according to himself, but then he missed five balls in a row. When he looked around for help with a frustrated expression, Christopher waited until he asked politely before helping him position the bat and hit his first grounder. Leaving Noah swinging at the balls, Christopher stepped back outside with Emily to watch.

"Thanks," she murmured as she watched her son with a frightened expression.

"He's doing fine. Don't worry," Christopher whispered.

Just then Noah hit his first ball. "Holy shit! Did you see that?" he exclaimed.

"Watch your language," Emily said with narrowed eyes.

"Good swing! Keep the bat level when you hit and don't rest it on your shoulder between balls."

"We can't stay too long. I need to cook something for dinner."

"Let me take you guys out. How about that drive-in place across the street?"

"You've done enough for us."

He noted her clenching jaw when she spoke. "You gotta eat, I gotta eat, and Doctor Jenks is picking up the tab."

She thought about it and shook her head. "I hate taking charity."

"It ain't charity, it's dinner." The laugh that followed obviously irritated her because she glared up at him.

"You're not going to give up, are you?"

"Think of it as an extra therapy session for Noah. It's just business."

When the last ball bounced back down the slope to the pitching machine, Noah had worked up a good sweat and was wincing as he rotated his left shoulder.

"Sore?" Christopher asked as he took the bat and helmet from the boy.

"Yeah," he admitted. "The scar pulls when I move it, but it's okay."

"Would a hot dog and cherry slushy fix you up?" Emily asked with a smile.

"Two hot dogs?" he bargained with an excited grin.

"I'll meet you over there," Christopher said as he returned the bat and helmet to the bored employee in the booth.

They ate dinner outside at a round concrete table with an umbrella to shade the hot afternoon sun. Noah was excited to get back to see his friends at school, but dismissed his mother's worry about being so far behind in his work. He stated plainly that he was already a better reader and speller than anyone in his class. His comment didn't sound like a brag, just a statement of fact, so as far as he was concerned, they were just catching up to him.

Listening to Emily describe all the things coming up in her week made him appreciate how hard she worked. Between a full time job, a mother with Parkinson's Disease who needed care in an expensive assisted living facility, a precocious son who got into trouble all the time, Christopher wasn't sure he could do half as well as she was doing.

"It sounds exhausting," he said at last. "So what do you do for yourself?"

She laughed. "I'm a working single mother! There's no time left for me. And speaking of no time, are you finished with your food, son-of-mine?"

"Yup," he answered as he crammed the last few fries in his mouth.

"Thanks again for everything," she said to Christopher as he stood with them.

"Let me check my schedule for next week and I'll brainstorm about what we can do to keep Noah off the couch."

"I'll do the same," she said as she threw away the trash and took Noah by the hand. "Say goodbye, Noah."

"I had so much fun," Noah said. "I can't wait to tell Tommy I hit three in a row tomorrow!"

"I want a good report from your Mom or I'm gonna make you run laps instead of playing next time."

"Yes, sir," he said with an irrepressible grin. "Thanks, Christopher."

"You're both welcome, and I'll pass it on to Doctor Jenks as well."

* * *

Sitting on his couch with a cold beer, Christopher picked up his phone and scrolled to Charlotte's entry with a grin. It was late enough she should have gotten back to Lafayette and had some time to work on her paper. As he placed the call, he took a sip of beer.

"Hi," she answered with a happy tone in her voice. "How was work?"

"Unbelievable," he said, really wanting to share what happened with her. "Did I ever mention a kid named Noah on my floor?"

"I don't think so," she answered, sounding interested.

"He's seven years old and was in for a pacemaker upgrade. He was born with a congenital heart defect and has to get new pacemakers as he grows. Anyway, the kid is smart and bored, so I got him a couple of Harry Potter books while he was there."

"Isn't that a little advanced for seven?"

"Trust me, this kid has an IQ out the roof. He finished *Prisoner of Azkaban* in a week."

"Wow!" Charlotte shifted around noisily.

"His Mom, Emily, was never around when I was there, but not for the reasons you might think. She's early-thirties maybe, and a widow. Her husband was a Marine and died overseas four years ago. So after Noah got out on Saturday, he complained that his pacemaker was shocking him all Saturday night."

"Is he okay?" she asked.

"Yeah, the little rat faked it so he could come see me during my shift on Sunday."

Her amused chuckle warmed him up. "And let me guess... to introduce you to his mom?"

Christopher smiled and decided to just lay it out there. "Yeah, probably, but I'm seeing someone now. Anyway, his surgeon, Doctor Rebecca Jenks, has been reading my reports on his—"

"Wait, seeing who?" she asked, sounding startled.

"You, of course. So Doctor Jenks has been reading my reports and asked me if I would be willing to work with him outside of the hospital. He's been having a hard time with the move to Houston and making new friends, but he needs to stay active to help his condition."

"I see," she said with an amused tone.

"It was so great, Charlotte. We took him to some batting cages down I-10 this afternoon and he absolutely rocked it."

"That sounds like fun. What did his mother think about all that?"

"She loved the help, but I feel for her. Her mom has Parkinson's and lives in an assisted living center now that her father is gone. Between working full time and taking care of both her kid and mom, she's getting pretty worn out." He paused for a moment to think then said, "Can I ask you a huge favor?"

"Sure," she replied with a hesitant pause.

"Would you ask your Aunt Julie and Polly if they would include her on your next girls night out? I'll sit with Noah for her if you guys can take her out to blow off a little steam. She's only been in Houston a few months and doesn't have many friends yet."

"Of course," Charlotte responded immediately. "It's so sweet of you to think of doing that."

"Y'all may not hit it off, so don't feel obligated to invite her again unless you want to. This is strictly a one-off to see if it will help her a little."

"Hey, I have an idea! Noah's the same age as Jen, so why don't I ask Uncle Jack if you guys can go over there Friday night to watch a movie or something."

"That's perfect," he said. "Let me know after you talk to everyone so I can let Emily know."

Charlotte was silent for a moment. "We make a pretty good team."

"Yeah," he said and took another sip of beer, trying not to jinx the mood.

"So we're going out now?" she asked with a nervous laugh.

"I want to, but it's really up to you at this point." He didn't want to open the wounds between them by bringing up what they'd both said and done.

"I want to try." She sighed then and asked, "What about Ashley?"

His stomach twisted a little, but he kept to the truth. "Ashley is a friend I met in college. She wants to be a lawyer more than anything else, and doesn't want to get married or have kids. It would never work out between us because I definitely do. We get along okay and when I'm not dating anyone we hook up sometimes, but it's nothing serious at all."

"Are you still going to see her?" she whispered.

"No, not like that," he said, then chuckled. "Hell, she was the one who told me to go see you on Saturday."

"Why?" The surprise was clear in her voice.

"I was never with her again after New Years Eve and she saw how happy I was with you. Then when she saw how miserable I was after Mardi Gras she just wanted me to be happy again."

Charlotte was quiet for a long time. "I'm sorry I got so scared. Thank you for being patient with me and giving me another chance."

"I just want to get to know you better," He put the beer down and got up off the couch. "Can I call you again tomorrow?"

"I'd like that."

* * *

Every evening Christopher called Charlotte to share his day with her. He talked about the kids he worked with, the hospital staff, and answered her questions. She was curious about the differences between Lafayette General and Southwest Hospital, so he asked Deborah questions on her behalf. When it came out that she was coming on staff after she graduated in May, Deborah teased him mercilessly about all the heartbroken nurses and volunteers he would be leaving in his wake.

Charlotte shared details of her own days and seemed more relaxed each time they spoke. There were tales about her two roommates, Tiffany and Adele, that made him chuckle. Her classes seemed interesting and he offered to give her reports another set of eyes, allowing him to see how her mind worked through her words. So he spent afternoons red-lining her papers over a few beers and felt even closer to her as a result.

By Wednesday, Charlotte had arranged things with her friends and Uncle Jack, so after his daily call with her he gave Emily a ring.

"Hello?" she answered with a weary sigh.

"Hey Emily, this is Christopher. Ya' got a minute?"

"Christopher! Of course, what do you need?"

"I was wondering if you'd let me take Noah off your hands Friday afternoon and evening. Do you guys have any plans?"

"No, just the usual routine. What did you want to do?"

"Well, the girl I'm seeing, Charlotte Guidry, has an Uncle Jack on your side of town with three kids, including a girl Noah's age named Jen. I was talking with her and brainstorming for fun things to do when she suggested I take them all on a bounce house play date and movie night on Friday after Noah gets out of school."

"Oh, he would love that! He's been bugging me to call you, but I told him he can't unless he comes home from school with his behavior on green or better all week. It's been working so far! He's even doing his physical therapy exercises, if you can believe that."

Christopher chuckled at her strategy. "I'm glad to be of service. Hey, there was one more thing. Charlotte has a group of friends that do a girls' night out on Friday nights. She wanted to call and invite you to come out with them for dinner and drinks while I've got Noah."

"Oh, no, I couldn't intrude like that," she protested.

"Well, she's dying to meet you after hearing about you and Noah from me. Would you at least consider it? You don't have to decide right now. When you come to drop off Noah you can meet her Aunt Julie and get a feel for things."

"Let me think about it and I'll let you know."

When he got off the phone with Emily he immediately called Charlotte back. She answered with an excited, "How'd it go?"

"The outing with Noah was a slam dunk. She said she's going to think about the girls' night out, but once she meets your Aunt Julie, I think she'll go. I can't thank you enough."

"I'm just glad to help." She got quiet for a while. "Are you doing anything on Saturday?"

"Laundry at some point, but I'm not working this weekend. Did you have something in mind?"

"Kurt will be gone over the weekend, so Polly wanted to go hang out at the mall and maybe see a movie. When I mentioned we were… seeing each other, she suggested I invite you along. Wanna come?"

"I'd love to." He smiled to himself at the nervous way she asked. "I'm beat now. Lemme talk to you tomorrow."

"Me too. Sweet dreams."

"Good night."

Chapter 11: Charlotte

Charlotte put her cell phone back on its charging base next to her bed. Talking with Christopher every night helped so much, especially because he avoided discussing their potential relationship unless she brought it up, focusing instead on his work. Hearing about what he did at work made her feel connected to him in a deeper way and she had begun to anticipate their talks more every day.

She'd told no one about what had happened until Monday when Polly called to check on her. Her first question was to ask if they'd used protection, then she began asking more general questions like how she felt about what had happened. Eventually the whole story poured out, with Charlotte sharing more of the intimate details than she intended and asking Polly questions about the things that confused her.

After talking for over an hour, Charlotte felt more confident hearing her friend's perspective. One point of discussion was that Charlotte take advantage of the campus clinic's offer for inexpensive birth control. After researching the topic extensively for a class report she had already determined her best option was probably an IUD if she could afford one.

Despite being careful, her roommates noticed a change in her attitude early in the week. When she finally shared that she and Christopher were going to be seeing each other again, they had an impromptu celebration with pizza and wine. Without going into as many details as she had with Polly, she explained that she had finally conquered her fear with his help. The friendly ribbing she got from them made her feel more normal than she had felt in years.

On Thursday afternoon, she drove out to Morgan City to pick up another small load of her things at her parent's house. Her mother was still struggling with the empty nest, so Charlotte invited her to come stay one weekend to see Kurt and Uncle Jack's family. Giving her mother something to look forward to made getting away easier. She didn't have the nerve to mention Christopher after what happened at Mardi Gras, but her secret happiness was getting harder not to share with her Mama.

The trip to Houston on Friday seemed to take forever. Polly was working late as usual, so Charlotte had time to unpack, shower, and get dressed before their night out. She decided to wear a slinky black skirt and emerald green top, pulling her hair back in an artful tangle. Her mother had given her emerald earrings one year for Easter to which Meemee Claire had added a matching pendant necklace. The color green fit her complexion, she decided as she looked in the mirror when Polly came through the front door.

"Holy crap," Polly said from the bathroom doorway. "You look fantastic!"

The compliment brought a blush to her cheeks as she smiled at her friend. "Thanks," she said. "Are we still meeting at Uncle Jack's house?"

"Yeah, Julie wanted to let Emily see how the kids were doing before we head out for the night."

"I haven't heard from Christopher all day. I hope he's okay with all the kids."

"Julie called me to say the girls started calling him Uncle Christopher now, so it's official." That made her laugh, but before she could say anything, Polly dashed off to change. "Be right back!"

By the time Polly was dressed for the evening, Charlotte was pacing around the living room trying to calm herself down. When Polly came in, she immediately noticed the tension and grinned. Charlotte gave her a dirty look and said, "Shut up."

"You don't need to be nervous. He's the same guy he's always been and now you know how much he likes you."

Taking a deep breath, she grabbed her purse. "Let's go."

Polly drove to Uncle Jack's house, leaving Charlotte with nothing to do but look out the window. "Did you make it to the clinic this week?" Polly asked.

"Yup. I decided on the hormone IUD and got it in on Wednesday. It hurt like hell when they put it in and I had to take some ibuprofen. I'm still a little sore, but I can't really feel it now."

"Still use a condom though. The first couple of months are risky until you know it won't come out accidentally." Charlotte shot her a look with an arched eyebrow. "Sorry, I forget you probably know more about that stuff than I do at this point."

"It's fine, I'm just nervous about seeing him." The panic was less since she knew what to expect, but now she worried about how little practical knowledge she had compared to the other girls he'd been with, like Ashley. *What if he doesn't want to wait for me to figure things out?*

"You look like you're chewing nails. Talk it out with me," Polly said. "We've got time."

"I've got so much to catch up on. Did I mention I've been watching amature porn all week? I'm taking notes like it's a class lecture. There are also Youtube instructional videos for all *kinds* of sexual things."

Polly grinned at her. "That's probably not a bad way to approach it. When I first started having sex with Bobby, we used to watch porn to get ideas, but most of those positions only work for the camera and suck in real life."

"That's why I was sticking to the amateur stuff. I found this one site that had a collection of videos made by real couples. I have to admit, that was the first time I ever got super hot watching porn." Admitting it made her face warm, but Polly had heard worse that week.

After a moment, Polly asked her quietly, "Why didn't you tell him you'd never had sex before?"

"The last time I told a guy I was a virgin, he broke up with me and started telling everyone on campus." She thought for a minute more and said, "I'm glad you all stopped me at the club. On Friday night I was drunk and stupid, but when Christopher came over on Saturday and kissed me, nothing else mattered. He wanted me and I wanted him. And that was enough to get me through it."

"And now?"

"I want him again. Maybe I'm greedy, but I don't care," she said, then shivered as her flesh prickled. *I want to taste him and feel him inside me.*

Polly pulled over and stopped in front of Uncle Jack's house. "Let's go see him then."

* * *

Jack and Julie's house was a riot of noise with kids running wild. Little Jackson was having a hard time keeping up with the bigger kids, but he yelled all the louder to make up for it. Christopher, a cute Hispanic boy, and Jackson all charged against Jack and the two girls hiding behind the couch with soft dart guns blasting.

"I got you!" Jen yelled at the boy who had to be Noah. *He's utterly adorable*, Charlotte thought. He was small for his age and thin as a whip, but his open face and bright smile seemed to light up the room.

"No you didn't," he crowed back, firing his last bullets and missing her completely.

Jack stood up and unloaded a double barrel full of darts right at his stomach and added sound effects of explosions with his mouth. "I got him for sure that time!"

Noah took the moment to create an elaborate death scene, throwing himself down in slow motion to roll around on the ground until he uttered a last, "Urgh!"

Jackson laughed loud as he imitated him, then landed across his stomach making a pile of giggling death. That brought a victory cry from the girls as Jack led the final charge to bring Christopher to his knees next to his fallen comrades in arms.

"Victory," Jack yelled as he put a foot on the fallen Christopher's chest, glancing up to see Polly and Charlotte holding on to each other and laughing. "Wait, I see reinforcements! Get 'em girls!"

The kids ran over to get their hugs from Aunt Charlotte and Aunt Polly, all except for Noah who climbed into Christopher's lap glancing at them as he whispered in Christopher's ear. After dispensing hugs and kisses, Charlotte moved toward Christopher as he lifted the boy to stand, then stood up himself. His wide eyes took her in from shoes to hair.

"You look like you're having fun," she said as she opened her arms for a hug.

"You look fantastic," he whispered as he hugged her hello. Before he pulled away, she kissed him on the lips and breathed in his warm personal scent. His face, already flushed from playing with the kids, grew a darker shade of red. "It's been a blast so far and we haven't even gotten to the movie yet."

Aunt Julie came out with a woman older than them that Charlotte assumed was Noah's mother, Emily. She was pretty, but looked tired. Taking the initiative to make her feel welcome, Charlotte stepped closer and asked, "Emily?" After a nod confirming her guess, she extended her hand and said, "I'm Charlotte Guidry."

"Oh yes, Christopher's told me so much about you. Thank you so much for introducing me to your aunt, but I can't see how it's true! You both look the same age to me."

"It was a little weird for us as well at first. She's only three years older than me, but as far as I'm concerned Uncle Jack picked a winner. This is our good friend Polly Makutsi."

Polly stepped forward and shook her hand as well. "Nice to meet you. Your son Noah is *adorable*."

"And he knows it," she laughed. "Thanks, and nice to meet you both."

* * *

Before the next battle in the war of the children could draw them in, the ladies all retreated to the dining room to wait for Bonnie and Cathy. After getting some beers and soft drinks, they settled to visit and get to know each other.

Charlotte decided she liked Emily straight away. She wasn't the most talkative person, but she had an expressive face that showed her feelings as the conversation drifted around the usual topics of work, home, and how everyone met. By the time Bonnie and Cathy arrived and everyone was ready to go, Jack and Christopher had the kids settled down to watch their movie. Walking through the dim living room, the kids had draped themselves over and around the two men sitting on opposite ends of the couch.

"Noah, you be good for Mr. Christopher and Mr. Jack," Emily warned as she stopped at the front door. "I want a good report or we won't do this again."

"Yes, ma'am," he said as he munched popcorn from the bowl in his lap. "Have fun, Mom!"

Charlotte gave Christopher a smile and a wave as he snuggled down on the couch with Noah. That prompted him to pantomime a kiss with a cheeky grin as she closed the door.

The destination for the evening was a local Tex-Mex restaurant with fantastic margaritas and live Mariachi music. The six women sat around a large table covered with baskets of tortilla chips, salsa, and pitchers of icy margaritas. It didn't take long before the elixir worked its magic to melt the ice and make fast friends of them all.

Emily took the longest to loosen up, but she finally leaned back with a wide, easy grin and said, "Oh my God, y'all have no idea how bad I needed this."

Julie spoke for them all when she said, "I bet we do. It's why we do it every week."

"And with Noah having so much fun today, I don't even feel guilty." She took another sip from her stemmed glass and sighed.

"Never feel guilty for taking some time for yourself," Julie said. "It's one of the first lessons I learned after getting married. I love my husband, and I love our kids, but I'm no good to them if I'm a burned out wreck."

"And I am burned out," she said as she drew her finger through the condensation on her glass. "I don't want to be. Hell, I can't afford to be, but the truth is, I am."

"How's your mom doing?" Charlotte asked.

"It's not a good situation. Her Parkinson's hit her hard right when she turned fifty. Dad kept her at home for a decade and did everything he could, but his family has a history of bad hearts and the stress from Mom's situation didn't help. He died just after Christmas. We had to sell the house to get her into the assisted living center she's in."

"I'm so sorry." Charlotte wanted to do more than just sympathize. "What about those surgical treatments using deep brain stimulation?"

"It's an option we've discussed with her doctor, but it's not always effective with the more aggressive forms of the disease. The current medicines aren't helping much either. And because she doesn't have insurance, we're forced to rely on Medicaid and the little I can afford to do for her."

"Let me do some research so I can ask better questions. Maybe I could come help you with her after I move here full time."

"Thank you," she said as she patted Charlotte on her hand. "I'd appreciate all the help I can get."

Polly jumped in to ask, "So, are you seeing anyone?"

Emily laughed and said, "A woman with a kid and a sick parent? Are you crazy? I might as well be invisible to men. My last date was with my late husband, God rest his soul."

The uncomfortable laughter that followed made Charlotte wince. Hearing the reality of the situation was overwhelming, but watching Emily wipe her eyes with a sad chuckle hit her even harder. She suddenly understood why Christopher had been so moved to help her and Noah.

"I can sympathize. My mom raised me alone." Julie looked down in her glass. "Maybe Noah is better off, though. I always wished Mom hadn't dated as much as she did."

"It's okay, I can still dream about the future," Emily said. "Someday, when Noah is off at college and I've got no responsibilities, I'm gonna find me a strong man and wear him down like a pencil in a sharpener." She grinned around the table at everyone. "And in the mean time I've got high-speed Internet and a lock on my bedroom door."

Cathy laughed and clapped her hands. "Oh you should have been with us a few weeks ago! After dinner we took a field trip to the Erotic Boutique. I had to lock my door every night for a week after that."

They all laughed, but Emily blushed deeply. "I've never had the nerve to go to one of those places alone."

"Well, that sounds like a perfect excuse to go back," Bonnie said. The amused smile on her face made her eyes twinkle.

After sharing mounds of fajitas and a few more pitchers of margaritas, the happy group piled back into Julie's van to pay another visit to the Erotic Boutique. Charlotte found herself more excited than nervous this time.

Walking through the store again, Charlotte looked at everything with a new perspective. She ran her fingers along some of the sheer negligée and wondered what Christopher's reaction would be if she wore it for him. One caught her eye, made of a sheer black fabric with deep green lace at the edges. The matching panties were open in the crotch and she tingled when she slipped her fingers through the hole.

"You gonna get that?" Polly whispered from over her shoulder.

Startled at first, Charlotte nodded and gave an embarrassed chuckle. "I think so. Do you think he'll like it?"

"Are you kidding?" Polly laughed. "He's gonna be like a kid at Christmas."

As they made their way around to look at other things, Polly seemed fascinated with a set of silk binding sashes. Picking up the piece of the red silk, she raised it to her cheek with a wicked grin.

"Do you and Kurt…" Charlotte started to ask, but lost her nerve.

"Sometimes he tries to hold me down and I fight to stop him. It's just a game we play, but when he forces me, I get so hot." She took a deep breath and picked up a complete set from the shelf. "I think I want to try something new when he gets back."

Making their way to check out, they saw Julie and Emily laughing together over their purchases. Polly asked, "What did you get?"

"I'll never tell," Emily said with an embarrassed grin, then looked to Julie. "God, I can't believe you talked me into getting all this."

Julie put her arm around Emily's shoulders and laughed. "I'm a firm believer that every woman needs her own set of… tools."

"Well, God knows I need a tune up bad enough," Emily muttered as they made their way out of the store.

They arrived at Julie's house around midnight and got out of the van laughing and talking about their evening. Charlotte was happy to see Emily smiling with Bonnie and Cathy as they made their way to the front door. Following them inside she found Jack and Christopher asleep on the couch in the dim living room with the kids snoring softly beside them.

Emily knelt down next to the couch and gently roused Noah. "Come on. Time to go home."

"Don't wanna," he muttered and snuggled up closer to Christopher.

"You're too big for me to carry. Come on, Noah."

Christopher woke up, stretched, and said, "I've got him." He picked the boy up and carried him against his chest as he followed her outside.

Charlotte joined the other women standing in the middle of the room. "So what do you think?"

"I like her," Cathy said. "She's a fighter."

Bonnie nodded. "I agree. She's got my vote."

"Good," Julie said watching Polly nod her head as well. "I'll make sure to include her when we plan next week."

* * *

Christopher was standing at the curb as Emily and Noah drove off in an old, beat-up sedan. When Charlotte joined him there, he sighed and put his arm around her shoulders.

"She's so funny. And strong," Charlotte said as the car's broken tail light disappeared around a corner. "And sad."

"Then you understand," he whispered. She knew what he meant without him explaining anything.

"Yes." She leaned against his chest. "Thank you for letting me help."

"How did the night go?" He turned her around to look in her eyes.

"We all hit it off. Julie's gonna start inviting her for our nights out."

"Good," he said and pulled her close in a tight embrace. "I missed you."

"Why? We talk everyday," she said with a chuckle. He was breathing against her hair, taking in her scent as she did the same against his chest. It gave her the courage to ask, "Would you like to stay over tonight with me?"

"I was hoping you'd ask." After kissing her hair he pulled back. "Want me to drive you home?"

"Sure," she kissed his lips one more time then let him lead her to his truck.

The ride to her apartment flew by as she squeezed his hand tight and leaned into his shoulder. He parked in the visitor parking, then surprised her when he got a small duffel bag out from behind his seat.

"What's with the bag?" The humor came through when she asked and his eyes sparkled as he swung it around.

"Did I ever mention I was an Eagle Scout?"

"No," she laughed.

"The Scout motto is *Be Prepared*."

"Well, come on in," she said and took his hand to lead him to the door.

Polly was still over at Julie's house helping put the girls to bed, so the apartment was dark when she opened the door. Charlotte stopped in the kitchen long enough to grab a couple of glasses of ice water, while Christopher went to her bathroom.

The fluttery feeling in her stomach could have been fear or anticipation, but the slick feeling in her underwear was unmistakable. She put their water on the nightstands on either side of the bed, then kicked off her shoes in the closet. When Christopher came in wearing a pair of boxers and undershirt, she grabbed the bag from the Erotic Boutique and said, "Get comfortable. I'll be back in a few minutes."

After she got to the bathroom, she stripped down and tossed her damp panties in the dirty clothes hamper. Then she hung her bra and clothes on the hooks on the back of the bathroom door. Looking at herself in the mirror, she teased her nipples erect with a grin, then dumped the contents of the bag on the counter.

Using her nail clippers to get the tags off the negligée, she stepped into the panties and pulled them up to check the fit. They were a little loose, but framed her butt the way she'd hoped when she saw them in the store. The top was feather light and nearly transparent, allowing tantalizing glimpses of her breasts and aureola. After pulling it over her head, she used her palms to smooth the fabric and took a deep breath.

Walking back into the her bedroom, she noted only her bedside lamp was on. Christopher was reclining on the sheets with his hands behind his head. When she turned to face him after locking the door, he uttered a low whistle.

"Damn, Charlotte," he muttered and slowly sat up. "You look... damn."

His reaction was exactly what she'd hoped. "Thanks." Crossing to her side of the bed, she sat down and took his hand. "I'd like to play around for a while, unless you're too tired?"

The smile he gave her in response helped her relax as they came together to kiss. Shutting her eyes, she felt his hand cup her breast through the fabric, his thumb rubbing circles over her erect nipples. It made her kiss him deeper and whimper against his mouth.

When his hand slid down her stomach, the tickling touch made her muscles contract and pull away. The previous week he'd never really touched her like that, he'd just slipped himself inside. Now as she felt his fingers explore her mons, she nervously gripped his shirt in her fists and opened her legs slightly.

"You're so wet," he murmured. "I have to taste you."

"Please." Letting his shirt go, she pushed at his shoulders. "I have to know."

In seconds he had her legs apart and was tracing her flesh with his tongue through the opening in her panties until she gasped his name. The sensation was like nothing she'd ever experienced. The texture of his lips and tongue were softer than fingers and more arousing than her vibrator. Then his finger pushed deep inside making her moan out loud and push against him.

"Tell me what you like," he whispered as his breath tickled along her wet skin.

"It's perfect," she confessed. "Just don't stop."

It was impossible to imagine what he was doing with his mouth and fingers that could elicit the sensations she felt. Nothing she'd ever done had prompted the uncontrolled, writhing ecstasy she experienced in those brief minutes before her world exploded and she cried out. It was over far too soon, but the pulsing satisfaction was undeniable.

He seemed to know just when to stop before it became too sensitive, moving to allow her to curl up in a ball as her body shook and spasmed. Spooning against her back, he kissed her shoulders as he held her close.

She couldn't speak at first and he didn't seem to need words to understand what he'd done for her. Caressing her hair, he continued to hold her until she relaxed. Turning in his arms to face him at last, she kissed him with her own flavor on his lips.

"I'd like to return the favor," she purred.

"I'm all yours."

His erect head was poking out the fly of his white boxers, already leaking a few slick drops. Pushing him to lay on his back, Charlotte knelt to pull his cock all the way out through his fly. He was circumcised, with a dark pink head above his stiffening shaft. She pushed his legs apart and reached inside his underwear to cup his large sack. It was lightly haired and soft as satin as she gently rolled his balls in her hand.

"That feels so good," he whispered.

Gripping his shaft in her fist, she lowered her mouth to lick his head like an ice cream cone. After he began to twitch, she took him between her lips and tasted him in her mouth. The groan he made was her first reward.

Keeping the pace slow, her hand followed her lips while she dribbled spit and precum out to lubricate his shaft. Every few strokes she'd take him all the way into the back of her throat to test how far she could go using the techniques she'd read about online. When she did it, his legs straightened and he gripped the sheet into his fists.

"If you keep doing that, I'm gonna cum," he whispered.

Taking a break to use her hands alone, she looked up at his sweaty face. "I want you to."

"Fuck," he said with his eyes closed tight. "As long as you don't mind."

Taking him back between her lips, she alternated between going shallow and deep until he began holding his breath. The balls in her hand seemed to move on their own as he strained against the sensations she gave him. It was a powerful feeling, she realized. Giving him pleasure this way and feeling his reaction was more exciting and satisfying for her than she'd imagined.

"Now," he muttered, warning her just as she felt the pulses moving up his shaft to eject his hot seed on her tongue. It didn't have much taste, but she hummed as she swallowed it down like it was a rich chocolate sauce. The rapid pulses slowed as he collapsed against the damp sheets to pant after holding his breath for so long. With one last lick and swallow, she let him slip out of her mouth.

He reached down with a sigh to smooth her hair. "Come up here," he whispered.

She climbed up to rest her head on his shoulder and caress his chest with her palm. "That was yummy."

"That was amazing," he chuckled, then turned his head to kiss her hair.

"Are you sleepy?" she asked.

"Yeah I am, but I'd like to wake you up later if you don't mind."

"I'd like that."

Sitting up for a moment, she got a drink of water to get the slick taste out of her mouth. She turned off the bedside lamp then pulled up the sheet to cover them both. While he made her the little spoon, her mind was buzzing as she considered everything that just happened. *He made me cum with his mouth and I let him cum in mine*, she thought, shocked at her own boldness. He brought out a part of her she barely recognized.

There was no question he liked what she'd done, but she wondered if he knew she had no idea what she was doing. After bringing her to orgasm with the utter confidence of an experienced lover, she felt lucky she hadn't ruined everything by gagging or hurting him accidentally.

It shamed her to be glad he was too tired for sex so she could avoid having to pretend she wanted it just then. The soreness from the IUD worried her and she just wanted some more time to get used to the idea of having sex with him again. And despite how comforting it was to be held by him, she fell into a troubled sleep where a faceless Ashley appeared like a jack-in-the-box whenever they kissed in her dreams.

Chapter 12: Christopher

The dim sunlight was just beginning to filter its way through the window when Christopher woke. He was laying on his side with his face buried in Charlotte's fragrant brown hair, his hand resting on her hip. Feeling the sheer fabric under his palm, he rubbed along her side and leg until she stirred and arched her back against his chest.

"Mornin'," she yawned as she rolled over to face him.

He brushed the hair out of her face and kissed her, taking deep breaths of her warm scent. She hummed against his lips as her hand moved down to grip his ass and pull his morning wood against her mons. He pressed harder, then broke the kiss with a grin, "Sorry, I gotta go pee first."

"Fine," she pouted and let him go. He reluctantly left the comfort of the warm bed and tiptoed across the hall to the bathroom. As he sat to force his semi- erect penis to point downward, he smiled at the memory of their evening together.

She was a totally different person than the previous weekend. Confident, assured, incredibly vocal and responsive, and she had given him the best blowjob of his life. Ashley might have the advantage of knowing his cheat codes after years of practice, but Charlotte seemed to instinctively know how to please him. He only hoped she enjoyed his efforts as much.

Her body was amazing, soft and curved in all the right places, and the negligée she wore had been the icing on the cake. She had more hair down below than anyone he'd been with before, but it was neatly trimmed and softer than silk. The scent of her, that clean, musky smell, was addictive and he already wanted to taste her again.

After washing his hands, Christopher crept back into her room and locked the door back. When he turned, she was laying against the pillows and gently stroking herself through the opening in her panties wearing a wicked grin.

"How did you know I was in the mood for breakfast?"

"I didn't, but I'm glad you are," Charlotte laughed as he climbed up from the bottom of the bed. "I want your mouth again. Is that okay?" He nodded with his eyes focused on her offering.

She raised her knees as he approached, so he slipped his arms under her thighs to hold her closer. Approaching her wet opening, he again picked up her tantalizing scent. It made him hum deep in his chest as he pressed his lips to hers.

"I just can't get over how good that feels," she whispered with her fingers sliding through his hair.

"I *love* doing this," he said, then proved his words.

He teased her by pulling her lips out to suck one at a time. They were the perfect size, he thought, big enough to take into his mouth but they didn't get in the way when be probed her with his fingers or tongue. The soft skin was pink closer to her center, then darkened to a caramel color at the edges. He made a long meal of them to her delight.

In return she made encouraging sounds, gasping when he did something she especially liked. At one point she began to lift her hips, giving him access to her fully. He took advantage and pressed in close to give his tongue deeper reach. When she began to beg, pulling at his hair to direct his attention at her swollen nub, he finally stopped teasing and began to satisfy.

At first he pressed his lips together to kiss the top of her slit, making her tremble in response and open her legs even wider. Her heat and impatience were plain, but when he sucked lightly to pull her nub between his lips, she gasped and gripped his hair hard enough to make him wince.

Ignoring the pain, Christopher began to suck and relax rhythmically, almost like he was giving head to the small bump. It stilled her, her breath stopped by what he was doing until he feared she would pass out. When he began to use his tongue, she released the breath in a long hiss.

"I need to feel you inside me," Charlotte gasped.

Moving his hand under his chin, he slowly penetrated her with his middle finger while keeping the same pace with his mouth. She panted and gasped the whole time, but stopped instantly when he reached her g-spot. Rubbing circles inside with his finger, she began to whine and shake, then she cried out as her thighs closed tight around his head.

He could feel the pulses of her orgasm against his finger and lips, but he didn't stop until she began to relax slightly. Not wanting to overstimulate her, he withdrew his finger and let her close her legs together.

"How can you do that to me?" she whispered. "I've never even imagined it could be that good."

He smiled at her reaction while climbing up to hold her. "I told you, I love doing that."

After a moment to catch her breath she said. "Don't laugh. I'm just going to come out and say it. I'm dying to feel you cum inside me again. Can you get us a condom? I can't move right now."

He was glad to use a condom since they still didn't know each other that well, plus it helped him last longer. Rolling over, he got one out of the drawer and grabbed the little bottle of lube he found there as well. Then he noticed a bottle of massage oil there.

"How about a massage?" he asked, holding up the oil.

"Why not both?" she chuckled and covered her face. "God, I feel so greedy. I'm sorry. Nevermind."

"I wouldn't have offered if I didn't want to. Take off your nightie. I don't want to ruin it."

She sat up long enough to take off her negligée and panties, then dropped them on the floor. His own boxers and undershirt followed, then he sat across her legs after she lay down on her stomach.

Rubbing the oil to warm it between his hands, he said, "I love the rosemary scent this has."

"I didn't expect it to smell like that when I got it, but it's grown on me. I've only used it on my legs and feet so far, but it made my skin so soft afterward.

He began to work the oil into the skin of her back as she moaned. After covering her back and shoulders, he did the same to her arms and legs moving around the bed to reach everywhere. Then he whispered, "Roll over and put this pillow under your hips."

As he sat between her raised knees, he warmed more oil between his hands and then started rubbing her legs, stomach, and breasts. When he finished the massage, she was limp. However, Charlotte's body had one spot that was practically humming with tension. Christopher picked up the condom and tore open the package.

"Yes," she murmured without opening her eyes. "Oh God, I'm so ready for this now."

He coated the condom with extra lube and moved himself closer. With a pillow under her hips, he knelt between her thighs and penetrated her slowly as she gasped affirmations. He continued massaging her stomach, breasts and thighs as he moved inside of her, and she writhed on the bed underneath him.

"I can feel everything so much better this way," she whispered between hisses and hums.

"It's the pillow. It keeps you at the right angle so I can hit your g-spot." As he said that, he pressed more firmly inside to show her what he meant.

"Oh, fuck," she moaned. "Do that some more."

Christopher stepped up his pace, holding her hips to keep her from sliding off the pillow. He varied his motion and speed based on her reactions, and she made it clear what was working for her. He noticed that she was taking quite a while to get off, but he reminded himself that some girls don't cum from sex alone. Wanting her to orgasm again, he used his thumb to stimulate her more directly. As he touched her, her moans and gasps got louder.

He was having a hard time holding back as he watched her enjoy herself for a couple of minutes. "I'm gonna need to stop for a minute."

"No," she demanded. "I want to feel you cum this way. This is perfect for me. I can feel everything."

He held on as long as he could hoping she might finish with him, but it wasn't going to happen. Shutting his eyes, he bent down to kiss her at the end. She reached around to squeeze him against her chest and wrapped her legs around his thighs, kissing him wildly as he cried out. Panting together, she continued to kiss his face and lips tenderly as he recovered.

"Thank you," she whispered between kisses. "Thank you."

When he opened his eyes at last, he saw she had tears in her eyes. "What is it?"

"Nothing," she said as she wiped her eyes, smiling through the tears. "I'm just being silly."

He realized she was keeping something from him as he watched her compose herself. This was more than just the two of them getting to know each other for her, more than the beginning of their physical relationship. Recalling the way she ended things after Mardi Gras, he was worried about what that secret was.

"What?" she asked, looking a little embarrassed by his scrutiny.

"Nothing," he said as he reached down to hold the condom and pull out. After throwing it away, he rolled back over to face her. She pulled the pillow out from under her butt and made a face at the wet spot.

"What's that look for?"

"I thought I'd seen the last wet spot on a pillow," she chuckled.

"What do you mean?"

She blushed a deep red and refused to look him in the eye. "I shouldn't be embarrassed discussing things with a guy who makes me cum with his mouth." She laughed again. "When I was younger, I only used to be able to orgasm if I masturbated with a pillow. I started doing my own laundry at home because I didn't want Mama to find out."

"How do you masturbate with a pillow?" he asked, utterly confused.

She looked at his perplexed expression, then suddenly got a wicked expression of her own. "Want me to show you?"

"Yes," he said, hoping she meant it.

"Well, it may not look like much is going on." She put the pillow on the bed folded in half, then lay on top of it so the lump was under her mons. "I just push against it like this," she said as she stared in his eyes.

Watching her do this private, intimate thing in front of him was fantastic. Her eyebrows moved as she pushed against the pillow until she finally took his hand and squeezed it hard. Watching her ass tense and relax, he reached over with his other hand to trace along her skin as she worked her way along.

"Watching you is so hot." Impulsively, he asked, "Do you ever think about me when you do it?"

"Yeah, all the time lately," she gasped. "I'm so close now. Will you kiss me?"

He lay down beside her and moved close, watching the tiny beads of sweat appear along her forehead. He kissed her then as she panted at the finish, straining hard with her eyes closed as she let herself go. He brushed the hair out of her face and kept kissing her softly as she recovered.

"I've thought about you a lot, too." His thoughts went to those evenings he'd spent with a Tenga cup, edging himself along as he imagined being with her. Thinking down that path reminded him of the more painful memories when Charlotte had ended things before. Her peaceful smile faded as he continued to touch her lightly. Eventually she fell back to sleep, snoring softly, but he was too keyed up to rest again.

Getting up carefully to avoid waking her, he put on his boxers and undershirt then slipped on a pair of shorts from his overnight bag. When he stepped out of the room, he smelled coffee and was irresistibly drawn to the kitchen. Polly was there in a thin cotton robe filling a mug with the steaming liquid.

She smiled when she saw him and said, "Good morning."

"Good morning," he said, reaching up to straighten his wild morning hair.

"Did you sleep well?" she asked, unable to hide the amusement in her voice.

"Yeah," he said. "And Charlotte still is."

"I bet. Want some coffee?" she asked, nodding to the two other cups sitting out next to the pot. She stepped out of the way and leaned against the counter to sip her steaming cup.

While he poured and sweetened his mug, he could feel her watching him. "Sorry if we kept you up."

"Woke me up, more like," she chuckled. "I didn't hear anything last night."

He shook his head. "She's very... expressive."

"I knew I should have stayed over in Kurt's apartment," she said with a definite blush.

"We'll try to keep it down next time."

"No, don't make her self-conscious about it. Please."

It was the *please* that piqued his curiosity. It sounded almost desperate. Polly looked like she wanted to say something else but pinched her lips tight. He wished he could ask Polly the questions he feared to ask Charlotte. *What was she so afraid of? What had changed when he kissed her last week? What was she hiding from him?*

The truth was he didn't know what he wanted from Charlotte yet. He liked her, but she'd hurt him and he still didn't know why. Without understanding, it worried him to risk his heart more than his obsession with her demanded. So instead of asking Polly anything, he sipped his coffee in silence.

A few minutes later, Charlotte came yawning into the kitchen wearing a robe. "Mornin'," she said as she went straight for the coffee pot to pour herself a cup. "Anyone in the mood for breakfast? I'm starved."

The apartment kitchen was too small for everyone to work together, so Christopher grabbed a knife and some fruit to cut up at the table while Polly made toast and Charlotte started the bacon.

The conversation stayed light as the girls told Christopher how much fun they had with Emily. In turn, he told them about his day with the kids. Noah and Jen had hit off a friendly rivalry that fueled their play all day long while Lisa struggled to get attention from both of them. She eventually complained to her father that it wasn't fair and she wanted a boyfriend to come over and play with her, too.

* * *

That afternoon the three of them hung out together at the mall. Christopher was happy when Charlotte took his hand occasionally as they strolled, but he wished he knew what she was thinking when she got that faraway look in her eyes.

Polly was a good distraction, offering a rolling commentary on the people and things they saw. When they started getting hungry in the afternoon, Charlotte suggested eating dinner in the mall and going to see a movie afterward. While they all ate chicken sandwiches, the discussion focused on which movie to see. Christopher pressed for *Need for Speed*, but the girls outvoted him to see *Muppets Most Wanted*.

"My only rule is that you two don't get freaky in the theater." Polly gave them both a look that dared them to challenge her. "That would not be Kermit-ed."

"Jeez, Polly." Charlotte groaned.

"I've gotta go to the bathroom," Polly said as she ran off laughing.

Charlotte shook her head, then the lost expression he'd seen off and on all day returned as she stared at the crowd. After a few moments of silence, Christopher asked, "Is everything okay?"

She smiled and nodded, taking a sip of her lemonade. "Just a little tired."

"You seemed to sleep okay."

"I had bad dreams and kept waking up when you moved." She hesitated for a second, then added, "I've never actually slept with anyone before."

Trying to defuse the tension with a joke, he said, "That's not technically true, you slept with me last week, too." He found himself laughing alone.

She looked up with an anxious expression. "That was my first time."

Still laughing uncomfortably for a moment as he tried to figure out the joke, he suddenly realized she was serious. "Wait. What?"

"That was my first time sleeping with somebody... Sorry, I didn't mean to spring it on you like that." She looked away again, her cheeks flushed crimson.

"Your first time... you were a virgin?" he asked as he tried to make sense of what she was telling him. The revelation set off a chain reaction in his head as every memory of her over the previous three months shifted subtly. His first reaction was confusion, then panic, and finally anger. "Why the hell didn't you tell me?" he asked with more passion than he intended.

She paled and pinched her lips as her eyes snapped back to meet his. "Because it was none of your business."

"None of my business? Maybe if I was some guy you picked up at a bar, but we've been dating since New Years! How could you not tell me?"

Her eyes narrowed as spots of color appeared on her cheeks again. "It was my virginity and my business. You wanted me. I wanted you. That's all that mattered."

"No, it's not. Not for me." His heart hammered in his chest as he tried to put a muzzle on his temper.

"Are the rules different for you? I didn't hear you share your detailed sexual history when we started dating. I never asked or expected you to tell me. Why didn't you ever mention *Ashley* before?" The tears in her eyes spilled over, but her face was red and twisted in rage.

"That's not the same at all! I told you that she and I never dated, we were just friends who hooked up sometimes. Why would I tell you who I was sleeping with?"

"Why would I tell you I've never slept with anyone? It's exactly the same. How long did you wait to fuck her again when you got home from Morgan City? A day?"

The shock of her accurate guess hit him like cold water down his neck and he must have given something away in his expression.

"Oh my God, you did…"

That pushed him over the edge and he put up his hands in surrender. "I'm done," he said as he stood. "I'll call someone for a ride to my car."

Shocked to silence, she sat there with eyes wide open as Christopher stalked away. Pulling out his cell phone he called his buddy Ryan for a lift, but got his voicemail. Joe didn't answer either, Kurt was out of town, so he called Ashley with an annoyed grunt.

"What's up? Long time no speak," she said.

"Are you busy? I need a lift." It was hard to keep his voice under control.

"Whoa, what lit you up?" she asked with real concern in her voice.

"Sorry, I just need to get a ride back to my car. I'll explain later."

"I'm driving into work now, but I should have time for a quick pick up and drop off. Where are you?"

They arranged to meet at the mall entrance near the popular food court carousel. He watched the kids spinning around on the brightly colored animals while he wrestled with his anger. Despite knowing he wasn't being entirely rational about the situation, he couldn't stop feeling used and lied to.

Some people dreamed about taking a virgin to bed. He'd been the first sexual partner for two other girls over the years and neither had worked out well for him. The first had become obsessed, attaching herself to his life and suffocating him until he was forced to end it. The other one never learned to relax, so sex with her remained a frustrating ordeal to the end.

All he wanted was a relationship with an adult, in the true sense of the word. Someone who knew their own body, who knew what they wanted in bed and in life. The endless drama of dating was why he'd sought out the relationship he had with Ashley in the first place.

Thinking of Ashley seemed to summon her as her car pulled up to the curb. He was headed out the door when he heard Polly calling after him. "Christopher," Polly shouted as she ran up to him. "Christopher, wait."

"Sorry, I need to get away before I say something I regret." He kept walking.

"What happened? Everything was going fine! Charlotte wouldn't explain." The heartbroken expression on her face stopped him for a moment.

"It's not for me to say," he said as he backed away. "Apparently it's none of my business." Polly looked past him and frowned at Ashley's dim profile in the car's window. He wanted to say something, but his thoughts were flying too fast to settle on anything. "I gotta go."

Sitting down in Ashley's car, he shut the door and said, "Drive." In the side mirror he saw Charlotte jog up as Polly gestured broadly towards them as they pulled away.

"Wanna talk about it?" Ashley said as she pulled out of the mall parking lot.

"Head west down I-10," he said. "I figured out why Charlotte dumped me after Mardi Gras."

"Oh yeah?"

"She was still a virgin."

"Oh." Ashley seemed puzzled, then asked, "So what happened?"

"She's not anymore. I found out over dinner tonight that I apparently did the deed last week without ever knowing."

"What? Why the hell didn't she tell you before?"

"She said it was none of my business."

"But you guys have been dating for months! That doesn't make any sense," she said as she turned on the feeder road.

"Preach it, sister. I don't care, I dodged a bullet with that one. I'm done."

"No, hold on, you can't break up with her over this."

"Watch me." He looked out the window at the passing scenery, intending to drop the subject.

"No, I'm serious. Did you find out why she did it?"

"She went off on me when I asked her why and then started yelling about you. I don't need this shit. Take the next exit."

"How the hell did *I* get dragged into your mess?"

From the look on her face, Ashley was pissed at him as well. "Fuck my life," he whispered to himself.

"Forget it. I don't want to know. It really is none of my business, but I know you. In a week you're going to be miserable. Cool off, give her some time, then work it out."

"Turn there, then get in the left lane." They were silent the rest of the trip while Christopher worked to get his anger under control. When he got out of her car he still hadn't managed it. "Thanks for the lift. I'll talk to you later."

Chapter 13: Charlotte

"What the hell just happened? I was gone for ten minutes!" Polly yelled at Charlotte as she gestured to the car Christopher had just gotten into.

Watching it drive away made the rage Charlotte felt grow into a wildfire. There was a girl driving the car. *It was Ashley*, she told herself. *He called Ashley to come get him*.

"Fuck him," she muttered. "Can we go home?"

Polly stared at her like she was insane. "Are you going to tell me what just happened or not?"

"I don't want to talk about it." *It was just sex.* That's what everyone always said, anyway.

"I'm not taking you anywhere until you explain this to me."

"It's none of your fuckin' business!" Charlotte had clenched her hands into fists and was glaring at her friend, daring her to ask again.

Polly looked away with an expression of disgust on her face. "Fine. Whatever."

She began stalking towards her car digging the keys out of her purse while Charlotte followed at her heels. The ride home was tense and silent, ending with Polly pulling up next to their apartment.

"Are you coming in?" Charlotte asked.

"No, I'm going to spend the day with a friend." She glared until Charlotte closed the door, then sped off, bouncing hard over the speed bumps in the parking lot. Christopher's car was already gone, she realized as she looked around.

After getting her keys out, she let herself inside the apartment. The smell of bacon was still in the air from breakfast as she locked the door again. Walking into her bedroom, she was stopped by the scent of sex wafting from the tangled sheets.

She screamed, dragging the sheets off the bed, pulling the pillows from the pillowcases in a frantic rage. Grabbing them all, she stormed out to the hallway where the stackable washer and dryer were hidden behind a louvered door. She put in the linens then watched the churning water, it surprised her when a tear fell off her chin. Polly had warned her, sex made you feel connected, but Charlotte hadn't realized what that really meant until today. The pleasure he'd brought her in the early morning had come with a cost.

It wasn't just sex, whatever conventional wisdom said. He had opened her up and found his way to her heart before she was ready for it. Watching porn all week had focused her on the mechanics of the act. The people in the videos hadn't mention the scents or tastes, or the way she would crave him to cum inside her. It was so much more intense and personal than she'd imagined sex would be, despite having imagined it regularly for over a decade.

Her first time with him the previous week had helped with her fear, but that had also overshadowed her response to the act itself. That morning he'd worshiped her body and made her feel like the most beautiful woman in the world. The massage, the amazing sensations his mouth had given her, and then the intense pleasure of having sex with him had changed everything.

Shutting the door on the noisy washing machine, she went to sit on the couch in the silent living room. *It wasn't just sex.* Her reaction was about how vulnerable it felt to be with him and how much she had to trust him. The truth was, she wasn't sure she could trust him now even if she wanted to.

When she had tried to talk to Christopher about how she felt at the mall, his reaction was a complete surprise. His outrage had sparked her own anger and then things spun completely out of control. It still made no sense why her virginity had mattered so much to him one way or the other. She stared at the dark television and waited for the soap and water to wash his scent off of her sheets.

* * *

Polly slipped back in late and came to stand in Charlotte's door while she put the clean sheets back on the bed. "You ready to talk about it yet?"

Charlotte finished folding back the top sheet and turned to face her friend. "I'm sorry I was rude."

Polly came in nodding and went to the other side of the bed to help stuff the pillows into the pillowcases. "So what happened?"

"You were right," she sighed as she tucked the pillow under her chin. "Being with him was completely different than I expected."

"Yeah, it's hard to explain before you find out for yourself. It sounded like you were having fun this morning. What went wrong?"

She sat on the bed and said, "I screwed up, I guess. I told him he was my first, and then he got mad."

Polly finished with the pillow and tossed it at the head of the bed. "I could understand him being surprised, but why would that make him mad?"

"He said he deserved to know before we hooked up last week, but I got mad and said it was none of his business."

"Seems reasonable," Polly said. "So why'd he leave?"

She looked her friend in the eyes. "He made me feel so special, but I know he's been with other girls the same way he was with me. He accidentally mentioned being with someone else last week and claimed they were just friends who hooked up sometimes. It's making me crazy, but I can't stop myself imagining them together. When I asked him why I had to tell him I was a virgin when he never told me about *Ashley*, he said he was done and left. I think she was the one who was driving the car." She twisted up her face to keep from crying about it again.

Polly smiled sadly. "I guess I was lucky Bobby and I were both virgins."

"How do you handle knowing Kurt's been with half the girls in Morgan City?" she asked, then instantly regretted it when Polly winced. "Sorry."

"Wow," she said as she looked away. "I so didn't need to hear that."

"So I'm not the only one who feels this way?"

"Not by a long shot," she said. "I just try not to think about it. Kurt's with me now and what we have together is special, no matter who we've been with before."

"Well you guys are practically engaged at this point. I don't even know what Christopher and I are… or were. Fuck it." She lay back and stared at the ceiling. "When I was in junior high, Rory Abernathy passed a note to ask if I'd go with him. That's what we called it back then. There were little check boxes for yes and no. When I checked yes, I was his girlfriend until I caught him kissing that slut Shelly Suderman under the big tree behind his house. Why can't it still be that easy?"

Polly chuckled and mussed Charlotte's hair. "Have you talked to Christopher about what he wants?"

"Shit, Polly, I can't figure out what I want. Besides, he broke up with me. I think he just wants me to go away at this point."

"Don't be too sure of that," Polly said with a knowing grin.

Chapter 14: Christopher

On Sunday, Christopher called up his buddies Ryan and Joe to go shoot at the gun range. They knew he was hot about something, but allowed him to simmer in peace. A few hundred rounds later, Christopher felt like he could breathe again, so he let them take him to the ice house near their range. Watching the Rockets lose to the Clippers wasn't fun, but they got him through the evening and poured him safely home afterwards.

Going into work on Monday, his anger had become a bruise he felt every time he thought of Charlotte. The kids on his floor fixed him, though. Working with them blew away his funk and helped him find his center again. Some were only able to smile at his jokes, but he counted each one as a victory.

On Wednesday, after finishing his paperwork in the afternoon, he was heading down to the cafeteria for a late lunch when Doctor Jenks stepped up to walk with him.

"Hey, Doc," he said, then dug his wallet out of his back pocket. "Do you just want the receipts or is there some kind of report I need to fill out?"

"The receipts are fine," she said taking the slips from his hand. "How did it go?"

"Well, last Sunday he hit a bunch of balls at some batting cages and ate two hot dogs for dinner. Emily used me as a motivator to help his behavior and keep him on task all week. She said he actually did his physical therapy exercises during the week without too much complaining. And as a reward, on Friday I took him over to play with some new friends at a bounce house place and watch a movie while Emily went for a girls' night out."

"Wow, that's fantastic!" Her smile was broad and warm as she looked at him. "Are you heading to lunch?"

"Yup," he said, wondering what she really wanted.

"Let me pick up the tab and run something by you."

Going through the line, Christopher grabbed a sandwich and bowl of soup while Doctor Jenks put together a salad from the salad bar. After grabbing a couple of bottles of water, she paid for it all on their way to a table.

"You can call me Becca when we're off the clock, by the way," she said. "I'm impressed with your work."

"Thanks, Becca." He was intrigued, but hadn't figured out her angle.

"You already know I've got a small trust that I use to help people in need, but I have a confession to make." She looked around the room and leaned over the table. "It may be small now, but I've got larger ambitions."

He was instantly fascinated. "What's that got to do with me?"

"Healthcare sucks. The rich people are moving to concierge care because it's cheaper to pay doctors directly than deal with insurance. Whatever Obama thinks he's doing, it's not going to work so well for the poor. I've got a pretty good perspective to see where things are headed and I think I can make a difference, for some people at least."

"Something like a free clinic?"

"In a way." She moved around her salad with her fork. "Right now I'm still trying to figure things out. Most free clinics focus on triage rather than prevention and send their patients home as soon as the bleeding stops. Can you imagine what happens to a kid with Noah's condition without the VA picking up the tab?"

Her words struck home, but he'd thought similar things before. "What's your angle?"

"Like I said, I'm still figuring the details out. I don't know if it will work, or scale up if it does. What I *do* know is that I can't bear to turn away kids I know how to help."

"So what do you want from me?"

"Right now I'd like your help with some other kids in your off time like you did with Noah. I can't pay you very much, but I can promise that these kids and their families *desperately* need your skills. The work may be hit and miss for now, but there may be much more later."

"Noah was a special case for me. I'd have helped him anyway." He thought about it for a moment and nodded. "Let's start small. Maybe one or two kids to see how we work together."

"Thank you," she said, taking her first bite of salad at last. After she took a sip of her water, she said, "I appreciate your discretion as well. This isn't something I want getting out yet."

Christopher ate a bite of his sandwich and thought some more about what she'd said. She was an influential doctor and had a formidable reputation of going to the mat for her patients. Her passion was something he could identify with.

"Some of my friends already knew you asked me to help Noah, but I won't mention it anymore."

"I appreciate it. Maybe someday I can return the favor and do something to help you."

He smiled to himself as he considered her words. Having a big-time doctor owing him a favor might pay off someday.

* * *

On Wednesday evening, Christopher realized he was losing his mind. Neither Joe nor Ryan were up for a round of video games, Kurt was off on a boat somewhere in the gulf, and Ashley only wanted to know if he'd called Charlotte yet. Work helped get his mind off of her, but as soon as he wasn't occupied with the kids in the hospital, his thoughts trailed back to her. He tried drinking her out of his system, gone for marathon runs to exhaust himself, but nothing helped. It had gotten so bad that he was alone in his apartment arguing out loud. After drinking most of a six pack, he picked up his phone and stared at her picture.

"You're gonna hang up on me, aren't you?" he said to the phone. "Why didn't you just tell me?"

Her phantom whispered in his mind, *You didn't tell me about Ashley.*

"She's just a friend! God damn it, you light me up like a bon fire. She's not even close."

He paced around the living room and stared at her face. *It was my decision.*

"I know it was your decision, but you why couldn't just let me know? I would have been more careful, tried to make it special for you!" He threw the phone on the couch and paced around the room again, finishing off his beer. "Fuck it. Fuck it." He picked up the phone and pressed the button before he lost his nerve. "Fuck it!"

Chapter 15: Charlotte

The week passed slowly. Between school and her shifts at Lafayette General, Charlotte spent her time trying to answer the question at the root of everything. She was fast approaching graduation, transitioning to living in Houston, and worried about her new job starting in a few weeks. In the middle of all that stress, she had conquered her fear of sex. But underneath was a deeper fear that Christopher had brought to light.

She could love him. Not the kind of infatuated romantic love she had always imagined as a girl, but an overwhelming, life-changing love that could make confetti of her heart if she wasn't careful. Giving up some of her hard-won independence for him wasn't a decision she could just make once and forget. She would have to learn to trust him, and to trust herself to not get lost in what they made together.

By Wednesday she reached the end of her endurance. She craved him like someone lost in a desert craved water. As she sat in her bed late at night, she held her cellphone and dared herself to call him, to explain what had happened. As if by magic, her phone rang and the picture she'd taken of his smiling face appeared on the screen.

Answering the phone, she shut her eyes and said, "Thank God you called. I was just sitting here looking at my phone and trying to work up the nerve."

He was silent for so long she thought she'd made a mistake, but then he chuckled. "I was expecting you to still be mad at me. I've been practicing all these things I'd say, talking to myself like a crazy person." He took a deep breath. "I miss you."

"I miss you so much," she echoed as the relief made her skin prickle.

"Can we please try again? I know my temper gets me riled up sometimes, but I do care about you, no matter what I say."

"Yes," she whispered. "And I've got to explain what's been going on with me. It hasn't been fair keeping everything from you."

"I'm listening."

The story poured out of her in the same disjointed, confusing way her mind worked it out. Starting with her fear of sex, she explained about Peter coming out to her after prom, and then her cruel ex-boyfriend Brian who still continued to torment her on campus. From there she told him about how supportive her friends had been as she struggled with the attraction she felt towards him and the fear that had followed.

Talking about Mardi Gras prompted a few questions from Christopher, and he followed her answers to tell how confusing the situation had been for him. Then she detailed how she'd finally overcome some of her fear alone over the last few weeks, followed by her heartbreak over his rejection when she'd called to explain.

"Damn it, Charlotte, I wish I'd let you explain all this to me after Mardi Gras. I feel like shit for that now." His voice sounded as anguished as his words.

"It's fine. You came over anyway the next day and it all worked out."

"But I still wish I'd known! I'd have done things so differently." The tone of his voice showed why he cared so much about her being a virgin; he had obviously wanted to make it special for her. That made her tear up a little, but she had to explain the truth to him.

"It was exactly what I needed, though. I would've lost my nerve if we'd waited too long and I would *never* have been able to relax and enjoy that first time the way I did last weekend."

"Then why did you go off on me at the mall?"

She gathered her thoughts and opened up to him despite her fear. "I've never had an experience like that before in my life. No one has ever made me cum. No one has ever cum inside me. And I never expected it to make me feel as close to you as it did."

He was quiet for a time. "I see."

"I know it's not fair, but when you mentioned Ashley to me, it got into my head. That afternoon at the mall I kept thinking about you being with her like you'd been with me. It was *killing* me. I didn't know how to handle feeling that way so I pushed you away. I'm sorry."

"Damn," he said. She could hear him shifting around. "I hadn't thought of that."

"I know I'm inexperienced, but I don't know how to stop being jealous. Other people can say *it's just sex*, but I'm not one of them. I'm sorry."

"So, what are you saying?" he asked in a tense whisper.

She wanted to chicken out and say, *I don't know*. Instead she took a deep breath and said, "You don't have to give me an answer now or anything, but if we're going to stay together I want to be exclusive with you. Officially."

"Wait, you want to be my girlfriend?" he asked with an amused tone that sounded like he was mocking her.

"Nevermind," she said as her pulse doubled and her face got hot. Just as she was going to drop the call, he started shouting excitedly.

"No! I mean Yes! Wait, don't get mad!" He let out a joyful laugh.

"What?"

"I would love to be your boyfriend! Holy shit, Charlotte, I thought you were about to dump me!"

That made her laugh along with him until they both sounded giddy from relief. "I promise I'll explain when I feel scared or jealous instead of shutting you out."

"And I promise to work on my temper. Thank you for telling me all this. I swear this will be the first decent night of sleep I've had this week."

"Me, too. Will you call me tomorrow night?"

"Yes. I'll be over at Jack's with Noah on Friday. Maybe I can stay over Friday night?"

It made her wince when she said, "Sorry, Mama is coming over for the weekend to stay with me and visit everyone. Hey, want to come over to Uncle Jack's on Saturday? I hear he bought a smoker and wants to slow cook some briskets."

"That sounds like fun."

"Talk to you tomorrow, then."

When they'd said goodbye, she sighed for one moment, then immediately called Polly to share the news that she officially had a boyfriend.

* * *

"You're in a good mood," Noëlle said from the passenger seat of Charlotte's car. The ride to Houston had been a pleasant diversion for Charlotte as she listened to her mother share all the family gossip she'd missed the last few weeks.

Her cousin Trey still hadn't shown his face around Morgan City, especially since Kendall acknowledged he was the one who'd gotten her pregnant. Claire Thibodeaux, Trey's eighteen year old sister, had broken with her family over it. After Trey's antics had made her miss her first year on the family Mardi Gras float, she had moved in with Pawpaw Garson and Meemee Claire and transferred to graduate from Morgan City High School.

Charlotte hadn't told her mother about Christopher yet. In fact, other than Polly, she hadn't mentioned their new, *official* relationship to anyone. There was joy in keeping it secret for a while, but the time had come to share.

"Aren't you gonna tell me why?" Noëlle looked at her daughter with an expectant smile. "Or you gonna make me guess?"

"What would you guess?" she asked with a teasing smile.

"Is it Christopher, perhaps?"

Charlotte laughed and nodded, keeping her eyes on the road.

"So tell me everything!"

"You know we had a bumpy patch back at Mardi Gras, but he's been very... persistent. Since then we've seen each other off and on, but as of Wednesday, he's officially my boyfriend."

Her mother clapped her hands together and looked up. "Oh, *Dieu merci!* I have been praying so hard for you, sha."

Charlotte felt her face heat at her mother's happy response. "Don't go crazy or anything like you did with Kendall and Kurt, we're still just dating."

"I'm so happy for you. Your papa and I both like him so much. Is he gonna come by tomorrow to visit?"

Charlotte nodded. "Yeah, Uncle Jack invited him already and we'll also see him tonight since he's helping watch the kids when we go out." Her mother turned to look out the window with a sigh, but Charlotte saw her wiping her eyes. "What, Mama?"

"Oh, nothin'. I'm jus' bein' silly." She put on a smile, but her damp cheeks told a different story.

"Tell me," Charlotte demanded.

"I know you was embarrassed to talk to your Mama about things, but I could tell you was strugglin' with the boys you went out with the last few years."

Charlotte nodded. "I couldn't figure out why I was so afraid. I jus' was."

"I was too." Noëlle confessed. "Back in the '80s when I was your age, it seemed like everyone jus' went crazy. Your uncles spent the weekends in New Orleans or Houston going to clubs. Your Aunt Laurie went along and sometimes didn't come home with 'em. She was the wild one of us girls and made fun of me because I wouldn't go, too."

Charlotte tried to picture her uncles and aunt going to clubs like she did with her friends and had to laugh. "Did they wear parachute pants and vans like the old videos on VH1?"

That made her mother laugh as well. "Yes, God help 'em. Your Aunt Laurie had a short wedge haircut like Pat Benatar and wore this awful purple glittery eye shadow. And sometimes your Uncle Oscar wore more makeup than she did!"

Charlotte laughed with her mother at the thought of fat Uncle Oscar wearing tight pants and makeup. "Please tell me there are pictures somewhere."

"There are! I keep some of the old scrapbooks I made as insurance."

"So if you didn't go clubbin' with them, what did you do?"

"Same thing I do now. I started working at the meat market the summer after I graduated high school. I met your Papa when he came in to pick up meat for delivery runs. He was a little older than me and looked so good it made me feel weak in the knees."

"Papa?" Charlotte laughed. "He's bald and has a belly."

"Oh, he didn't always look like he does now, child. Every hair he lost was from worrying about us. He got a belly driving his truck all these years to pay for our house and put you through school. When I see him now, I can only see how much he loves us. I hope you're lucky enough to find a man that loves you like he does."

Charlotte smiled to herself at her mother's words. "I hope so, too."

"Now talkin' about bein' afraid." Her mother pinched her lips and got a faraway look in her eyes. "When I was about thirteen, we had a confirmation class with Sister Benedicta. To my eyes back then, she seemed about a hundred years old, but she was as hard as flint and quick with a ruler if you acted up."

"I'm glad I got Father Pierre. He was so nice."

"Sister Benedicta spent more time talking about sin than salvation, especially sexual sins. Looking back I suppose she'd been abused or something because she was always on about how girls shouldn't lead men on by dressing wild or bein' too friendly. Then one day your Aunt Laurie whispers a little too loud, asking someone why that dried up old stick was always goin' on about sex."

"I bet that set her off," Charlotte said.

"It got really strange. Sister Benedicta grabbed Laurie's hand–now remember she was about twelve–and smelled her fingers right there in the classroom. Then she started screaming about how she could smell the sin on her, then went on about self-abuse and how bad sex hurts girls. Laurie was trying to pull her hand back and screamin' about telling Papa. Then Sister Benedicta dragged her out of her desk and said, 'Let's call him right now so I can tell him about you abusin' yourself.'"

"Oh my God, Mama, what the fuck?" Charlotte had goose bumps and a sick feeling in her stomach from the story her mother was telling.

"Well, Laurie must have really been doin' it because she started cryin' and beggin' Sister Benedicta not to tell Papa. The rest of us didn't know what to do, so we sat there while this twisted old woman poured out horrible stories about the devil makin' us sick if we kept doing it, and how bein' with a man would tear you up inside and hurt 'til you wanted to die."

"You should have reported her to someone." Charlotte was livid at the idea of someone doing that to a young girl, let alone someone in her family.

"None of us said a word. We was kids and this woman was a nun. Now I can feel some sympathy for the poor old bitch. She was probably raped young and joined the orders to feel safer. But back then, hearin' her was like hearin' God himself talking and I never doubted what she said. Like I tol' you, sha, I understand bein' afraid."

"Nothing like that ever happened to me."

"I was careful to make sure it didn't. Maybe I was too careful and put my own fear inside you somehow."

"No, Mama, wherever it came from, it wasn't you. I think it grew over time because when I first started dating Peter, I was just uneasy. Later it was much worse, and I wouldn't even kiss anyone anymore. It wasn't until Christopher that I had the courage to face it. He was so gentle with me, Mama." Even dancing around the topic made her uncomfortable, but she wanted to share that little bit.

Noëlle nodded and smiled. "Your father was too, and he was patient with me over the years as we worked through things. He's always treated me like a precious gift and I love him so much for that. I promise it'll get better if you let it, child."

"Thank you for sharing that with me," Charlotte said.

"And you, sha." After a moment she looked away. "Y'all bein' careful?" Noëlle asked, blushing pink from embarrassment at her question.

"Yes, Ma'am," she answered, equally embarrassed. "Very careful."

"Well then, that's enough on that subject," she said with obvious relief.

* * *

Charlotte, Noëlle, and Polly arrived at Uncle Jack's house at dusk. Charlotte was wearing a bright yellow sun dress that stopped mid-thigh, while her mother had on a more conservative lavender skirt and top set. Polly wore some long shorts and a short top that let her smooth stomach peek out when she moved. She'd said Kurt found her navel irresistible, so she took every opportunity to torture him.

The house was a zoo with the kids running in and out, playing some kind of chasing game. It mostly seemed to involve the girls and Jackson running from Noah and making loud squeals and giggles when he got too close. Kurt and Christopher were sitting on the couch when they came in, but stood immediately to greet them.

"Mama," Kurt said as he came to hug Noëlle. "I missed you!"

Charlotte slipped her arms around Christopher's waist to rest her head against his chest. "Hey."

He kissed the top of her head and squeezed her tight. "Hey."

After a long hug, she drew back and grinned up at him. "You remember Mama."

He turned, leaving an arm around Charlotte's shoulders to extend his hand to Noëlle. "Mrs. Guidry, nice to see you again."

"Call me Noëlle." She shook his hand, then got a sly glint in her eye. "Or you can call me Mama if you want."

"Mama!" Charlotte protested with wide eyes as Polly and Kurt laughed at her reaction.

That made Christopher laugh loudly and squeeze Charlotte when he said, "You got it, Mama. Come on, y'all might as well come meet Dad."

"Your father's here?" Charlotte asked as a thrill shivered down her back.

Christopher led them out to the patio. "Yeah, Jack picked up a used smoker and asked if I knew anyone who could help him check it out. Dad's hobby is competing in barbeque cook-offs, so he offered to come by when I mentioned it to him."

Charlotte saw Uncle Jack with an older man who shared Christopher's build and features. The two of them were engrossed inspecting a metal cylinder on thin legs when Christopher interrupted.

"Dad, I've got someone I'd like you to meet." When the man looked up and saw Christopher holding Charlotte's hand he smiled broadly. "Dad, this is Charlotte Guidry, her mother Noëlle, and her friend Polly. Ladies, This is my father, Roger Dunlop."

"You didn't tell me how pretty they'd be," he said to his son before addressing them directly. "Nice to meet y'all." Shaking hands all around, Charlotte noticed his eye lingering on her mother with amusement. "All I've heard about for the last few months from Christopher has been your family and little Noah. I'm glad to finally put some faces to your names."

"It's nice to meet you too, Mr. Dunlop." Charlotte shook his hand while he gave her a penetrating look.

"I've heard the most about you, young lady." His voice was pitched low, like it was a secret between them. "And I like what I hear. Christopher tells me you've been helping with little Noah and his mother."

"I didn't do that much." Her face warmed from his compliments and attention.

Christopher spoke up then and said, "Just introduced them to her family and made Emily feel welcome with her friends."

"I hope to get to know you better," Roger said, releasing her hand at last.

Noëlle chuckled. "My husband, Gerome, and I feel the same way about your son, Christopher. I hope you'll be joining us tomorrow."

"I wouldn't miss it. It looks like Jack, here, picked up a good smoker and I'm looking forward to helping him eat some of that brisket he bought."

Emily came out the sliding glass door with Bonnie and Cathy trailing behind her. "There you all are," she said as she joined them. "I thought I heard you come in."

Another round of introductions followed as Roger continued to work his magic. She could see where Christopher got some of his mannerisms and charm. Then the kids came out with Julie, raising their voices as they asked questions about the large smoker. Roger knelt down and showed them where the fire would go and how the smoke would flow, patiently answering all their questions.

"We ready to go?" Polly asked when the conversation lulled.

"We should get going or we'll miss our reservation," Julie said as she rubbed her hands together.

"You want me to drive your van?" Cathy asked Julie. "You've done your share of driving lately."

"Sure!" Julie said and tossed the keys over. "We'll see you guys later. Have fun kids!"

"Bye, Mom!" the girls exclaimed, but little Jackson started crying immediately.

"Oh, it's okay," Julie said as she knelt to hug her little boy. "Mama's coming back soon and I'll give you a kiss when I get back if you go to bed for Daddy. Okay?"

"No!" he insisted, his pudgy fists clenched in anger.

Jack scooped him up and occupied him until Julie and the rest could make their escape. Christopher came with Noah so he could say goodbye to his mother out front. While they were saying goodbye, Christopher pulled Charlotte close and kissed her deeply.

His soft lips made her hungry as she clung to his arms. They parted at last to rest their foreheads together.

"I already miss you," he whispered.

"Maybe we can go for a walk or something during the day tomorrow."

"Or something," he grinned.

She touched his face and stared in his eyes. "Or something," she agreed.

Cathy started the van and honked the horn. "Come on, I'm starving!"

"I'll see you later!" Charlotte said as she danced away to the van.

Chapter 16: Christopher

Christopher was sitting near the smoker as the fragrant scent of cooking meat filled the air. He'd come early, while it was still dark, to help Jack get the briskets out of the brine bath they'd been soaking in and start the fire in the smoker. There was something wrong with the way it drew smoke, but he finally got the temperature steady where it needed to be by changing the charcoal and wood mix.

Afterward, he stuck around for breakfast with the kids while Julie and Jack worked together to set out a great spread featuring bacon, eggs, and pancakes. He watched the two of them with a smile and a bit of envy. They had a good rhythm in their life together with balanced priorities that kept the family first, but their own relationship a close second. It was obvious to Christopher that they were crazy about each other from the occasional smile, loving touch, or quick kiss.

The previous couple of weeks had been a wild ride, but he'd deemed it worth the trouble in the end. Just seeing Charlotte for a few minutes the night before had been enough to keep his obsession under control. He still couldn't explain to himself how she'd gotten under his skin so quickly, but decided he didn't care anymore; they were a couple now. It was his first real relationship in years, but he liked where things were headed.

He was still thinking of Charlotte a while later when she surprised him by walking out through the sliding glass doors. She wore jean shorts and a light pink t-shirt with her long brown hair pulled back in a ponytail.

"Hey," he said as he stood to greet her. He grinned at the playful sparkle in her eyes. "Did ya miss me?"

She didn't say a word, just put her arms around his neck to kiss him deeply. He began to kiss her back, opening his mouth to let her minty tongue tickle along his lips. As she pressed her body against him, his hands slipped down to pull her hips tight so he could press his growing erection against her stomach. "I need you," she whispered at last.

"This is gonna be a long day," he whispered against her cheek.

"You have no idea," she whispered back, but didn't explain her secretive smile.

As the house filled with family and friends, Charlotte stayed close by. She would take his hand at times or touch his shoulder when others were around, but when they found themselves alone she'd attack him like a starving animal. His body was in a constant state of arousal as she teased him all morning. The feeling of frustration built and he thought he'd have to lock himself in the bathroom for some private relief until he saw her heading out the garage door with a sly look over her shoulder.

Slipping out behind her, he closed the door quietly. "You're making me insane."

She glanced back with a knowing grin. "Good." Rather than turning to embrace him, she backed up against him and turned her face for a kiss over her shoulder.

He held her close while leaning against the door to prevent someone from opening it and catching them. While his hands caressed her breasts and stomach, she pushed her ass against his rock-hard erection. He couldn't stop his fingers slipping down inside the waistband of her shorts then continuing under the elastic of her panties to reach her warm, furry mons.

She gasped when his fingers reached her damp hair and soaked panties. With one hand on her breasts and the other massaging her roughly, he ground his cock against her and panted in her ear, "Cum for me."

"I can't! Someone will catch us," she gasped as her body writhed against him.

"Not if you're fast. One of us has to get some relief. I want to feel it."

With their lips touching as they breathed together, his focus remained solely on getting her off. She pushed hard against his hand, whimpering as he squeezed inside to rub more directly beneath her swollen nub. "Oh fuck," she whispered, her eyes squeezed shut against the sensation.

"God, you're so wet. I wish I could have you in my mouth."

She moaned and pushed harder against his fingers. "Tell me what you would do."

"I'd lick along here," he said as he traced around her opening. "Then I'd suck these into my mouth." He pulled her soft lips open and ran his finger back and forth. "And at the end, I'd focus right here." Then he focused his assault on her swollen bud.

At his words she froze suddenly, her weight falling against his arms and body, then she strained hard as she raised her hand to her lips to hold back a muffled cry. Feeling the rapid pulses against his fingertips told him all he needed to know before she relaxed against him and shivered.

"God, I want you," she whispered with her cheek against his. "I've never wanted anyone like this. I swear I feel like I'm going crazy."

"You're going crazy? You've been teasing me all day," he chuckled into her hair. After kissing her neck, he carefully removed his hand from inside her shorts. She stepped away and turned around as he lifted his slick fingers to his lips. "And I've loved it."

She watched for a moment with a hungry expression on her face, then she surprised him when she grabbed his hand to lick the last two fingers clean herself. With his fingers still on her lips she said, "We need an excuse to go back to the apartment. I'll tell Julie to ask us to go to the store for something. I need to have you."

"Good plan," he said, kissing her again to taste her lips. "I'll drive."

* * *

As they walked through the door of her apartment, they were already pulling at each other's clothes. In moments, Christopher had Charlotte's shorts down and her t-shirt off, letting her slip off her bra and panties while he dug a condom out of his wallet.

"Maybe next month we won't need those anymore," she said with a grin.

"Really?" he asked, surprised.

"I got an IUD, but we need to make sure it stays in first." She ran her hands over her breasts while he rolled it on. "It makes me so hot when you cum. I can't wait to feel you cum inside me without one."

He grabbed her and kissed her roughly, then turned her around and pushed her down to put one knee on the couch. "I won't last long this time."

"I don't care," she said looking back over her shoulder at him. "I need you."

He lifted her hips slightly and slid in slowly while she pushed back against him with a happy sound of welcome. "You're so wet," he groaned.

"I love the way you feel inside," she said, reaching between her own legs to cup his balls. "Give it all to me."

He increased the pace slowly to enjoy the experience, then gripped her hips hard to go even faster. She was vocal as he drove himself quickly along. Despite being teased all day, he was surprised at his self-control while she continued to beg and roll his balls in her hand.

He reached around to her stomach, trying to stimulate her manually and bring her off with him. She had to let go of his balls then to hold herself up. Only the side of her face was visible, but she had her eyes squeezed tight and her mouth wide open. Gasping harder, she squeezed the couch cushions and bowed her back to open herself to him even more.

It was finally too much. Pressing all the way inside while holding her hips tight, the spasms racked his body as he emptied himself with a low growl. "Oh, fuck," he muttered at the end, then caressed her ass and lower back tenderly. "Oh, baby."

She collapsed slowly on the couch while he held onto the condom. "I could feel it building up this time," she whispered. "I think I'll be able to cum with you inside me someday. But even if I never do, it feels *so good* when you let go."

He tossed the condom in the kitchen trash and wiped off with a paper towel. By the time he got back to the couch she was relaxing into sleep. "Don't fall asleep. We're supposed to be going to the store." He sat down on the carpet in front of the couch with a sigh.

She smiled when he brushed the hair out of her face. "I keep thinking it's as good as it can get, but it keeps getting better."

"I'm glad," he said and kissed her.

"There are so many things I want to try."

"Like what?"

"Different positions. Different places. I want to get you off like you did me today. It made me so hot knowing everyone was on the other side of the garage wall." She covered her face and laughed. "God, I'm so weird."

"That's not weird. It was hot as hell!"

"And somethin' Polly said got me thinkin'. Sometimes Kurt holds her down and makes her have sex while they're play fightin'. She even got some soft sashes for him to tie her up in bed."

"You guys talk about sex like that?" he asked. He and his buddies never mentioned specifics when girls came up in conversation. The fact that she'd shared things like that with Polly bothered him a little.

"Not details. He *is* my brother after all and that would definitely be weird. Polly offered to answer questions about things for me. I didn't really say anything to her about us. I just don't know what's weird or not. All I've ever had is the Internet and that's not exactly a good measure."

"True." He rested his chin in front of her face, and she stared at his features, eyes darting around with a slight smile fixed on her lips. "What are you thinking?" he asked.

"I wish I lived here already."

"It's only a couple more months."

"I know. What about you?"

"I'm enjoying the afterglow and wondering if you'd let me taste you again."

Her face blushed a deep pink, but the speed she sat up and scooted to the edge of the couch made him chuckle. *"Bon Appetit,"* she said in her soft French accent.

The sight and scent of her stirred his heart rate as he pushed her knees further apart. She had trimmed since their last time and he could see a little sexy razor stubble at the edges. The soft brown hair was already slick from her arousal when he parted the hair along her slit. Leaning closer, he blew warm air over it slowly to make her shiver.

"Yes," she moaned as her fingers went through his hair. When his lips touched hers, she hissed and leaned back against the couch. "You have a magic mouth."

The taste was like licking a penny, clean and bright despite his earlier intrusion. Most people had stiff, wiry pubic hair but Charlotte's was a soft as goose down. Before being with her, Christopher would have said he preferred smooth shaven. Now he rubbed his cheeks against her soft hair as he licked and kissed her into a frenzy.

Bringing his hand up, he penetrated her carefully with his finger to stimulate that sweet spot inside. When her hands gripped his hair in fists he began to rub circles there, letting it build until she froze.

He stopped then, knowing she was hovering on the edge. "*Merde*," she whined. "Don't stop."

"Do you remember the kitchen earlier today?" She had waited until Julie took Jackson out to change him, then kissed him while stroking the front of his jeans. He had begged her then, but she just laughed and skipped into the living room to play with the girls.

"I'm sorry, I was just playin'!" She began to move herself to try forcing his lips back to hers. When she growled at him, clearly upset at his denial, he began to kiss along her thighs and the creases along her slit.

Purring as he built her up again slowly, he brought her to the edge again and stopped. This time she gripped his hair and pulled harder, nearly crying as she begged, "*Pour le Dieu*! Oh fuck, I need to cum!"

"Beg," he commanded.

"I'll do anything you want," she whined.

"I want your mouth," he whispered.

"Yes, of course."

"Back at Jack's house this afternoon."

"No, we'll get caught!" She opened her eyes wide in shock.

"Maybe," he said. "I don't care."

"Mama is there," she said. "And your dad is coming this afternoon!"

"Well, then I guess I'm done here." He smiled as he sat back, watching her flex the muscles in her ass.

"Fine," she conceded, pulling his hair to bring his mouth back to her. "I'll do it. Just make me cum."

This time he brought her along as slowly as he could, spending more time with the edges than the middle. Scooting even further, she pulled up her knees to open herself completely. Christopher opened his mouth wide to cover her opening as much as he could, keeping his tongue soft as he gently licked around her swollen nub.

She froze again, shivering as she teetered on the edge, then she reached behind his head to hold him in place, locking her fingers together as she cried out. When the pulses began, he felt her squirt a bit of hot liquid in his mouth with each spasm. It tasted like her usual wetness, so he hummed deep in his chest and happily swallowed it down.

Her toes were curled up as she held them in the air, then she lowered her feet to rest against his shoulders. She relaxed the grip on his head when she collapsed back against the couch. "I can't feel my legs," she whispered.

He sat back and took one foot in his hands to massage her arch. "You came *hard*," he said, then kissed her ankle.

"It's never been like that. I saw bright sparks and felt like I was falling down a well. I can't move right now."

"Let me know when you recover. We need to get back soon."

"Why? You worried about missing the barbeque?" She chuckled warmly as he continued to massage her foot.

"No," he said as he put one foot back on his shoulder and took the other into his hands. "I'm looking forward to giving you dessert."

She covered her face with her hands. "I can't believe you made me promise to do that. If we get caught I'll never be able to show my face there again."

"After all this it won't take very long, I promise. It gets me so hot when you cum in my mouth. You tasted great when you shot off, by the way."

"What are you talking about?" she asked as she looked between her fingers.

"You came in my mouth," he repeated. "Little hot squirts."

"Female ejaculation is a myth," she said with a frown and dropped her hands.

"Tell that to your body," he said. "I know what just happened."

She opened her mouth to say something, but closed it again. Then she asked with a wrinkled brow, "Really?"

Christopher nodded and laughed, then kissed her foot. "And I liked it."

* * *

It took a few more minutes for Charlotte to recover, then they got dressed and swung by the store to pick up the cake Julie had ordered for dessert. When they made it back to Jack and Julie's house, the kids were throwing a football in the front yard with Jack.

"Where were you?" Noah yelled when he saw them get out of the car.

"Gettin' us some cake," Christopher said as he roughed the boys hair.

Lisa and Jen started jumping up and down. "Thanks, Uncle Christopher!"

Charlotte twisted her fingers in his and smiled up at him with a sigh. "That has a nice ring."

"Yeah," he said suddenly feeling his face warm.

Going back inside, Christopher noticed Charlotte had a relaxed glow. When Julie looked up as they entered the kitchen, she gave Charlotte a sly smile.

"Thanks for getting the cake," Julie purred. "Sorry it took so long for them to bake and decorate it." She nodded towards Noëlle who was stirring a pot of red beans on the stove.

"It was our pleasure," Charlotte said with a deliberate wink at her aunt.

"Good." Julie took the cake box and put it on the kitchen table. "Christopher, your father is out on the patio."

"Great, we'll head out there and say hi." Christopher noticed Noëlle smiling over her shoulder at them as they left the kitchen. "I think your Mom knows," he whispered as they passed through the sliding door.

"I know she does," Charlotte said, crossing to hug his dad. "Hi, Roger."

Christopher was left feeling shocked again at the speed things were moving.

"There she is," Roger said as he hugged Charlotte quickly. "I hope you don't mind me smelling like smoke. I keep having to stir the coals. I think I figured out why this thing was so cheap."

"Hey Dad." Christopher hugged his father as well. "Yeah, I saw it wasn't drawin' smoke right this morning. What's wrong with it?"

"I think the guy who made it didn't get the reverse flow calculations right. The chimney is too short and when I opened it to check on the meat a while ago, it looks like the double walls might be too narrow. There's not enough space to create the draw it needs." Roger took off his ball cap and scratched his wet hair.

"Think you can fix it?"

He put his hat back on and nodded. "Yeah, I think so. I need to take it to my shop so I can use my welder. Then I can move the baffle plates around and put in a longer chimney. We should still be okay for today. I'm keeping it hot enough by compensating with the wood and charcoal mix."

Charlotte watched the two of them with a puzzled expression on her face. "I guess smoking meat is more complicated than I thought."

"That's life," Roger said with a nod. "Lots of things seem straight forward until you get in deeper." The look he gave Christopher seemed to imply he was speaking about more than just smokers. "I'm out of beer. Any chance you could get me one?" he asked Charlotte.

"Sure. You want one too?" she asked Christopher.

"Love one." When they were alone, both men sat down and were silent for a while.

"She's takin' a real shine to you." Roger delivered the observation with a little worry in his tone.

"Yeah," Christopher said and leaned over to rest his elbows on his knees. "I'm takin' a shine to her as well."

"It's been a while for you."

"What're you gettin' at?"

"I like her and her family. I wouldn't want her to get hurt, is all."

Christopher clenched his jaw to keep from snapping back at his dad. "This ain't gonna end up like Steph."

"I never said it was, boy, but I know you. Just be sure of yourself before you get too deep. She seems real tender-hearted."

Christopher thought for a minute and nodded. His dad was right in a way. Part of the reason he'd liked being with Ashley was that things never got too complicated. Not that things were complicated with Charlotte, but he had to admit they were getting closer everyday.

Charlotte came back out carrying three bottles of beer with Polly and Emily following her out the door chatting.

"Seriously?" Polly asked Emily. "What did you say?"

"What else could I say? 'Yes, sir, I'll have it on your desk before I leave tonight.' I'm just glad my friend at Noah's after school program could stay an extra hour or I don't know what I'd have done."

Charlotte handed the men their beers then turned to talk with her friends.

Half listening, Christopher considered his situation with an eye to the future. He'd jumped at the chance to stay with Charlotte when she suggested making it official, but the reality was sinking in. His future plans had been so focused on getting through college and finding a job that he hadn't really considered what would come after.

With only himself to think of, he could just go to work and focus on the tactical parts of his life. Now with Charlotte coming to town in two months his extra time during the week would probably disappear, limiting how much extra work he could do for Doctor Jenks. The impromptu video game wars with Joe and Ryan probably wouldn't happen as often either.

Jack and Kurt came out and the kids swarmed out after the ball Jack threw into the yard. "Y'all go play by yourselves for a while. I'm gonna sit down and rest since you wore me out." They both collapsed into chairs with a sigh and Jack took a pull off his long neck bottle.

"Hey man, how you been?" Kurt asked Christopher as he raised his bottle.

"Great, how 'bout you?" Christopher asked and tapped their bottles together.

"Glad to be home," he said. "And glad to see you and Charlotte are still hangin' out."

That brought a nod and smile to Christopher's lips. "Yeah, me too."

"Hey," Jack interrupted. "I been meaning to ask y'all. Kurt and I were talking about goin' huntin' and wondered if y'all might want to tag along."

Roger nodded and said, "We own some woodlands about halfway between Dallas and San Antonio if you were lookin' for somewhere to go. It's about thirty acres with feral hogs all over it and you can bag them all year without a license in Texas."

Jack's eyes opened wide and glanced at Kurt. "We were thinkin' of going back to Louisiana, but that actually sounds like a better idea. Can we camp there?"

"Sure," Roger said. "We got a water well and a gas generator to pump it. There's a rough bathroom and outdoor kitchen there as well, for butcherin' mostly. One of these days I'm gonna build a cabin and move out there, but my youngest is still in high school."

"That beats Uncle Charlie's leaky old cabin by a mile and I ain't seen any hogs out there in years," Kurt said, nodding at the idea.

"I'd love for Jack to meet my buddies Joe and Ryan. Why don't we make a long weekend out of it?" Christopher thought the idea was sounding better and better.

"I wanna go!" Noah exclaimed from behind Christopher's chair. Then the men all turned to look as Noah sank until only his eyes and the top of his head were visible. "Please?"

Jack squinted at the boy for a moment. "You ever been camping?"

"No, sir."

"You ever shot a gun?"

"No, sir."

Jack pursed his lips thoughtfully and glanced around at the other men. When everyone had shrugged or nodded, he called out, "Hey, Emily?"

Christopher heard a whispered *Yes!* from behind his chair as Noah came around to stand by his knee. He reached over to rough the boy's hair and pat his back.

Emily came over with eyebrows raised. "What's up?"

"We were just planning a weekend hunting trip and wondered if we could take Noah with us."

"Who's going and where will you be?"

"Roger offered his family's woodlands up between Dallas and San Antonio. So far it's the four of us, plus maybe two more of Christopher's friends."

Noah had his hands clasped under his chin and a pleading look on his face. "Please, Mama, I swear I'll do all my physical therapy and homework without complaining ever again!"

She gave him a skeptical look and rolled her eyes. "Let me think about it. If someone can keep his behavior at school green or better between now and then I'll consider it more seriously."

"Whoo hoo!" Noah danced around, jumping in the air

"She didn't say yes," Jack warned.

"She didn't say no and that's almost as good!" Everyone laughed as he ran off, bragging to the girls.

"Thank you for thinking of him," Emily said quietly to them all, but especially to Jack. "I'll call you privately to discuss the details later this week. He has some medical conditions, but if Christopher's going, it should be fine."

* * *

It took a while to bang out the details. Since Easter was coming up in two weeks, they decided to plan it for the week after that. That far out everyone was confident they could get off for a three day weekend, leaving on Friday and coming back Sunday night. They discussed the logistics and gear until the meat was ready to come out of the smoker.

The meal was amazing, with fork-tender barbecued brisket and a delicious spicy sauce prepared by Roger. The girls made red beans and rice, potato salad, and some fried okra that was as crispy as popcorn. After eating until they were almost too full, Julie brought out the cake and coffee, and then put a movie on for the kids.

Christopher excused himself to the bathroom and was washing his hands when there was a quiet tap on the door. He unlocked it and looked out to find Charlotte standing in the doorway with a wicked grin on her face.

"That cake did nothing for me," she whispered and locked the door behind her.

With wide eyes, Christopher watched her kneel in front of him and open his jeans with trembling fingers. She pushed his pants and boxer briefs down past his hips so she could tease his soft head with her tongue.

"Oh, damn," he said as she looked up into his eyes.

It didn't take a second before he was fully erect and she wasted no time taking him into her mouth, running her hands over his balls, shaft, and stomach with a hungry growl. He couldn't stop himself from running his fingers through her hair to influence the pace and depth. Her smile as he did it made him moan.

Watching her lips sliding along his wet shaft was intensely erotic. He began to move his hips along with her, almost like he was fucking her mouth. The tingle in his balls gave him warning, and he said, "Now…"

She gripped his ass in both hands, took a deep breath, then sucked his full length into her mouth as he came. With his face turned up and his eyes squeezed shut, he gave her the dessert she craved. Both of them were silent except for their breathing. She let him slip out slowly after the pulses stopped, then helped pull his underwear and pants back up.

"Thank you," she whispered as she stood, then kissed him deeply.

The slick flavor didn't bother him at all as he opened her mouth with his tongue. Holding her face in his hands, he kissed her mouth, her cheeks, her closed eyes.

"Thank *you*," he whispered in return, then hugged her close. "That was the hottest thing I've ever done, but someone will come looking for us if we don't go."

"You go first, I still need to use the facilities." She kissed him again and stared in his eyes for a moment before moving out of the way.

The smile didn't leave his face the rest of the night.

* * *

During the week he'd find himself smiling again, recalling the long Saturday he'd spent with Charlotte and her family. Between working with the kids on his floor and picking up the extra work for Doctor Jenks, Christopher tried to figure out what shape his life was growing into. It would have been easy to keep rolling along like he always had, but with Charlotte's graduation just over a month away he had to figure some things out first.

There was no denying that for all the trouble they had getting started, the more time they spent together the deeper they connected. He could feel himself twisting as she braided herself into his heart and life. It felt odd, but not at all unwelcome. As his priorities shifted around to match hers, the new shape they made clicked together in a most satisfying way.

The speed everything was happening still made him nervous, as well as Charlotte's tendency to freak out over things that looked small to him. Her reaction over his relationship with Ashley had been a surprise until he reminded himself that she had no experience with hookups and casual sex. But despite her inexperience, she was so wonderfully enthusiastic with him, and that blend of sensual and innocent she possessed fired him up.

Lost in thought, Christopher was sitting at the nurses station and staring at the open chart in front of him without seeing the words he'd written. When a man cleared his throat to get his attention it startled him.

"Sorry, I didn't see you come up," Christopher said as he stood. The doctor had to be in his sixties, but was well preserved and looked fit. "Can I help you?"

"I'm looking for Christopher Dunlop," he said, but his expression said he already knew who he was talking to.

"That's me," Christopher said, glancing around to see if Deborah was nearby, but he was alone at the nurses station.

"I'm Doctor Elias Osborne," he said and extended his hand. "I'd like a word with you privately if you have the time."

"Sure, what's up?"

"I've been hearing good things about your work with the kids. Can you tell me a little about what made you want to get into clinical social work?"

Christopher frowned for a moment as he tried to figure out why some strange doctor was coming to talk to him like this. "I was a scout and taught soccer all through high school. I always wanted to help the kids I worked with that needed it, but serving in Afghanistan really showed me how bad some kids have it. I felt like I had to do something to help when I came back."

"You must know how rare it is that a young man like you would want to work in this field. Someone with your background could probably do very well in law enforcement or as a contractor overseas."

"What's your point?" he asked, having trouble keeping the impatience from his tone.

Doctor Osborne chuckled. "A friend who works in a large VA hospital in Atlanta has been looking for you for over a year and doesn't even know it yet. She works primarily with the families of deceased and wounded vets. Most of the kids in her program grew up on military bases with one or both parents in the service. It's made it hard for your average social worker to relate enough to help them."

Christopher nodded and said, "Yeah, I bet. Dad was a drill sergeant in the Marines for twenty-five years and we grew up moving every couple of years, all over the world. The people I went to school with would have been clueless dealing with the kids I grew up around."

"Then you know what I mean." He paused for a moment to give Christopher a hard look. "I'd like to introduce you two. I think you could help each other."

It all clicked then, this might be the dream job he'd been looking for. "I'd like to talk to him."

"Her," he corrected. "Can I have your personal contact information? And I'd appreciate if you didn't mention this to anyone around here."

Christopher wrote out his cell phone and email address on a slip of paper and handed it over. "I'm usually free after seven most evenings."

"I'm sure she'll be in touch in a day or two. It was nice meeting you."

After he left, Christopher sat and considered the implications of getting an offer to work in Atlanta. Even after traveling the world, he'd never wanted to live anywhere but Texas. His dad and brothers would miss him, but they'd understand. His buddies Joe and Ryan would, too. So would Ashley.

After spending time with Charlotte, he couldn't imagine she'd understand. Her identity was so firmly rooted in her family that she'd probably never consider moving. Just bringing it up would probably lead to another explosion of drama, so he decided to keep the potential opportunity to himself until he had more information.

* * *

That evening, he spoke to a Maggie Jensen from Atlanta for a couple of hours about her work and his background. By the end of the conversation he was even more excited about the opportunity and that made it harder to decide what to tell Charlotte without an offer. Maggie had ended the conversation saying she had a meeting of the board the following week and they would be discussing making him an offer then.

He and Charlotte spent the next weekend together with Kurt and Polly while the secret burned a hole in his chest. While he was with her, Charlotte's enthusiasm kept him from dwelling on it too much, at least until he tried to sleep with her next to him. Laying there, he couldn't help imagining how it would be when she moved to Houston in a few weeks and they'd be free to spend more time together. The thought should have made him happy, but in light of the potential job offer, it filled him with dread.

By Good Friday he hadn't heard anything from Maggie about the job. Charlotte had invited him to join her family for Easter since she wasn't coming to Houston over the holiday weekend. Kurt and Polly were going as well, along with Jack and his family. It was tempting, but he didn't want to be there obsessing about the job offer. So he declined saying he wanted to spend Easter with his dad and brothers, which was true enough.

In the afternoon on Easter Sunday, after a long day at church and hanging out with his family, he'd almost given up hope when the email came at last. He stared at his phone as the hairs on his arms rose. The subject line simply said *Offer*. He thumbed the notification and read Maggie's letter outlining her goals for the new position. He'd be organizing a department of social workers, developing training materials to help deal with the kinds of issues military kids faced, and then leading the treatment program himself. The salary was insane and the work was exactly the kind of thing he'd dreamed of doing.

He replied to thank her for the offer and ask how long he'd be allowed to consider it. She replied almost instantly saying she wanted to start on the first of June, so he could have until the last day of April to let her know.

His first thought was to call Charlotte, but she was in the middle of celebrating Easter with her family. He couldn't drop this on her long distance, especially since he hadn't told her anything about the opportunity at all.

His next thought was Ashley. After a quick call to find out if she was free, he arrived at their favorite little Thai place at the same time she did. She was wearing sweats and had her hair pulled back in a tight ponytail that reminded him of Charlotte. Ignoring his wince at that thought, he stopped in the parking lot to give her a quick hug and said, "Thanks for meeting me on such short notice."

"You sounded really fucked up on the phone. Did she dump you again?"

That made him wince even harder. "No, we're still seeing each other. Things are actually going really well."

"So what is it?"

"I got a job offer." They walked through the door and allowed the hostess to seat them before he continued. "It's a great opportunity doing exactly what I want to do." The waitress brought their usual Pad Thai with extra peanuts to share. After she left, they dug in while Christopher filled Ashley in on the details from the phone call, getting more excited about the opportunity as he described it to her.

"So what's the problem?" she asked as she sipped her jasmine tea.

"It's in Atlanta." He pressed his lips together. "I don't know what to do."

"You know what to do!" Ashley said with a laugh. "Pack up, Bitch! Congratulations! That job sounds like it was made for you."

"It's not that simple." He looked down into his tea. "Not anymore."

After a few moments she seemed to get it without him explaining. "Oh shit, you're falling for Charlotte, aren't you?"

Nodding twice, he looked up with a helpless laugh. "Why did I have to meet her now? What the fuck do I do?"

"You haven't told her, have you?" The sympathy in her expression stung his eyes like salt water.

"I didn't want to until I got the offer in case it fell through. I just got the offer tonight, but she's in Morgan City with her family. I've got to tell her, but she's a little panicky. I'm worried about how she'll take the news."

"Yeah," she nodded thoughtfully as she considered the situation. "It's too soon to ask her to come with you, but probably not long enough for a long distance relationship to work out."

"Exactly. God, it's like you can read my mind," he laughed. "I miss hangin' out with you."

"Yeah, well, you're the one who told me she couldn't handle it." She smiled sadly and shook her head. "I can't think of anything to make this easier. Either you stay for her or leave for the job. You're just gonna have to tell her and work it out, but you better do it soon."

He nodded. "You're right. I'll tell her tomorrow night when we talk."

"Well, you could wait until the weekend to do it face to face."

"I can't. A bunch of us guys are going camping all weekend and I won't see her until the weekend after. Maggie needs an answer before then because the job starts on the first of June."

Ashley patted his hand and said, "Call me if you need to."

Picking up the check for them both, Christopher said, "Thanks, Ash, I will."

Chapter 17: Charlotte

When Charlotte's phone rang, she turned away from her laptop and hopped on the bed, bouncing happily as she pulled the phone off of its charger and fell against her pillows. "Hey!"

"Hey yourself. Did ya have a fun Easter?"

"Yup! Everyone missed you. Meemee told me next time to invite your whole family so you don't have any excuse to miss it."

Christopher laughed warmly. "We had fun, too. Dad got Uncle Jack's smoker fixed up and we tested it with a few briskets on Sunday. I've got leftovers in the freezer when you come back. He wanted to send some home to your family."

"That was sweet, please thank him for me. Oh, hey, guess who's havin' a baby boy?"

He hummed for a moment while he thought. "Julie."

"How'd you know?" she exclaimed while he laughed.

"Just a guess. I'll have to pick up a box of those cigars Jack likes for the hunting trip this weekend. How was your day?"

"Finals are looming, but I've got it under control. How're the kids doing?"

"Amber, that girl I told you about with that bad infection, she lost her foot."

"Oh no!" Charlotte remembered it was that horrible antibiotic resistant staph infection. "Did they ever figure out where she picked it up?"

"Nope, no idea. I still think it was their community pool. She mentioned she'd already cut her heel when she went swimming and used the shower there."

"Poor baby," Charlotte said. "They do have better prosthetics these days. Remind her about the girl who got on that dancing show after losing both her lower legs."

He made a cute *humph* sound. "Really? I've never seen it."

"You've never seen it at all? Oh, we're gonna fix that when I move to town. I know a fun drinking game we can play when we watch it together. How's Noah doing?"

"He is *so* excited about going camping this weekend. Emily wants us to start goin' once a month to keep him in line."

That made Charlotte laugh. "She's excited about this weekend as well. Bonnie has been trying to set her up with a guy she works with and they are finally going out on Saturday for the first time."

"Good for her!" He sounded genuinely glad. "She deserves a little happiness."

"Emily swears she isn't interested in seeing anyone, but she didn't fight too hard when we ganged up on her." Charlotte paused while he chuckled. "I really like her. She's so strong. I can't imagine the pressure she's under, but she just keeps on going."

"Did I mention I met her mom? She's a tough old bird and knows about all of us from Emily and Noah. She said she wants to come by next time we do a barbeque at Jack's house if she's feeling up to it."

"Emily and I are already planning how I can help out with her mom when I finally move there." The impatience she felt made her stomach twist as she curled up with her phone. "God, I can't wait to be there with you! There are so many things I'm looking forward to. I want to cook you dinner after work and meet your brothers and maybe visit the church you grew up in. I like your dad so much, I can't wait to get to know him better." She realized what she was saying and got nervous. "Sorry, I don't mean to rush things."

"No, it's fine, really," he said with a sigh. His tone of voice didn't sound fine to her. "Listen, I need to tell—"

She got so nervous that she decided to change the subject and interrupted him. "Did I mention I got my paperwork from the hospital? I'm starting orientation the Monday after graduation. I can't believe it's only three weeks away!"

He didn't say anything for a moment, but then said, "Hey, uh… how serious are you about us being together long term?"

Christopher almost never brought up their relationship directly. She knew how strongly she felt about him and suspected he felt the same way, but they'd never actually come out and said it to each other. Taking a deep breath, she said exactly what she'd been thinking recently.

"I dream about being with you. You've changed my life so much that I can't imagine living it without you anymore." She closed her eyes and mentally chanted, *Please don't be scared. Please don't be scared.*

He cleared his throat. "Talking to you now, everything else seems unimportant."

When he didn't say anything for a long moment, Charlotte burned to know what he was thinking. "Why are you asking this now?"

"I've been thinking about the future. I was so focused on getting through school and starting work that I've never really thought about what happens next. You've made me rethink so many things." He chuckled to himself, but Charlotte didn't understand why. "The more I get to know you, the more my dreams change. I thought I knew what I wanted, but now all I want is to be with you."

She felt a thrill as his words confirmed her hopes. "Good. Once I move to Houston we'll see where things go. There's plenty of time to work out the details. I'm so happy you want to be with me, too."

"Yeah," he agreed. "We'll have plenty of time now." The tone of his voice sounded like he'd reached a decision about something. For the first time, it hit home how serious he was about them being together and it warmed her all the way through.

"If you were here right now I'd be kissing you so hard."

He laughed and said, "If I didn't have work tomorrow, I'd already be in my truck."

She sighed in frustration. "Talk to you tomorrow night?"

"Yeah," he sighed. "I'll call you when I get done with work."

After they hung up, Charlotte got off her bed with a laugh and locked the door, then pulled her toy out to dream about him again.

* * *

When Charlotte let herself in the apartment she shared with Polly, she found her roommate sitting on the couch already dressed for their girl's night out.

"Hey," Polly said as she sipped from a glass of red wine. She had on a dark red dress with matching heels toppled over on the floor in front of the couch. Her feet propped up on the coffee table and her legs were covered in patterned black hose. "How was the trip in?"

"I got a late start and hit traffic near Beaumont then again at I-10 and 610. Let me change real quick. Got any more wine?"

She put on a little black dress, black hose, and tall black heels, then joined Polly again as she put on her emerald earrings. Taking her glass from Polly's fingers, they clinked their glasses together.

"To Jack, Julie, and a safe delivery of baby James," Polly offered with a grin.

After taking a sip, Charlotte said, "I can't wait to see what Cathy's going to say. She nearly guessed after Mardi Gras, remember?"

"Speaking of Mardi Gras, did you tell Christopher about the baby?"

"Yeah, he said he's bringing up a box of Jack's favorite cigars this weekend to celebrate while they're hunting." Thinking of Christopher made her smile.

"What's that look for?"

"Nothin'."

"Don't you nothin' me. That wasn't nothin' 'cause I know somethin' when I see it!"

Charlotte sat down on the couch with Polly and leaned in a little to confide, "I think we're gettin' serious."

"Really?" Polly asked with a grin. "Kurt said something about him being a little distracted on Wednesday when they got together to play video games with Ryan and Joe."

"When he called on Monday, he asked how I felt about us being together long term."

"What did you tell him?"

"The truth; that I can't imagine life without him anymore." Charlotte took another drink to force the tightness in her throat away.

Polly nodded and sat back chuckling. "I knew it." She sat her empty glass down on the coffee table.

"Don't jinx it. I need to finish school and get here to see how things go first, but now I know we both want it to work out."

"I'm so happy for you," Polly said with a wrinkled smile as she clapped her hands.

"Thanks," Charlotte said, then finished off her wine in one long gulp. "Let's go!"

* * *

They got to Julie's house after everyone else had already arrived. Since Jack and Christopher were out hunting with the other men, Julie had sent Jackson away to spend the night with her mother, Lily, and the girls off with Jack's ex-wife, Sophie. With the house to themselves, Julie's plan was to have some drinks before dinner so she could share her good news with her friends.

"Come on in," Julie said as she opened the front door. "I was about to send out a search party."

"Sorry, I got stuck in traffic on the way into town," Charlotte said as she hugged her aunt.

They went to the dining room where Bonnie, Emily, and Cathy were already seated with their champagne flutes bubbling.

Bonnie gave them all an expectant look. "So *now* will you finally tell us what we're celebrating tonight?"

"I'm betting Kurt finally popped the question," Cathy guessed with a bold look in Polly's direction.

"Nope!" Polly laughed. "Not yet, anyway."

"Oh my God, was it Christopher?" Emily exclaimed, turning the attention to Charlotte.

She felt her face heat and shook her head. "Not me either."

Julie came in from the kitchen and filling her own fluted glass with ginger ale while everyone watched with open mouths.

Cathy slapped the table and exclaimed, "I knew you were pregnant again!"

"Ladies," Julie said as she raised the glass with glistening eyes. "To James Garson Brousard." Then she rested her other hand on her stomach and smiled.

The reaction was hugs and laughter as each woman in turn offered her congratulations to Julie. She answered all the usual questions about due dates and test results while passing around the small black and white sonogram images. The women sat to continue talking and finish off the bottles of champagne Julie had chilled for the occasion.

Charlotte found herself smiling into her glass, with bubbles rising through the amber liquid, when Cathy whispered, "You knew and covered for her that night last month, didn't you?"

Her offended tone made Charlotte chuckle. "What kind of nurse would I be if I couldn't tell when someone was four months along?"

"She is now, but she wasn't showing back then."

"I really just guessed." Charlotte took a sip of her champagne, then gave Cathy an embarrassed smile. "Besides, she didn't want everyone to know during her first trimester."

"There's more to you than meets the eye." Her warm smile didn't hide the wry look she gave Charlotte.

* * *

Julie drove her van as the women tried to guess where they were going. All they'd been told was to dress up for a nice dinner. Charlotte was in the back with Cathy where they quietly passed her flask of cranberry flavored vodka back and forth. The liquor was making her feel light headed and a bit frisky.

As they approached the Galleria area, Bonnie finally guessed they would be going to some upscale place called *Rubin's* and everyone gasped when Julie confirmed it. When Charlotte admitted she'd never heard of it, Cathy quickly explained the new restaurant was one of the hottest spots in town.

After they pulled up to the restaurant and Julie handed off the keys to the valet, the women followed Julie to the hostess waiting near the front door. They were immediately whisked away to a private dining room filled with colorful artwork around a large dining table.

"Now, all this is on me, so y'all order whatever you want." Julie drew her cloth napkin across her lap and reviewed the board of fare presented by the tall, slim waitress wearing a black dress.

As she gave each guest their own menu, the waitress said, "My name is Ashley and I'll be at your service this evening. If you have any questions, I will be happy to answer them. Just to let you know, our pace of service is deliberately slow to allow you time to savor your meal. If you need to leave by a specific time, just let me know and we'll accommodate your schedule."

Charlotte reviewed the menu of options, but stopped as soon as she saw they had a seafood section with fresh fish. They claimed all the fish was flown in daily, which made the Alaskan salmon seem especially appealing.

"What are you gonna have?" Polly whispered on her right. Cathy was on her other side and leaned in to hear as well.

"The salmon, but I can't decide on the sauce."

"If you do the fennel, I'll do the leek and lemon cream so we can share," Cathy suggested.

"Then I'll do the cedar plank salmon with dill so we can have a three way," Polly purred, then laughed at herself.

"Well, the boys *are* out of town," Cathy said with a glint in her eye. "Hey, wanna do a sleepover and watch old movies tonight? I don't have any plans in the morning."

"That sounds like fun," Charlotte said at once and glanced to see Polly nodding as well. "Our place?"

"Sure, why not," Polly said. "We need to take some pictures though so we can torture the guys." She looked to Charlotte with a serious expression. "Can we sleep in your room since you have the biggest bed?"

"Uh, you guys aren't serious, are you?" Charlotte was looking back and forth between them with a nervous tremble in her stomach.

"Hey, don't worry, Christopher won't care. Eating isn't cheating," Cathy insisted, but gave herself away when she started laughing. "Sorry, Polly, I couldn't keep a straight face when I saw Charlotte's expression."

"You rats!" Charlotte said and pushed them both. "I can't believe you did that to me!"

"All's fair in love and war." Cathy said with a smug tone. "Besides, you got me when you lied about Julie getting drunk at Mardi Gras."

Charlotte added a wedge salad to her salmon with fennel and ordered a cranberry juice with vodka. When the waitress corrected her by confirming she wanted a Cape Cod, Charlotte bit her tongue to keep from making a snarky comment.

The conversation flowed around the table as they enjoyed the appetizers that Julie had ordered for them all to share. Julie and Bonnie discussed the changes at their office as she got closer to term. Bonnie remarked that with the baby coming in their slower fall season it shouldn't be too hard to make the necessary adjustments.

Emily was clearly nervous about her impending date with Frank Lawson and they all tried putting her mind at ease. Bonnie passed around her phone with a picture of him from his real estate website. He was in his forties, a widow with two girls, and lived in a very nice neighborhood. The discussion was just starting to cross the line from racy to explicit when the waitress came back to their embarrassed silence.

As she directed the white-coated staff where to place the plates and platters, Charlotte finished off her drink. "Ma'am," she said to get the waitress' attention. "May I have another cranberry and vodka, please?"

"Please, it's just Ashley. I'll have another Cape Cod brought over right away." The condescending way she smiled when she said it irritated Charlotte again. "Anyone else care for another drink with dinner?"

Polly frowned and leaned close to whisper, "Wow, what a bitch."

"I hate people that think they're better than you."

The salmon was amazing, rare and flavorful, just as Charlotte liked it. After an initial bite and yummy noises all around, Cathy, Polly, and Charlotte each divided their portions into thirds to share with each other. After trying them all, Charlotte decided her favorite was the salmon with leek and lemon sauce that Cathy had chosen.

After the food was gone and the table cleared, Cathy swiped her glass and upended the flask to split the cranberry vodka between them. "Salud!" she said with a fake Spanish accent.

Charlotte was the first to review the dessert cart with an eye for something new and novel. One dessert particularly caught her eye. It was two white chocolate truffles with a single espresso bean on top of each one, all surrounded on the plate with a raspberry drizzle. It wasn't until the plate was sat before her that she realized they were actually sculpted to look like a lovely pair of breasts.

"Oh my," she whispered to herself.

Cathy leaned over to look and giggled.

"Stop it," Charlotte said. "I'm a mature adult and can eat my candy boobies if I want to."

That comment brought everyone's attention. Bonnie told the waitress, "I'll have that as well, but make mine bigger."

Julie laughed out loud. "I'll have to have them, too, I guess. Can I get some that lactate?"

Charlotte noted that the waitress' eyes narrowed, almost like she was judging them for daring to be silly in such a serious establishment. "I'll see what I can do. Would anyone else like them?"

"I want mine sprinkled with cocoa powder," Polly said as she looked down her top, holding back her laughter.

"I suppose I should have mine with cinnamon then," Emily said with a straight face. "But bring me an espresso as well."

Cathy was covering her mouth and nodding, but couldn't stop long enough to modify her order. Charlotte put her arm around her friend and said, "Cathy would like some just like mine."

That sent Cathy completely over the edge and she covered her face with her hands as the sound of stifled laughter followed the red-faced waitress out. When they were alone again, the whole group laughed until they had to pass around tissue to blow their noses and wipe their eyes.

"Oh my God, I have no idea how we're going to eat those with a straight face," Julie said as she fanned herself.

When they all had their desserts, Julie made them wait until she took pictures of each pair. The waitress was as good as her word and brought out each one as requested. Bonnie's were largest, sitting on top of a little pile of white chocolate shavings. Julie's had a cream drizzle instead of the raspberry. Polly's were evenly coated with cocoa powder and were surrounded by a dark chocolate drizzle. Emily's pair had a dusting of cinnamon with a coffee liqueur drizzle. And Cathy's were identical to Charlotte's pair, down to the orientation of the espresso bean and drizzle pattern.

Before she got the giggles again, Charlotte picked one of hers and popped it in her mouth. The white chocolate hid a creamy dark chocolate center that was rich without being too sweet. The crunchy espresso bean topped it off with a nice zing of coffee flavor that made her moan happily.

"That is so good," she whimpered. "I'm going to have to bring Christopher back here when they get back from their camping trip."

The waitress stopped and glanced back at Charlotte. "Did you mean Christopher Dunlop?"

Ashley, Charlotte thought in horror as she looked at the waitress with fresh eyes. She was tall and slim, but had a very nice figure. Her hair was a light shade of brown and straight all the way past her shoulders. She couldn't stop imagining Christopher kissing those lips. *Was she better in bed? Did he like being with her more? Oh fuck, I need to say something.* "Yes," she said quietly. "You must be his... friend, Ashley."

All conversation stopped around the table as the other women stared at them both.

"Yes," Ashley nodded, then seemed to think for a moment. "I'm glad you guys were able to work things out."

"What things?" Charlotte asked. She examined every word and expression for hidden meanings, fighting herself as she helplessly imagined Christopher being with her.

"About his new job in Atlanta. Are you going with him?"

"New job," she repeated as her face heated. "What *new job?*"

The look of horror on Ashley's face seemed genuine, but Charlotte thought she caught a glimmer of amusement in her eyes. "I'm sorry, I shouldn't have said anything." Then she immediately moved away, intending to leave the room.

"Wait," Polly said as she stood. "You can't just drop that on the table and leave."

"It's none of my business, I'm sorry, I just assumed he'd mentioned it."

Emily had some heat in her tone when she said, "He's currently treating my son and *I* don't know anything about a new job out of state either."

Julie said, "You can either tell us now or after I call the manager over."

Ashley glanced out into the restaurant, then leaned over the table. "On Sunday he took me out to dinner to talk about a job offer he got. It's to put together and run a team to help families of vets in Atlanta." Looking in Charlotte's eyes, she added, "He told me he was going to talk to you about it on Monday, but I didn't talk to him again this week. I'm so sorry."

Her dessert was threatening to come back up as her stomach clenched. "I need to go," Charlotte whispered as she got up. "Excuse me." Jogging outside, she ran past the valets and into the wet night. *What else did he not tell me?*

She grabbed her phone out of her purse and pressed Christopher's contact picture. As the phone rang she realized they probably didn't have cell phone coverage out in the woodlands. Listening to his voice announce his outgoing message made her hands shake, but after the beep she found she had no idea what to say.

"I met Ashley." She tried to force her thoughts into some kind of order. "Why didn't you tell me?" The rage and pain were pushing words out like a levee giving way against a flooded river. "You went out with her while I was out of town and never told me? You have a job in Atlanta? Why didn't you *tell me*?" She was lost in the torrent and vented her rage into the phone. "I don't want to see you anymore. I don't want to be your girlfriend anymore. Don't call me, I'll never answer. I *hate* you. I *hate* you. I *hate* you. I *hate* you."

When the second beep came indicating the message was full and disconnected the call, Charlotte was still standing in the rain sobbing into the dead phone, continuing her chant.

Chapter 18: Christopher

The campfire spat and crackled as the resinous chunks of wood burned. Smoke drifted up to obscure the stars while bright sparks floated up from the fire into the night sky. Christopher looked around the circle of friends and family sitting in camp chairs and released the fragrant cigar smoke in ringed puffs from his open mouth.

"God, I needed this," Jack muttered as he did the same from across the fire.

"I don't know why?" Roger teased. "After hearing how your year started from Kurt, I'm surprised you've survived to get here."

"Yeah, but hopefully the worst is behind us. I'm looking forward to a little uncomplicated pleasure this weekend." Jack took another draw off his fat cigar and blew the smoke out slowly. "Thanks again for inviting us up here. This place is amazing."

Christopher had been coming up with his family since he was a kid, so it felt like home to him, but watching Noah and the others helped him see it anew. The tall pecan and oak trees that covered their land made plenty of food for the feral hogs, deer, and wild turkey. His father had dug the well and poured the cement pad for the outdoor kitchen before he'd gotten married. After Christopher and his brothers were born, the family had spent many summers improving the campsite.

The creek that wandered across their land had been his favorite spot to play growing up. It made a sharp bend at one point with a nearly vertical bank on one side that was perfect for jumping off into the water. It also served as a good spot to hide and wait for wildlife coming down for a drink, which they would be taking advantage of in the morning before dawn.

Noah had slept on the three hour ride in and then spent most of the afternoon exploring and chasing grey squirrels. After spending the afternoon setting up tents and getting the generator going for the well pump, Christopher took Noah for a long walk to the bend in the creek, pointing out the hog prints in the soft dirt and the marks they left rubbing their bodies against the trees.

They ate dinner around the campfire and as night fell to darkness, Noah climbed into Christopher's lap and fell asleep. The conversation drifted quietly around the hunt and what they planned to do with all the meat. Kurt pulled out his guitar and played a few Cajun songs with Jack singing along. That wound things down until Christopher began to nod off himself, so he lifted the sleeping boy and carried him back to the tent they were sharing with Jack.

Noah woke up long enough to get into his pajamas and climb into his sleeping bag. Christopher left the battery powered lantern on low so Jack could find his own bag when he made it in. Just as he was getting into his own sleeping bag he saw Noah staring at him with a thoughtful expression on his face.

"You okay?" Christopher asked.

"Yeah," he said and took a slow breath. "Christopher, did you know Mom is going on a date?"

"She mentioned it," he said absently as he fluffed his pillow.

"She's never been on a date before," Noah frowned. His whole demeanor had changed as he lay there, growing sad and tense. "I mean, since Dad died."

"I heard he's a nice guy Miss Bonnie knows. How do you feel about it?"

"I wish it was you." The words came out so quietly Christopher wasn't sure he'd heard them at first.

"You and I are still gonna be friends, no matter what happens." Saying those words made him feel more confident about his decision to stay in Houston. Charlotte might be the main reason, but Noah and the other kids he worked with for Doctor Jenks were as well. Maybe someday he'd kick himself for letting his dream job go, but not with Noah's thin face shining over at him.

"But why don't you like Mom? I know she likes you."

Rather than trying to explain why there was just no spark between them, Christopher said, "I like her just fine, but she's a little older than me. And besides, Miss Charlotte and I are already going out."

Noah frowned. "But what if Mom likes that guy from the date? What if she *marries* him? I don't want someone else to be my dad."

"No one can replace your dad, Noah, not even me. I was only a little older than you when my mom died. Afterward I worried *my* dad would bring someone home and try to replace her. Then later on when I saw how sad he was, I began to hope he would find someone to help make him happy again."

"Mom wasn't very happy when we had to move here to take care of Nanna, but since we met you, it's been great." The hopeful look in his eye was hard to take.

"Yeah, but what else happened? She made some new friends and started going out with them. You got to meet Uncle Jack and Aunt Julie and hang out with their kids. There are lots of reasons she's happier now."

"I guess," he muttered, not sounding entirely convinced. "But they're not my real uncle and aunt."

"They still care about you, just like me. And you're also doing better in school. Doctor Jenks is giving her good reports since you've been working out more. I bet not having to worry about you so much has helped as well."

"She doesn't yell at me as much, that's for sure." The two of them settled down and the tent was silent for a while. "Thanks for talking to me."

"Anytime," he said and reached over to rough the boy's hair. "Let's get some sleep."

* * *

After a relaxing weekend of camping and hunting, the drive back to civilization gave Christopher time to reflect on what he had to do. He still needed to let Maggie Jensen know he was going to pass on the job. While it was frustrating to let the opportunity go, there would be other jobs. Charlotte felt like a one in a million chance he couldn't let get away.

Noah was drowsing in the middle seat of his father's Suburban while Roger drove them back to Houston. Just as they got back on I-45, Christopher's phone beeped. Realizing he had signal again, he looked down to see three voice mail messages waiting.

The first message was from Charlotte. When Christopher heard her say that she met Ashley, his stomach knotted in a ball of nerves. As Charlotte's words got louder and came out more heated, his heart dropped: she knew about the Atlanta job. The knife-to-the-chest pain came when he heard the message end with Charlotte repeating like a mantra, "I hate you" over and over again.

While he was still reeling from that, the second voice mail from Noah's mom, Emily, started playing. Her growl sounded like a protective mother bear as she dressed him down for not letting her know he was moving to Atlanta. She was upset about what it would do to Noah and berated him for being thoughtless about Charlotte's feelings. He was struggling to figure out how this cluster fuck had happened when the final message played.

Ashley sounded tense when she said, "Christopher, call me first. I screwed up. I'm sorry."

Glancing over his shoulder he saw Noah was sound asleep in his booster seat. "Dad, I need you to pull over for a bit."

"You okay?" he asked, looking concerned.

"No," he said with a catch in his voice. "I need to make some calls while we have signal here."

They pulled over at the next gas station and Christopher got out of the Suburban. He thumbed Ashley's contact and waited forever while the call connected and rang.

"I fucked up," she said as a greeting.

"Is that why I've got a voicemail from Charlotte that says she hates me?" he screamed.

"There was a big party of girls at work on Friday night celebrating one of them getting pregnant. I heard one girl mention her boyfriend Christopher had gone hunting this weekend, so I asked if it was you. When she said yes, I asked her about the job in Atlanta."

"Fuck me," he muttered as he leaned his head against his dad's Suburban. "Holy shit."

"I thought you were going to tell her this week!"

"There was no point! I decided to pass on the job and stay in Houston to be with her." He stretched his neck and walked in circles.

"Look, I know I screwed up. What can I do to help fix this?"

"You've done enough. I need to talk to Charlotte." He dropped the call and immediately touched Charlotte's contact to call her.

It didn't ring, just went straight to voicemail. "This is Charlotte. I'm not interested in talking right now. Leave me a message unless you're Christopher Dunlop. Christopher, lose my number. I have nothing to say to you."

There was something about her tone. Despite sounding more controlled than her voicemail had, her pain was even more evident somehow. He dropped the call and stared at the traffic passing them on the road for a long moment, then got back in the Suburban.

"Let's go home," Christopher said to his father.

"Wanna talk about it?" he asked as he put the Suburban in gear.

"Nope." Christopher sat back and studied the road as the pain slowly turned to rage. It wasn't his fault. He didn't do anything wrong. "Maybe."

Roger checked the rear view mirror and said, "The boy's asleep. Say what you need to."

"I got a job lead out of the blue. Some doctor heard about me at the hospital and put me in touch with a lady working with vets out in Atlanta. She wants me to develop a program to help their families, put together a team of people, and then run it for her."

"Wow! Okay, so what happened?"

"I finally got the offer letter last Sunday and asked for some time to think about it. You know I'm gettin' serious about Charlotte, but it's too soon to ask her to come with me and a long distance thing will kill it. I needed to talk to someone, and Charlotte was busy in Morgan City with her family, so I called Ashley."

Roger didn't say anything, but his sour expression when he glanced over spoke volumes.

"She's just a friend, Dad."

"Uh huh." His skeptical tone put Christopher's back up. "I bet Charlotte doesn't think so."

"Anyway, I planned on telling Charlotte about the job offer on Monday, but when I got her on the phone I realized I couldn't take the job and leave her."

Roger chewed on that for a moment and said, "So I take it something happened?"

"On Friday the girls went to the restaurant where Ashley works. She heard Charlotte mention me and asked about the job. Ashley spilled the rest and now Charlotte hates me."

Roger let out a long sigh. "So what are you gonna do?"

"I don't know. Charlotte won't talk to me now. Emily is mad because she thinks it's gonna hurt Noah. Fuck." His phone rang, displaying Kurt's name on the screen. He accepted the call and shut his eyes. "Hey man."

"Dude, you took a job out of town and slept around on my sister?" he growled.

"No, I was gonna turn it down. Look, you gotta help me straighten this—"

"So what's with this *Ashley* chick?" It was hard to control his temper with Kurt shouting at him.

"She's just a friend, but now that I'm seein'—"

"She ain't just a friend. Charlotte said you were still sleepin' with her between Mardi Gras and Easter."

"We hooked up sometimes, but not since—"

"What the fuck, man! I've had your back while you guys were working things out. Jesus, am I stupid or what?" He gave a bitter laugh. "Well, that's all over now. You stay the fuck away from my family, you hear me?"

"Loud and clear," Christopher growled back and dropped the call, muttering obscenities.

"Who was that?" Roger asked.

"Kurt," Christopher answered, swallowing down the bile in his throat. *Fuck the drama. If it's over, then let it be over.* "He told me to stay away from his family."

"Let it cool down for a day or two. Maybe call Jack up and explain what happened to him. I bet he'll help you work it out."

"I'm not explaining anything." The bitterness welled until he had to clench his fists to keep from pounding the dash. "I'm done."

"Don't make decisions when you're angry, son. You know what happened last time."

He and his first real girlfriend in high school, Steph, had planned to keep things going when she went away to the University of Texas at Austin. That had lasted a few weeks until he surprised her one Saturday morning and found a guy in her room. When he raced back to Houston, he stopped at the Marine Corp recruiting office on the way home and signed up on the spot.

It turned out her cousin had stopped over for a visit. Christopher had broken her heart and ruined what they had going over a misunderstanding, but this time he wasn't the one making snap decisions. Charlotte had stepped on his heart three times in as many months. He kept paying for her inexperience and irrational jealousy. It was obvious to him that their relationship wasn't going to work out after this latest blowup.

"Fuck her," he whispered. Checking the signal on his phone, he placed one more call.

Maggie Jensen answered, "Hey, I was hoping to hear from you today."

"I just wanted you to know I've thought about it and I'll take the job. I'll give you a call tomorrow night to work out the details, but I wanted to let you know today like I promised."

"Wonderful! I'll send the paperwork to your email address. Just print out the forms, sign them, and send them back. I'm so glad to have you aboard."

"Yeah, I can't wait to get to Atlanta," he said. "Talk to you tomorrow."

* * *

Going in to work at the hospital on Monday, Christopher was still boiling at how unfair Charlotte had been. He kept his mood to himself, but something must have leaked because his coworker, Deborah, was walking on eggshells around him all day.

Instead of going to lunch, he went down to the Human Resources department to file his letter of resignation effective the last Friday in May. The nice lady who took his form asked why he was leaving and smiled when he described the position he was leaving for.

That evening he spent over an hour on the phone with Maggie brainstorming and outlining what their program would look like. After he got off the phone, Christopher set up some shared documents online for his notes and immediately began to organize research to back up his ideas. Sipping a beer for dinner, he worked late into the night, then fell exhausted into bed, too tired to dwell on the ache he felt in his chest.

It took until Wednesday for the news of his departure to spread through the hospital. The unhappy reaction from the other staff members surprised him, but it was Doctor Rebecca Jenks' reaction that surprised him most.

"I thought we had a deal," Becca growled from over the nurses station counter. He had been finishing his reports for the day when she came up and startled him.

"What?" he asked, looking up with a confused expression.

"You couldn't come talk to me first? We had an understanding."

"You mean the after hours work? I thought I was just helping you out a little."

"I had plans for you." She sighed heavily and shook her head. "So how did you find this new job out of town?"

"Doctor Osborne said he heard I was doing a good job and referred me."

Becca's mouth compressed into a thin line and her eyes narrowed. "That fucker."

"What's going on?"

"Nothing that concerns you anymore, short-timer," she said and turned to walk away.

"Wait, are you saying this isn't a real job?" He went around the counter and chased her down the hallway.

"Oh it's real all right." She didn't stop until she got to the elevator and pressed the button.

"Stop! Talk to me. Why are you so pissed off?"

"Did you tell anyone you were working for me after hours?" she asked, her eyes zeroing in on his.

"No."

She studied his face for a moment. "Then he must have found out some other way." She stepped into the elevator as the doors opened.

"Who? Doctor Osborne?"

"Look, there's more going on than you know about and I don't care to explain it to you now. Congratulations on the job, but make sure you turn all your outstanding receipts to me before you go." The elevator door closed, blocking out her scowling face.

Utterly confused, Christopher wandered back to the nurses station to finish his reports before leaving for the day. He had his standing Wednesday session with Noah after work and dreaded dealing with Emily. As he drove over to their apartment he steeled himself to ignore her unfair judgment of him. When he knocked on their door, he heard the familiar thunderous footsteps of Noah running to open it.

"Hey. Mom wants to see you."

When Christopher went inside he saw Emily standing with her arms crossed. Ignoring her for a moment, he asked Noah, "How was school this week?"

"Good," he said with an uncharacteristic lack of energy.

"Let's get this over with," Emily said. "Do you want to tell him, or shall I?"

Christopher clenched his jaw until his temper cooled, then knelt down and beckoned him over. "Come here, Noah." Looking in his eyes, he put his hands on the boy's arms. "Something's come up. I got offered a job in Atlanta working with kids like you. I've decided to take it."

Noah didn't react at all. "Is that it?"

"I'm moving to Atlanta at the end of May."

"Okay. Can we go running now?" Christopher looked up at Emily and caught her anger melt into concern.

"Noah, do you understand?" his mother asked as she touched his back. "He won't be coming back after the end of May."

"Yeah." Without looking at either of them, he pulled away and walked towards the door. "Are you coming or not?"

Christopher stood and shrugged at Emily's confused expression. "Sure thing. Let's go."

After getting outside, Noah stepped into a slow jog while Christopher ran along with him across the green courtyard. The apartment buildings outlined the large parking lot and grassy play area where they ran. Christopher mulled over his little friend's reaction until Noah broke the silence.

"You'll come back to see your Dad sometimes, right?"

"Of course, and to see you as well if you want. Your mom has my number and you can call me anytime." After running a little further he added, "I'm sorry if this hurts you, Noah."

"It's not your fault. It's *hers*." A look of rage flashed across his face.

"Who?"

"Charlotte," he spat with a look of contempt that seemed far older than his years. "She did something to make you want to leave."

The eery insight startled Christopher enough that he slowed to a walk, then stopped. "What happened is grown up stuff. You wouldn't understand, but—."

"I heard Mom say she got mad at you and then you got mad at her. Everything's all fucked up now and it's her fault!"

Kneeling down to pull the crying boy close he whispered, "No, buddy, it's not really her fault, not like you think."

"Then why doesn't she want to be with you anymore?" The exchange with Noah had Christopher feeling punch drunk.

"I really don't know, but it's just not gonna work out, buddy, no matter how much I wanted it to." The boy cried on his shoulder for a minute, then backed up to wipe his eyes. "She thinks I did something, but I didn't do it. She won't let me explain and now everyone else is mad at me, too. If this was the first time something like this happened, I'd work it out somehow. But it's not the first time and I'm tired of trying. Besides, this job is something I've always wanted to do."

After nodding a few times, Noah said, "I still wish you would stay."

"I know you do, buddy."

They finished the run and workout, then Christopher left Noah after walking him into his apartment for dinner instead of staying like he normally did. The hard light in Emily's eyes followed him from their doorway until he got in his car and drove away.

* * *

Ashley called once to find out how he was, but when Christopher explained he was leaving Houston, she fell silent. It wasn't fair to blame her for the whole situation, but he couldn't stop his anger from showing through. In the end, she wished him luck and told him goodbye. It felt final.

Researching the treatment plans went from a distraction to a passion over that first week. What started as a collection of notes and ideas began to coalesce into something more. Every evening he would speak to Maggie for her feedback as she reviewed his documentation remotely. They developed a good working rapport, sharing ideas and refining their goals as the day of the move crept closer.

At first, a month felt like plenty of time to get ready to move, but soon Christopher was overwhelmed by the millions of things he had to do before he arrived in Atlanta. Some of them were purely tactical, like breaking his lease and packing up his apartment. The spartan furnishings and decor in his apartment required a surprising number of boxes. Maggie offered to find him an apartment in a good part of town, so he let her act as his agent while he signed the lease via fax. After he moved and got a feel for the area, he could pick his own place.

During the second week of May, Christopher started to comb through resumes to find the right kind of people for his team. After stalking the applicants on social media to get a feel for their personalities, he interviewed each one on the phone. Some of them seemed to get what the team was really going to be about and offered to help develop the plan, so he opened up his shared documents for their review and contributions.

By the end of of the fourth week, the team had been virtually assembled and Maggie had an excited tone in her voice when she called to check in on his last Thursday night in Houston.

"Are you ready to hit the ground running on Monday?" she asked.

"I really am," Christopher sighed as he sat back against his couch. He was in his usual position sitting on the floor in front of the coffee table with his laptop and documents spread out in front of him. There were boxes stacked near the front door ready to load up in the rental truck for the move on Saturday. "I can't believe how much we've gotten done."

"I've got to tell you, what you've accomplished over the last few weeks should count for your Master's degree. You did a fantastic job with the research and documentation, and your insight into the issues faced by the families of service members was a real education, even for me."

"Dad was a drill sergeant and we lived the life. Moving every couple of years, having friends in and out of your life, it's a different thing than growing up and always going to the same schools."

"You should be proud," she said. "When you get in town on Sunday, give me a call so my husband and friends can help you unload. I feel like I know you better than anyone I've *never* met before."

Christopher laughed and nodded. "I feel the same way."

After a pregnant pause, Maggie started to ask, "So about that situation you're leaving behind with the girl..."

"It's over." He reached over and grabbed his beer. "Nothing you need to worry about." It was, too. Charlotte had never called. After a week, his obsession faded from an ache to a bruise. She was too unstable, he told himself. The constant drama wasn't something he wanted to deal with long term anyway, no matter how compatible they were in other ways.

"What about that one boy you were working with. What was his name?"

"Noah. He's actually taking it better than anyone expected. He and his mom were from Atlanta before they moved here, so he wants to come visit after I get settled in."

"Well, from what you said, he and his mother are prime candidates for our program."

"They should be, considering I designed most of it around my experience working with them. That's why I pushed so hard for the support group component for the parents. Having the girls night out to blow off steam did so much for Emily's stress level. Did I mention she started dating again?"

"No," Maggie answered with a chuckle. "So, are we gonna start a dating service, too?"

That made Christopher laugh hard. "No, it's just an indication that she's getting some balance back in her life, that's all. Emily said the guy is really nice, so hopefully the little rat won't torpedo the situation for them."

"I'm glad you've got some closure then. It would be hard to leave if things were still up in the air."

"Yeah, I was worried about that at first. It's worked out though."

"Okay, then, call me when you get close to Atlanta and we'll meet you at your new apartment."

"Great," Christopher said. "I'll see you then."

After getting off the phone, he drank the rest of his beer, then climbed up on the couch and tried to go to sleep. His last day at the hospital had come early because he hadn't taken all his vacation days. He'd said his goodbyes to everyone who was still talking to him, but the impulse to try Charlotte one more time was hard to fight.

Knowing it was over and being at peace with it were two separate things. It didn't bother him that all of her friends believed what Charlotte had accused him of. If that was what it took to make a clean break, then there was no point contradicting her. It would be easier to simply let it go than point out her mistake and still leave anyway.

Just as he began to drift off to sleep, his cell phone rang showing Charlotte's picture. *Fucking perfect*, he thought to himself as his stomach boiled. He debated not answering, but swiped to accept the call just before it went to voicemail.

Chapter 19: Charlotte

Charlotte ducked into a closet to make the call. Just two weeks after starting at Southwest Hospital, she was already doing something that could get her fired. She trembled as the phone rang. *Please be there. Please pick up.*

"Hello?" Christopher mumbled.

"I'm working in the ER tonight. Emily and Noah were in a bad car accident. Can you go get her mother from the assisted living center? The doctors need a relative to make decisions. It's bad, Christopher." She lost control of her voice and ended with a sob.

"Fuck! Of course. I'll bring her as fast as I can get there. Can I call anyone else for you?"

Hearing his voice again brought back all the pain and confusion she'd banished weeks ago.

"Call Aunt Julie. I've got to get back before someone catches me."

She dropped the call and tucked her phone back in her pocket. Since he was the only other person who'd met Emily's mother, Maria, Charlotte had to call him. She couldn't deliver the news over the phone that her daughter had been crushed in a car accident and was probably going to die.

The tears came again and she couldn't stop them this time, blurring the screen as she input patient information gathered by the triage nurses. Wiping her eyes to keep up a professional demeanor, she noticed a worried looking doctor approach the nurses station. Charlotte glanced at her badge and saw her name was Rebecca Jenks.

"I'm looking for Noah Vasquez," she said. "He's my patient."

"He's in room twelve." As they looked into each other's eyes, Charlotte felt a moment of connection with the doctor.

"You know him, don't you?" Doctor Jenks guessed.

"Yes," she squeaked past her closing throat. "Please save him."

Nodding as she left, she said, "I'll do my best."

Charlotte found it hard to concentrate on her work, but pushed on as the minutes ticked by. The job to input notes taken by the triage nurse was just the latest in a series of boring assignments since she started work. After sitting through orientation, she'd been assigned to work in medical records, the dispensary, and was now doing data entry for admissions. It wasn't what she imagined her job would be like at all, but if she hadn't been there to identify Emily and Noah when they arrived, no one would have known who they were.

They had come in without identification because her car had been destroyed. Charlotte had been returning to the nurses station from her break when the paramedics rushed past. Emily was unconscious, strapped to the back board with her bloody leg bones poking through her skin. Little Noah looked almost as bad with a messy head wound and visibly broken arm.

When Charlotte cried out their names, the doctor running along with them sent her to pull their medical records. Having their blood types and other critical information would speed up the treatment process.

After doing as he asked, she returned to her post like a zombie, only slipping away long enough to call Christopher. Giving information about patients without permission was a clear violation of the hospital's privacy policy and health care laws. She didn't care; someone had to pray for her friends besides her.

"Are you just gonna sit there? We're backing up and need to move the patients along," Minh said. The older nurse was in charge of the triage process and her boss for the evening.

"Sorry," Charlotte whispered and returned to typing the admission notes into the computer.

The work was mindless and repetitive, allowing plenty of time to worry herself sick. Her thoughts looped continuously through visions of Emily and Noah on their gurneys to hearing Christopher's voice and reliving his heartbreaking betrayal. The cycle was enough to make the chicken sandwich she'd eaten for dinner come back to haunt her.

SOMETHING DIFFERENT

When it happened, no one could believe that Christopher was planning to move to Atlanta. Then Emily confirmed it after he told Noah he was leaving in front of her. Charlotte had trusted him but it had all been a lie. Now in the middle of this horrible crisis, she was going to have to face him. She vowed he wouldn't get the chance to lie to her again.

After getting caught up with the data entry, Charlotte looked up to see Christopher pushing Maria into the lobby in her wheelchair. Maria was pale and trembling, but Charlotte couldn't tell if it was from worry or her advanced Parkinson's disease. Christopher nodded to her as he pushed Maria to the nurses station counter. He looked as handsome as ever despite his wrinkled clothes and tousled hair.

"My daughter," Maria gasped. "My Noah."

"The doctor's are working on them now. I'll let them know you're here."

"Did Doctor Jenks get notified?" Christopher asked.

"Yes, I saw her come in about thirty minutes ago."

He sighed in relief and nodded. "Good. We'll wait over there."

After taking the message that next of kin was available, Charlotte returned to share what she'd learned. "Both Emily and Noah are being prepped for surgery. I told the nurses you were here. Someone will probably come with more information in a bit."

"How bad is it?" Christopher asked.

"I only got a glimpse of them on their way in. Emily had compound fractures in both legs. Noah had a broken left forearm and a head injury. The charts haven't been updated except for the orders to prep for surgery."

Maria covered her face and sobbed while Christopher looked sick. "Thanks for calling me."

"Did you call Aunt Julie?"

"Yeah, she's gonna leave the kids with Jack and come in. She also mentioned calling Bonnie to pass the word to Frank."

"Oh God, I didn't even think about him. They've only been out a few times but I know they were hitting it off. Damn." Charlotte felt the tears rising again. It wasn't fair that Emily just started to find happiness only to have her new life torn from her.

There was a tap on her shoulder as she stood there. When Charlotte turned she saw Minh glaring at her. "Don't you have work to do?"

"Sorry. This is Maria Lopez, the mother of the crash victim and her son. I was just giving her an update."

"That's not your job! Don't leave the nurses station again without speaking to me first."

Charlotte walked away as a gnawing pain in her stomach made her feel weak. Back at the computer she found the stack of notes had grown again, so she began entering them while Minh stayed to talk to Christopher and Maria.

Minh returned to the nurses station with a scowl. "You were the one who called them?"

Now the chicken sandwich was pressing against the back of her throat. "Yes. I know the woman and the boy from the crash. They were brought in without identification so I told the doctor who they were and called her mother."

"Do you *want* to be fired? You can't do that!" Minh rolled her eyes and shook her head. "I'm gonna have to report you now or *I'll* be fired. Jeez. Just do your damn job, would you?"

Biting her tongue, Charlotte pounded the keys as she entered the stack of notes next to the computer. Now her cycle of worry included a stop in Human Resources along with Emily, Noah, and Christopher. Sweat beaded on her lip and forehead as she imagined losing her friend, her boyfriend, and her job all in the same month.

She was still busy when Julie came in wearing sweats and a t-shirt with her hair in disarray. She went straight to Christopher and Maria, hugging the older woman as they both sobbed. A few minutes later, Bonnie and a man she assumed was Frank came in as well. They all shook hands or hugged, then spoke for a few minutes before sitting down to wait.

The minutes became hours. Small bits of information came out of surgery, but nothing significant until a sad looking doctor came out and invited them to one of the private rooms off the waiting area. Charlotte knew what that meant and brought up Emily's record on the computer. *Time of death: 02:14 A.M.*

The welling horror of that message on the computer screen made her break down and sob. Her friend Emily, who'd been through so much struggle and heartache was gone. And her son, Noah, the bright funny boy she'd grown to love was now alone. Charlotte pushed away from the desk and ran to the bathroom to lock herself into a stall and threw up her chicken sandwich.

Alone, she imagined the doctor's careful words to her friends. Maria was too ill to care for the boy, and his deceased father's family hadn't stayed in contact at all. Charlotte knew that the pain of losing her child and being unable to care for her grandson would be searing to Maria. That poor woman, that poor boy. It all poured out along with her own grief at losing someone she'd grown so close to.

"Charlotte?" Minh called from the door. "I told you not to leave unless you speak to me first."

"My friend in the car accident just *died*!"

"Welcome to the real world! There are patients out here who may die if you don't do your fucking job! So put on your big girl panties and get back to work."

The surge of rage was so strong that Charlotte feared she might end her brief career in the back of a police car. By the time she got out of the stall, Minh was gone. *What a bitch...* Then the rage flashed out and left a black despair that took her tears and breath away. She returned to her computer and silently entered patient notes until the end of her shift.

* * *

Wrung out after her all night shift, Charlotte padded along the busy hallway on her way to Noah's room. The dawn light shown through the open windows until she reached his doorway. Christopher and Maria were sitting in the dark room with the shades drawn. Noah looked so small in the bed with wires and tubes tying him to the wall.

"Hey," she said as she stepped through the door. "How's he doing?"

Christopher looked up with dark circles under his eyes. "Concussion. Broken arm. Becca said his heart's okay, though, and the pacemaker is still working, thank God."

"Becca?" she asked as she crossed to the bed to look at Noah. His visible skin was a mottled purple, but he was breathing evenly.

"Noah's pediatric surgeon, Doctor Jenks."

"I met her tonight. Last night. Whatever." She touched Noah's face with the back of her fingers and moved his hair off his forehead. "Has he woken up yet?"

"No." Christopher looked over at Maria who was snoring softly in her wheelchair. "The anesthesia wore off hours ago. Becca says he could wake up anytime."

"Do you mind if I wait with you?"

"Knock yourself out."

Charlotte sat down in the chair next to Christopher's and chewed on her fingernails. She'd bitten them all off during her shift as the stress brought the childhood habit back. Her beautiful nails were gone along with the polish she'd chipped off. Now her fingers looked stubby and raw.

Christopher's phone buzzed and he took the call. "Hey Maggie."

Maggie? How many women does he string along at once? She ripped off another bit of nail while he listened to whatever Maggie was saying.

"Thanks for understanding. I know this puts you in a bind. For what it's worth, I think Antoine would be a good choice to replace me. He had some good ideas the last couple of weeks and really seemed to get what we were going for. Plus he was a military brat like me."

The meaning of his words made her arms prickle. *Could he be giving up the job in Atlanta?*

"Okay, I will. I'll keep you updated. Bye." When he'd put his phone back in his pocket, he glanced over and caught her staring.

"Sorry, I didn't mean to intrude," she said.

"No big deal," he sighed and returned his attention to the boy in the bed.

"You're not taking the job?"

"No."

When he didn't elaborate, she returned to destroying her nail beds until the need to understand drove her to speak. "Why?" she whispered.

"He's gonna need me." Getting up, he walked over to the bed to look at the boy. "How could I leave?"

It felt like a slap in the face. Hadn't she meant anything to him? Hadn't she needed him, too? "You were going to leave me," she said impulsively.

"No, I wasn't, not until you broke your promise."

"What promise?" she growled, offended by the implications.

"You promised to talk to me and not shut me out." He looked over at her with a tired expression. "I really don't want to get into this right now."

"You lied to me," she hissed.

"What lie?" he asked with a red face and hard eyes.

She couldn't believe he had the nerve to ask. "You were with Ashley again."

His lips thinned and his temples flared. "We had dinner and talked about you. We also discussed a job offer I'd gotten. In the end, I decided to stay here in Houston and pass on the job to be with you, but then you flew off the handle. Again. You didn't break up with me, Charlotte, I broke up with *you*."

She couldn't breathe. All the air was sucked out of the room. It couldn't be true, he had to be lying or twisting the truth but she couldn't see how. Getting up, she stumbled through the door feeling like her head was a balloon tied on by a string.

When she got to the nurses station one of the doctors standing at the counter approached her. "Are you the duty nurse?" Doctor Jenks asked as she finished signing off on a chart.

She realized she was still wearing her scrubs and badge. "No, sorry, I'm off duty."

Doctor Jenks looked up and seemed to recognize her. "You were in the emergency room last night. You know Noah."

She nodded. "Emily was a close friend."

"Mine, too." She said as tears welled in her eyes. "Wanna get a cup of coffee? I don't feel like being alone right now."

"Me neither." *Could it be true? Did I make him leave?* Forcing thoughts of Christopher away, she extended her hand and smiled weakly. "I'm Charlotte."

"I'm Becca."

* * *

The cafeteria was bustling with employees and visitors eating breakfast while Charlotte and Becca got their coffee. Finding a table off to the side, the two women sat down together in silence for a moment.

"How did you meet Emily?" Becca asked.

Charlotte couldn't stop the sad smile from touching her lips. "Christopher."

"I thought that was you." Becca said with a wry expression. "He used to talk about you all the time."

The smile slipped away. "Yeah."

"Sorry. I didn't mean to bring up a sore subject."

She shrugged it off and changed the subject. "Did you find out what happened to cause the accident?"

Becca grimaced. "Drunk driver. He ran a red light and drove his big ass pickup into the drivers side of her car."

"Fucker," Charlotte growled.

"He wasn't even hurt." After an ironic laugh Becca leaned closer and whispered, "He's lucky I wasn't his attending physician when they brought him in or he would have been."

After the brief moment of dark humor, Charlotte wilted again. "Poor Emily."

"She had been crushed. There was never really any hope. But Noah will pull through just fine."

"What about the concussion?" she asked, taking a sip of her coffee.

"The CT scan didn't show any bleeding, so I'm hopeful it'll heal without complications." Leaning back in her chair, she sighed and closed her eyes. "The brain is very resilient. I was more concerned about his heart, but thankfully it looked just fine."

"What'll happen with Noah? His grandmother can't take care of him. She needs as much help as he does."

"Christopher stepped up." Becca smiled and opened her eyes to whisper, "Oh, if I was only twenty years younger… and I wasn't married… and he was Jewish." She winced at Charlotte's uncomfortable reaction. "Sorry, I was trying to be funny."

"It's fine." Except it wasn't fine. Christopher's words kept circling in her brain, forcing her to reexamine every memory of that awful week after Easter. She had been so positive she was right, that he'd betrayed her. Hearing his perspective suddenly made her doubt herself and everything she thought she knew.

"Hey, you wanna talk about it?" Becca seemed sympathetic and trustworthy. It was so tempting.

"I wouldn't know where to begin." Wiping her eyes, she leaned on her elbows and put her hands around the warm cup.

"Christopher told me a little about you. He mentioned how much you have in common when it comes to your career plans. And I know how much you helped Emily because she talked about you and your friends as well. What happened?"

After a deep breath to gather her thoughts, Charlotte said, "I was jealous of a girl he'd been with. When I ran into her one night, she mentioned seeing him, but he hadn't said anything to me about it. She also knew about his job in Atlanta and he'd never told me."

"Don't feel bad, he never told me either," Becca murmured in a grumpy tone.

"Why would he have told you?" The only connection she knew about was Noah, and Christopher had never mentioned Doctor Jenks except in passing.

Becca's cheeks turned pink. "He never told you about our arrangement?"

Charlotte felt her stomach drop and face get hot at her insinuation of their relationship. "I think we're done here."

"No, Charlotte, wait!" She reached over and grasped her wrist. "He did extra work for my patients like Noah outside of the hospital. That's all!"

"Oh," she said as she sat again slowly. "He never mentioned that to me."

"I asked him not to. I've been working on something on the side and didn't want anyone around here to know."

Chuckling at herself, Charlotte said, "And there is my problem in a nutshell. I don't trust him, not in my heart anyway. I believed Ashley immediately. When he planned on moving, I assumed I was right to mistrust him. Now I'm not so sure and it's too late."

"Ah," Becca said and took a sip of her coffee. "I've been there. *My* husband is rather... popular as well."

"What? With women?" Charlotte asked, trying to figure out the enigmatic smile on her face.

"Have you ever heard of the band *Hijinks*?"

"Sure, who hasn't? I grew up with Mom playing *I Wanna Be Your Man* and dancin' around the living room with my brother and me."

"That's my husband, Robert Jenks."

"Are you fucking kidding me?" Charlotte tried to imagine this dowdy doctor married to one of the '80s great dance club musicians.

Her reaction must have tickled Becca, who smiled and shrugged. "He farts in his sleep and I have to shave his ears these days."

"Oh my God, don't tell me that!" After the moment passed, she got serious again. "How did you get over being jealous?"

"I'm not gonna lie to you, it's hard. Communication is the key. You have to be willing to ask questions and listen to the answers without jumping to your own conclusions. If you allow the seed of doubt to grow, you're doomed."

"That's the opposite of what I did," Charlotte said with a weary shake of her head. "I was so scared of the truth that I cut him off before he could hurt me more. The insane thing is that I got mad because he didn't try to talk to me after cutting him off. It turns out *he* might have dumped *me* for spazzing out again and took the job in Atlanta to get away from me."

"That actually fits what I know from the bits and pieces he's let slip." Becca said it with a wince and reached over to pat her hand.

"And that probably means I've lost him for good." The realization stole what little energy she had left. "This coffee isn't helping."

"I wish I had some Irish whiskey to spice it up." Becca took a sip and stared off for a moment.

"So, Christopher is gonna take care of Noah?" Charlotte prompted after a few moments of silence. It was just like him to want to do it, but it was hard to imagine Maria trusting her grandson to someone she barely knows.

"I found Christopher and Maria in the private room with three other people after I got out of surgery. It wasn't that long after they'd heard we lost Emily. Maria was nearly hysterical about what to do with Noah. She said she has some family in west Texas and New Mexico, but no one around here. Noah's father was an illegal immigrant who got amnesty by serving in the Marines, but his family is all south of the border."

"God, what a mess."

"Yeah, but in the middle of her rant, Christopher quietly said he would stay in Houston and help her. She actually tried to talk him out of it at first, but he was adamant about staying. He said he could move back in with his father for a bit, then find a place with a good school district in the summer. Another woman said she and her husband would help him as well."

"That would be Aunt Julie."

"Anyway, they all started brainstorming about what they needed to do to help Christopher become Noah's legal guardian. I could actually see the weight lift off of Maria's shoulders."

"I'm going to help as well." Charlotte resolved.

Becca's phone interrupted playing the happy refrain from *I Wanna Be Your Man*. She dug it out of her lab coat and lifted it to her ear. "This is Doctor Jenks." She paused and smiled. "I'll be right up." After ending the call she said, "Noah's waking up."

Chapter 20: Christopher

Christopher was standing near Noah's bed when Becca and Charlotte returned to the room. The fact that he'd lost his temper and blurted out the truth about their situation made him even more uncomfortable around her. His heart ached for Noah and he didn't want to deal with her bullshit in the midst of everything. Except it was too late, he realized, as her eyes lingered sadly on his face. He looked back to Noah and pushed her out of his mind.

"Hey Noah," Becca said as she smiled and felt his forehead. "How are you?"

"Did I need another pacemaker?" he whispered. His tongue ran along his cracked lips as he blinked slowly at the people around the bed.

"No, we checked it out and it's working perfectly."

"Why's my arm hurt?" he muttered as he tried to turn his head to see it.

"There was an accident, but you're going to be just fine." Becca kept her tone light despite the weariness in her face. Christopher felt a surge of admiration for her after performing surgery and being up all night with her patient. "Do you want some water?"

"Yeah."

Christopher filled a styrofoam cup with ice water from the pitcher near his bed and put a bendy straw in it for Becca to give him a drink.

"Here you go." She held the straw to his lips. "You can sleep some more if you feel like it."

"Okay," he said after he finished drinking and slowly shut his eyes again.

Becca went to sit by Maria in her wheelchair. Noah's grandmother had bowed her head and was whispering what sounded like prayers. Christopher went to the other side and knelt down next to her as well.

"That is a very good sign," Becca whispered to her. "He was attentive and responded to questions appropriately. He tracked my face with both eyes and even drank a little. I think I can get some sleep now. So should you." Becca looked up significantly at Christopher to solicit some support.

"I agree, Maria," he said. "Let's get you back home to rest for a while and you can come back here to see Noah later today." Christopher saw her shake her head, but it quickly went from a determined motion to a tremulous symptom of her Parkinson's disease.

"I don't want to leave, but I can't keep going," she admitted with an angry scowl. "I hate being old and sick."

"I'll take her home if you want," Charlotte said from behind Becca. "I need to get some sleep after my shift. Her assisted living center isn't that far out of my way."

Christopher was relieved. He didn't have to leave Noah yet. At some point the questions would come about what happened and his mother. That was going to be a hard conversation, but Christopher was determined to be there for him. "Thank you," he said and gave Charlotte a weak smile.

"Let me go down and get my stuff out of my locker. I'll be right back."

As she left, Christopher noticed the way her scrubs fit and it raised his blood pressure. He adjusted his involuntary reaction to her body with a grimace, cursing himself to keep his attention on the problem at hand.

Standing back up, he picked up Maria's purse and blanket off of the back of the wheelchair and put them in her lap. "Do you need to go to the restroom or get a drink before you go?" he asked her.

"No, I'll be fine until I get home." Her chin quivered a bit as she looked up at him. "I can't thank you. I have no words. That you would give up your job, your life for him. For me."

"Stop. We've been through this. Dad will help us until I can find a job and you'll be with us every step of the way. We're all gonna do this together." Christopher felt the weight of the responsibility, but he couldn't leave Noah to fend for himself in the foster care system. If he hadn't offered to help, that's exactly what would have happened when the hospital's social workers got involved. "I'm just glad you're willing to trust me as his guardian."

"Oh, *mija*, why did God take you away from me?" she asked the ceiling as the tears came again. After a moment, she looked back at Christopher and said, "Still, I give Him thanks He gave *you* to us, *mijo*. I don't know what I would have done without you today."

By the time Charlotte came back with her backpack, Christopher was fighting off sleep himself. After they said goodbye and left, he reclined the chair and covered up with a sheet to watch Noah. He woke when the nurses came in to check Noah's vitals, but the boy slept through it all.

* * *

When he woke up later in the afternoon, Charlotte was sitting next to him in the other chair watching Noah sleep. Between them on the small side table was a sandwich and can of soda. After glancing at his watch to see it was a little after three in the afternoon, Christopher sat up and rubbed his face.

"Hey," he muttered. "Sorry I was a dick earlier."

"You were right," she said without looking at him. "I brought you something to eat in case you're hungry."

"Thanks," he said as he unwrapped the roast beef sandwich. "I didn't have to be a dick about it, especially after you called to tell me about Emily and Noah."

"Forget about it." She finally turned to look at him with a sad smile.

After washing a bite down, he asked, "Did you bring Maria back with you?"

"Yeah, she's still eating down in the cafeteria with Julie and Cathy. They sent me to scout things out before they came up. Has he woken up yet?"

As she finished speaking, Noah moaned softly and reached up to scratch his left shoulder where the cast started. "Mom?" he whispered.

Christopher felt the butterflies start as he walked over to the bed. "Hey," he said and tried to smile.

"I thought you were movin' to Atlanta," Noah said with a frown. "We said goodbye and everything."

"Somethin' came up. How're you feeling?"

"Like I've been hit by a truck," he said and coughed out a laugh. "Ow, that hurts. What happened?"

His comment made Christopher shiver. "What's the last thing you remember?"

"Mom and I had dinner with Nanna. She made enchiladas. Then I woke up here."

"You and your mom were in a bad car accident last night."

"Is Mom okay?" he asked, his lip already trembling.

When Christopher hesitated, the look of concern on Noah's face grew into panic. "I'm so sorry, Noah," he said as he took the boy's hand, his own eyes filling with tears. "She's gone."

"No," Noah whispered as his face crumpled. "No, Mommy!"

As the sobs poured out, he reached up with his good right arm and Christopher held the boy. He cried along with Noah while Charlotte quietly stepped out of the room and closed the door.

* * *

There were so many details to take care of that all Christopher could do was to keep a list and work on whatever task was at the top. He helped Maria with the funeral arrangements, worked on his legal guardian paperwork, coordinated his father and friends to move his stuff back to his father's house so he could spend as much time with Noah as possible.

When she wasn't working, Charlotte quietly supported him by making sure he ate and picking up the small tasks he couldn't find time for. He was especially grateful that she picked up and dropped off Maria each day. Working together with her again felt as natural as breathing, but he had to work at keeping his old obsession at bay.

The funeral was held on Wednesday at a memorial garden Maria had selected on her side of town. Christopher had to unpack half the boxes in his father's garage to find his suit, long-sleeved shirt, dress shoes, and belt. When he went back into the house, his father was tying his tie in front of his dresser mirror.

"Matt wants to come, too," Roger said cautiously as Christopher carried his clothes past the open door of his room.

Stopping for a moment, he watched his father finish with the tie and put on his coat. "I never said he couldn't, I just figured a seventeen-year-old would have better things to do on a Wednesday night than attend the funeral of someone he's never even met."

Roger grinned and shrugged. "I think he's actually excited to have a little brother to hang around with for a while."

"That won't last," Christopher said with a laugh. "I've had two and they're nothing to write home about."

Continuing to the bathroom he shared with his brother, Christopher changed and brushed his hair. So far the week had been a crazy mixture of stress, pain, and, oddly, humor. His father had agreed instantly when Christopher told him the situation, making room in the garage to store all his boxes and furniture until he could find a more permanent place to live. There was no way to predict he'd be twenty-seven years old and living again in the room he'd grown up in.

Charlotte and the girls had helped Maria empty Emily's apartment and move Noah's things into Tyler's old room. Christopher rarely left Noah alone in the hospital, so he only saw Charlotte in passing, but he could smell her perfume in the house when he stumbled into bed. He found it equally distracting and comforting.

"You about ready?" Roger called from the hallway.

"Yup," he said as he opened the door.

Matt was standing next to his father dressed in dark pants, a long-sleeved shirt, and tie. "Me, too."

The drive to the memorial garden in his father's Suburban was spent in quiet contemplation. Christopher had been to more than his share of funerals after joining the Marines. They never got easier, but they did help bring closure. When they arrived, the three of them were directed to the memorial wall where the small service would be held.

Maria was there in her wheelchair, wearing a black crepe dress. Charlotte had brought her and was standing behind her dressed in a black skirt and top. His father approached first and offered his hand and condolences, then introduced Matt to her. His brother made Christopher proud when he skipped the handshake and embraced the frail woman, then whispered something that made her smile.

Charlotte must have heard because she laughed and looked up to smile at Christopher. The moment their eyes met, he couldn't help smiling at her in return. She nodded once to greet him, then looked away as her smile faded.

"Christopher," Maria called.

When he approached and hugged her, he said, "I'm so sorry."

"She will rest easier knowing you are watching over her son."

Jack and Julie arrived with their kids, then Bonnie and Frank came up. Cathy had to work, but had sent a lovely standing display of yellow roses. Polly came last with apologies that Kurt couldn't make it because he was out in the gulf all week. Christopher was reading the cards on another large display when he recognized a name.

"Unbelievable," he muttered under his breath.

"What?" Roger asked and peered over his shoulder.

"This one is from the family of the guy who killed her." He indicated the largest standing display of lilies and mums.

Maria must have heard because she wheeled herself over and glared at it. "What does the card say?"

"Sincere condolences and sorrow for your loss," Christopher paraphrased and handed her the card.

After Maria read it, she began to mutter a torrent of Spanish as she tore the card into tiny bits. Christopher knew some Spanish from his time in the service and was surprised to hear almost all the curses he knew before she was finished creating confetti.

"I will go to his trial and testify about what he stole from me and my grandson," Maria vowed through tears, then turned herself and rolled back to the spot in the wall where her daughter would be placed.

The last to arrive was a priest who introduced himself as Father Williams. The way Julie and Jack greeted him seemed to imply they went to his church. He was an older man, but had the kind of presence that commanded respect and attention. Christopher found himself mentally comparing him to his own Pastor Cole and decided they were two of a kind.

After calling them to prayer, Father Williams offered a heartfelt eulogy and ended with asking God to protect Noah in the days and weeks to come. The funeral director had come with the plain ceramic urn containing Emily's ashes and solemnly placed it in the niche below where her name engraved on a brass plaque.

There was a reception at Jack and Julie's house afterward that everyone attended. Christopher kept to the edges, already itching to get back to the hospital to check on Noah. The women mostly stayed in the living room listening to Maria share stories about Emily. Christopher walked out to the patio to join his father, Jack, Matt, and Frank sitting around the cold fire pit drinking beer.

"I was wonderin' where you got off to," Roger said as he pulled the last beer out of the six pack on the table. Twisting off the top, he held it out for Christopher.

He took the beer and pulled a long swallow before sitting down with them. "I missed this place," he said looking around Jack's backyard.

"We missed you," Jack said with a sad smile. "Well, I did anyway."

"Yeah." He shook his head. "I didn't plan on everything falling apart like that."

"If it's not too personal..." Jack prompted, not asking the rest of the obvious question.

"It's not a big secret. Ashley was just an old friend. I talked to her about Charlotte and the job offer because she knows me really well. When I decided to pass on the job, I didn't see any reason to bring it up. If anything, I didn't want to put pressure on Charlotte knowing I'd passed on my dream job to be with her."

Jack chuckled. "Kurt owes me a bottle of scotch when he gets back from his run. I'm thinkin' Ardbeg."

"What are you talkin' about?"

"I told him there was a reasonable explanation." Jack shrugged. "I'm just glad we can hang out again."

"Me, too."

Frank shifted around and said, "Christopher, I've got to tell you how much I admire you for what you're doing. I never got the chance to meet Noah before..." He clenched his jaw and paused while he got himself under control. "My wife died six years ago, and now Emily. I didn't get to know her well, but I sure liked her."

"God, that sucks for you," Christopher agreed. "Was Emily the first person you'd dated?"

He nodded. "I had my two girls to think about, but Emily was in the same boat. When Bonnie set it up, I thought it would never work out, but we hit it off so well it was scary."

"I lost my wife a decade ago," Roger said. "I really feel for you right now."

The conversation flowed around Christopher as he sat back and drank his beer. His brother was texting continuously, but occasionally joined in as well. Listening to the other men talk about life and loss was soothing in a way. Eventually, Jack and Roger must have had enough and started telling some dirty jokes that kept Frank in stitches until Bonnie came out to see what the commotion was.

When it came time to leave, Christopher ran into Charlotte coming out of the bathroom. That brought to mind the last time they had been in there together which made heat rise in his face. Charlotte must have been thinking the same thing, because she blanched and looked away.

"Excuse me," she whispered as she stepped past him into the living room.

He went into the bathroom, closed the door, and looked in the mirror. He decided he looked like shit. There were dark circles under his eyes where his skin sagged. "What the fuck am I doing?" he muttered, then washed his hands and splashed water on his face.

* * *

After getting to the hospital on Thursday, Christopher approached the Human Resources department about returning to his old job. They welcomed him back immediately. It was embarrassing to see the fuss the staff made about him helping Noah, but was happy to have his job back. By arranging to start the following week, he gave himself time to make the final living arrangements for himself and Noah at his father's house.

On Friday, a week after the accident, Noah was finally released from the hospital. He sat quiet as the nurse pushed him outside in a wheelchair, but Christopher could see him struggling with the new reality he faced. His grandmother was already waiting in his father's Suburban when the nurse stopped to help him stand up.

"Can you climb up in there?" Christopher asked.

Noah had his left arm strapped against his chest, but that didn't slow him down much. "I got it," he said and pulled himself up into the seat next to his grandmother Maria.

"Here, let me help you buckle up," Maria said.

"I can do it," he growled and jerked the buckle out of her hands.

Christopher noted the wounded look in her eyes, but held his tongue. Noah had been snapping at everyone all week, especially Charlotte. Anytime he brought it up, Noah would shut down and stop talking entirely.

"Well," said Roger. "I guess we'll be headin' home then."

Christopher said goodbye to the nurse and got into the passenger seat while his father climbed behind the wheel. He heard Maria trying to comfort Noah, telling him how everyone had helped decorate his new room.

Noah whined, "Why can't I just go home to my old room?"

"We had to move all your toys and things in with Roger and his family for now," Maria explained. "Christopher is going to help take care of you with me."

"I've got my boy Matt keepin' an eye on the smoker this afternoon," Roger said. "He's lookin' forward to meetin' you, Noah. We'll have a good barbeque dinner together to welcome you home."

Noah sighed heavily but didn't say anything else on the trip.

As Christopher looked out the window the reality of the situation came crushing down hard. He had worked with kids for years, but this was so different. The snap decision he'd made to take responsibility for Noah still felt right, but now it was tempered with a healthy dose of fear. *Please don't let me fuck this up.*

Charlotte's car was parked in the street in front of his father's house. She'd been so helpful setting up Noah's things in his brother Tyler's old room. When his father invited her to celebrate Noah's homecoming with them, he couldn't object. They'd probably spent more time together the past week than he had in all the months he'd known her. Sometimes he forgot things were different between them now and had to stop himself from touching her or taking her hand.

When they stopped by the garage, Christopher jumped out and got Maria's wheelchair from the back of the Suburban. While his father helped her down, Christopher grabbed Noah's bag and walked him towards the back door of the house. The large yard had a detached garage and an outdoor kitchen off the patio. His brother Matt was standing next to the smoker feeding wood into the fire box.

"Hey Matt, I'd like you to meet Noah." Christopher led them over and watched Noah's expressionless face as Matt extended his hand.

"Good to meet ya, Noah," he said and shook the boy's hand like he was made of china. "I hear you're gonna be staying with us for a while."

"Yeah," he said, but didn't seem excited about it.

"Wanna play some video games?

That brought a small spark to his eyes. "Whatcha got?"

"Wii and Xbox. I bet you could do bowling one handed."

"Sure," he said, not letting his excitement show too much. "I guess that would be okay." Then he looked up at Christopher as if seeking permission.

"Fine by me, just take it easy and let me know if your arm starts to hurt. I've got your pain pills if you need them." He lifted the bag from the hospital.

Watching Matt lead Noah off made him let out a long breath. *Maybe it really will be okay,* he told himself.

Charlotte came out carrying a beer bottle and handed it to him. "Welcome home."

"Thanks. How'd the room turn out?"

"It's still a little cramped but we got everything in. You guys can move things around later if you want to. Let me have his bag and I'll go put his things from the hospital away."

"Thanks. Can you put the pain medicine up high in the medicine cabinet in our bathroom? I don't want him getting it himself."

"Sure will," she said as she went into the house. His eyes followed her figure again and he wondered what to do about her for the millionth time. She had been so amazing to be around, he was sorely tempted to open himself up to her again. *If I could just trust her to talk to me when she gets upset.*

Sitting down near the smoker in one of his family's faded patio chairs, he watched his father push Maria to the table. They were chatting about his barbeque competitions, which could keep his dad talking for hours. Maria was still wearing black, but seemed to be bearing up well. Her tremors would get worse when she was stressed or tired, but the new medicine the doctor had just started her on seemed to be working much better than the last.

The cold beer wet his throat and put out the fire in his stomach. Letting his thoughts drift, he shut his eyes for a moment and tried not to think about the thousands of things he was leaving undone. Maggie reported things were going well, so he didn't feel too bad about the situation he'd left her with in Atlanta. He had to go back to work in a few days, but he even pushed that away to just enjoy doing nothing for a moment.

The tinny sound of video game music grew when Charlotte opened the back door. "Can I get y'all anything?" she asked Maria and his dad, waving the beer in her hand.

"I'd love a glass of water if it's no trouble," Maria said and thanked her with a nod.

"This is my house, let me get it," Roger said as he stood up. "You have a seat young lady, you've done more than enough helping me this week."

Charlotte sat down between Maria and Christopher and took a long sip of her beer. "That barbeque smells wonderful," she said as she lowered her bottle.

"I can't wait to taste it," Maria said. "When Emily told me about the barbeque at your Uncle Jack's house the other month, I was so sorry to have missed it." She smiled at the memory for a moment, but it faded to sadness. "You were so kind to her and Noah."

"We were friends," Charlotte said. "The way you say it makes it feel like we were doing her a favor. She was my friend and helped me as much as I helped her. After Easter…" She stopped suddenly with an embarrassed look toward Christopher. "She helped me with my share of problems as well, trust me."

Christopher realized she was referring to her misconception about his job in Atlanta. Taking another sip of beer, he wisely kept his mouth shut.

"I am still going through all her papers and trying to figure out her bank accounts and what she had for insurance. I did find Noah's insurance information finally. Since his father died in the service, he gets a monthly benefit now as well as some financial assistance when it's time for college. As soon as I get it all straightened out, we'll go over everything together. In the mean time, I need to write you a check for his expenses."

"No," Christopher said with an emphatic shake of his head. "We can meet with a financial planner to help manage his income and savings, but I'll take care of whatever he needs day-to-day."

"I can't let you do that," Maria said. "You don't know how expensive it is yet. He grows out of his shoes every two months, his medical bills are insane even with insurance, and when he gets in a growth spurt, he'll eat you out of house and home."

"We've got some experience around here with growing boys," Roger said as he appeared with her glass of water and sat down next to her. "I think we can manage."

"I want to help. Even Emily let me help. Please." She had her purse open on the table and a desperate look on her face.

"I know how expensive the funeral was for you. Let me track his expenses for now and we'll settle up later. That way we can all see what it costs and make things fair."

She finally nodded and closed her purse with a sigh. "You're right, it was more expensive than I thought. But you just let me know if you need anything."

"I imagine I'll need your famous enchiladas about twice a week. Hugs are good, too." Christopher smiled as he took another pull of his beer.

That made them all chuckle and Charlotte even reached over to take his hand. He was tempted to pull away, but it was so obviously an unconscious gesture on her part that he couldn't bring himself to hurt her. When she realized what she'd done, her cheeks flushed pink as she quickly pulled her hand away without looking his direction.

"When's dinner?" Christopher asked his father.

"Let me check. It shouldn't be long now." He got up to inspect the briskets, releasing billows of smoke. "Okay, it looks done to me. Let's set the table."

Charlotte and Christopher went into the house to get plates and utensils. He noticed Matt and Noah were both laughing about the game they were playing and smiled to himself. Charlotte opened the refrigerator to get the covered bowls of potato salad and baked beans. While she popped the beans into the microwave, Christopher got down the plates.

"Thanks again for all your help," he said as she stared at the spinning bowl through the microwave's window.

"My pleasure," she said. "I like the little guy, too, you know." He couldn't see her face, but the amusement in her voice made him smile.

"Yeah, I do know," he said as he carried the stack of plates and utensils out to begin setting the table. As he placed the plates and flatware around the table, he impulsively moved Charlotte's beer over to the spot next to his.

They met at the doorway as she came out with the food. He let her pass, then went inside to the living room. "Dinner's ready. What do you guys want to drink?"

"I'll take iced tea," Matt said as he rolled a virtual ball down the lane.

"Me, too," Noah said as he rubbed his shoulder.

"Your arm feelin' okay?" Christopher asked him.

"Yeah, it's fine. Just itches."

"Pause the game and get out there before Dad starts yellin'."

After herding the boys out the door to the patio, Christopher headed back in to grab their drinks. When he came back out there was some tension at the table between Charlotte and Noah.

"I said, *I* want to sit next to Christopher," he said with his face screwed up like he was gonna cry.

"It's fine, Noah," Charlotte said as she picked up her beer. "You only had to ask."

"Why is she even here anyway?" he said to Christopher with tears streaming down his face. "It was her fault you were gonna leave and now Mom's dead. She ruins everything!"

Charlotte covered her mouth and stood, rushing toward the driveway. "I'm sorry," she muttered to Christopher as she passed him.

"Noah!" Maria exclaimed. "You apologize at once!"

"You can't make me! I hate her!" he shouted as he ran past Christopher into the house and slammed the door.

Christopher was torn, but went after Charlotte before she could get away. "Hey, wait a minute."

She was panicked, her eyes wild and lost. "No, this was all a mistake. I should never have tried again. We're better off apart."

"Stop, please," he said, but she pulled away and ran to her car. Short of physically restraining her, he couldn't make her stop and listen. In moments, she was gone, and he felt her loss like a hole in his heart.

Chapter 21: Charlotte

"I thought you were having dinner with Christopher and his family?" Polly asked when Charlotte came through the door to their apartment.

"Y'all still goin' out tonight?" Charlotte asked in return, ignoring her question.

"Yeah, Julie wants to go back to that Tex-Mex place we took Emily to the first time."

"Gimme a minute to change."

She stripped down to her underwear and bra, then pulled a bright green dress out of her closet and laid it across her bed. She sat to pull on some black hose while sniffing back her tears.

It wasn't Noah's fault. He'd just lost his mother after all. And in a strange twist, it turned out he was right about her driving Christopher away to Atlanta. Wiping her eyes, she stood to straighten her hose then pulled the dress over her head.

When she looked back, Polly was standing in her doorway watching her dress with an inscrutable expression. "Don't just stand there," Charlotte growled and turned away. "Zip me up."

Polly sighed and zipped her. "You're not gonna talk about it?"

"No," she said with some heat, then cooled fast. "Sorry. Let me fix my face."

Walking past Polly to her bathroom, she brushed her hair quickly then began to apply green eye shadow to her eyelids. Polly followed and stared at her face in the mirror.

"Julie said you were following Christopher around like a puppy all week. I thought you hated him?" Polly hadn't been convinced that he'd slept with Ashley over Easter and never let Charlotte forget it.

Opening her mouth to apply her red lipstick, Charlotte continued to ignore the questions. She hadn't told anyone what Christopher had said that morning in the hospital; he'd broken up with her instead of the other way around. Once she realized her mistake, she spent every spare minute trying to make it up to him, to repair some of the damage she'd caused.

There were moments during the week when things between them felt almost normal. He would smile at her again or would start to reach for her. Then at the table with Roger and Maria, she had foolishly taken his hand when he made a funny comment. He'd ignored it completely, making her feel even more embarrassed.

"I'm ready. Let's go." Charlotte faced her roommate with a grim smile.

Polly stared at her for a moment, like she was trying to read her eyes. "Fine. You drive."

* * *

Julie raised her glass of sparkling apple juice. "To Emily."

Charlotte looked around at Polly, Bonnie, and Cathy as she raised her own glass and repeated with them, "To Emily."

"Damn," Bonnie said after her sip of champagne. "Frank is crushed. He told me he wanted to do something to help last week, but felt too weird since he barely knew her and hadn't even met Noah yet."

"They only went out four times, right?" Cathy asked.

"Yeah, I think so," Charlotte said. "Were they... intimate?"

"Oh yeah," Julie said as she swirled the juice in her champagne flute. "He rang her bell quite a few times, apparently." She sighed deeply and raised her eyebrows. "I don't suppose anyone else has been considering their own mortality this week?"

"I actually updated my will and trust, which I'd been putting off forever," Bonnie said. "It was particularly morbid deciding what to do with my remains. I ended up buying a little niche next to Emily and prepaid all my arrangements today."

"God, Bonnie!" Cathy laughed in shock. "What the fuck?"

Bonnie drained her glass of wine and waved the empty glass at Julie who had the bottle of champagne at her end of the table. "I'm not gonna waste any more time. When I finally join Emily on that shelf, I'm going to have lived three more lives. At least."

"I'd be happy with one," Charlotte murmured drawing their eyes to her again.

Bonnie raised a questioning eyebrow. "I thought you were going to spend the evening with Christopher and his family."

Steeling herself, she finished off her champagne and thumped the glass on the table. "I was wrong about Christopher."

"Oh, thank fuck!" Cathy said and flagged down their waitress. "Ma'am? Could you bring us all a round of tequila shots please?"

"Not me," Julie added.

"Bring her one anyway. Charlotte can drink two to celebrate not being an idiot anymore."

Rage shot through her like a bullet. "What the fuck does that mean?"

Cathy returned the glare with an amused expression. "It means maybe, just maybe, you'll stop being such a mopey bitch now. God, *everyone* knows he's crazy about you but you."

The words struck like a lightning bolt. "He can't stand me. It was *my fault* he was leaving for Atlanta!" The pain of admitting her failure to her friends made her blink back tears. "He's the one who couldn't trust me, not the other way around."

"Sweetie, we've all been there." Polly swirled the last few drops of champagne around her glass. "If I got what I deserved, I'd have ended up like Kendall back in Morgan City instead of having Kurt love me. Forgive yourself, then ask him to forgive you, too. You may be surprised by his answer."

It was hard to catch her breath as everyone at the table nodded at Polly's words. "I'm such a spaz, though. I don't know how to be his girlfriend without screwing everything up. I suck at it!"

"Then just be his friend," Cathy said as the waitress came back with a tray full of shots and little plates of limes. After everyone had theirs except Julie, Cathy raised the shot. "To being friends."

The conversation wound around work and pregnancy, returning to remember Emily on occasion, but each time with a little more laughter and a little less pain. They discussed Noah and Christopher, barbeques and planned summer trips, and by the time the food was gone and the bill was paid, Charlotte felt herself relaxing for the first time in over a month.

* * *

After returning to Julie's house, she and Polly drove back to their apartment complex to find Christopher sitting on the back gate of his truck. He looked miserable before he noticed them driving up, but gave a thin smile as their headlights splashed over him as they parked.

"See?" Polly said with teasing tone of voice. "I bet this won't be bad news."

"Oh shit, what do I do?"

"Be his friend." Polly patted her leg and got out of the car. "Hi Christopher! Bye Christopher!" She laughed as she passed him, jingling her keys when she got to the door then slipped inside, leaving them alone in the parking lot.

Charlotte approached him sitting there, but stopped just out of reach. "What's up?"

His face twitched as he looked down between his knees. "It's not a mistake."

Her last words to him coming back that way felt like a cooling salve. "What do you mean?" she asked, not wanting to assume too much.

"You trying again. It's not a mistake. After you left, I talked to Noah. He has it in his head that if his Mom and I had been together, she wouldn't have died. I had to explain that wasn't true. I also told him I still care about you and that you're going to be a part of my life just like he is."

Her hand moved by itself to cover her mouth. "Christopher…"

"Please don't stop trying." He sat there looking at her with his eyes full of pain. "Please."

She stepped closer and tucked his head under her chin, surrounding him with her arms. His breath hitched as he hugged her close, his arms squeezing her tight around the middle. It felt like coming home when she kissed his hair. His scent warmed her and made her knees feel weak. The tender moment filled her with peace until she caught Polly peeking out of their front window and started to giggle.

Christopher drew back with a confused look on his face. "What?"

"Look," she said, nodding to the window just as Polly dropped the curtain and disappeared. "Sorry, Polly was spying on us."

"Oh," he said with a sheepish grin. "I'm just glad it wasn't Kurt."

"Why?"

He pulled her close again and sighed. "I thought you knew. He threatened me to stay away from your family."

"He did what?" She had to pull back to make certain he wasn't making a bad joke.

"He called and threatened me to stay away from you and your family on the way back from our hunting weekend. That was the point I figured I'd better just cut my losses."

Cursing her own stupidity again, she groaned and pressed her face against his shoulder. "I'm so sorry, Christopher. I screwed up so many times, I can't see why you still want me around."

He whispered in her hair, "When you're with me, I don't feel the hole inside me anymore."

She recognized his sincere sentiment, but he set up for such a funny reply that Charlotte couldn't resist giggling, "That's funny. When you're with me, all I can think about is you filling the hole inside me."

He sputtered at first, then began to laugh so hard he fell backwards in the bed of the truck and banged the back of his head. "Damn it," he muttered as he rolled over holding his head, still chuckling between moans.

"Sorry!" Charlotte climbed into the bed of the truck to feel his head for bumps or blood. When he tickled her unexpectedly, she flopped down next to him and suddenly found herself being kissed deeply. After a moment, she kissed him back with a rising heat that matched his. As things slowed, she murmured, "Come inside so I can put some ice on that bump."

"I can't stay too long." Sitting up, he helped her down then hopped down himself. Their hands came together naturally as they walked towards the door.

After making him a Ziploc ice pack and sitting him down at the kitchen table, Charlotte slipped down the hallway. She'd seen Polly duck into her room as they came in, so Charlotte tapped on it and whispered, "Christopher came in for a minute. I had to put some ice on his head."

Polly opened the door with a big grin on her face. "What did you do? Knock him out?"

"You should know, you were spying on us!"

"You have to tell me *everything* when he leaves. Wake me up, no matter what time it is."

"Stop it, it's no big deal." The heat in her face betrayed her hopes, but Polly just laughed and shut the door.

Christopher was still sitting at the table with an amused expression on his face. After their funny moment of intimacy outside, she was suddenly nervous. The warm feeling in her center and damp feeling in her underwear didn't help.

He put the ice pack down and felt his head with a chuckle before speaking. "Look, this has been a hellish week for all of us. I don't want you to feel pressured. We haven't had time to talk about anything or work out the mess from last month. Just knowing you're gonna keep trying is all I really wanted tonight, and—"

"Stop," she said and took his hands. "I'm a spaz and will probably screw things up again. I overreact about stupid crap because I'm scared and have no idea what I'm doing. I feel like I don't know how to be a girlfriend, and when I'm with you, I'm terrified I'm going to get hurt somehow."

He frowned and started to say, "I'm not—"

"Let me finish. Please." She looked up in his loving, worried eyes. "I finally realized I didn't trust you enough. I was so afraid that I forgot why I wanted to be with you in the first place. You are so amazing." She choked up, then laughed at herself. "And for some reason you still want to be with me." She stood then, pulling at his hand. "And tonight I *really* want to be with you."

He chuckled in return as she pulled him into her room and shut the door. "Have I told you yet how beautiful that dress looks on you?"

"If you like it now, wait till you see it on the floor by the bed." She turned so he could help with the zipper. His hands pushed the dress off to puddle at her feet while he kissed her shoulders from behind. Sparks shot all over her body as his breath tickled her skin. "Oh, I missed this."

"Me, too." His hands moved forward to cup her breasts as she reached back to run her fingers through his hair. Her bra was open before she knew it and his fingers were on her skin, teasing her nipples into hard points.

His erection pressing into her back made her turn around to run her hands down the front of his jeans. He gasped in her mouth. The zipper and button took seconds to open, then his jeans joined her dress on the floor. Before she could slip her fingers inside the elastic of his boxer briefs, he lifted her with a growl and placed her on the bed. They tore each other's clothes off then, humming with frustration until their underwear littered the floor.

"You don't need to use a condom anymore if you don't want to," she whispered in his ear. The follow-up appointment just before graduation confirmed her IUD was staying put.

"I won't last long," he warned, kissing her neck and ears.

Drawing him in between her legs she said, "I don't care. I just want to feel you inside me again. God, I missed this!"

In seconds, she was full of him. The sensation without a condom was so much better that she actually cried out. The slippery feeling of being skin-to-skin intensified the experience. She pushed hard against his thrusts and encouraged him with kisses and moans.

"I've got to stop," he begged, holding himself still. "I don't want this to end right away."

"No," she whined against his cheek. "Give it to me. I want to feel you."

She pushed herself onto him all the way, grinding against him until he cried out into her hair. Holding him tight, she felt the pulses that signaled his release. It kept going on and on, far longer than it ever had before. He continued to strain and push until he collapsed on top of her.

His weight bearing down was comforting. Lying there with him still inside of her body provided a kind of intense satisfaction. As his breathing slowed, she dragged her fingertips up and down his back, relaxing with him as he recovered.

She could feel a tickle as he shrunk inside of her. The slow movement of his shaft left room for his seed to spill out, but she didn't care about the mess they made. She was at peace with everything now.

When he finally moved, it was to turn his head so he could kiss her cheek. She hummed deep in her throat and kissed his face in return. They started again slow, passionate, and warm, but the heat increased as their lips and tongues began to tease. With each breath, the passion grew until he was devouring her lips and chin.

To her delight, he began to grow again inside her. Encouraged by the movement she felt, she reached down his back to pull at his hips. While it wasn't the iron rod he'd had at the beginning, he was able to tease her along with small thrusts as they continued to kiss.

"That's a neat trick," she gasped when he kissed along her neck to her ear. The feeling of fullness returned as he rocked inside her. "I thought we had to wait for you to recover."

"It's never happened before." The whispers tickled her damp skin where he'd been kissing. "I blame you."

"Can I get on top?" she asked. When he slipped out it left her feeling empty and cold. She moved out of the way so he could lie down on his back. They were so wet and slippery it took both of them working and laughing to get him back inside.

She sat up and rode him slowly, fanning her breasts and stomach to dry off a little. He was staring at her breasts, then reached up to cup them. "Your body is so amazing."

"It kinda likes you, too," she said with an arched eyebrow. Rolling her hips, she kept them both sighing and moaning. While he squeezed her breasts, she reached down and slipped her fingers between them to feel their joining.

Touching his shaft moving inside made her tremble. She leaned forward a little and closed her eyes as she pressed her fingertips against her mons. Rubbing definitely helped. She could feel her orgasm build while she pushed against her fingers and his cock.

"Is this better?" he whispered. He'd moved his hands to her hips and was pulling her down harder with each thrust. She nodded and put one hand down on the bed next to his shoulder so she could lean over further.

"Getting closer now," she whispered. "Oh, that feels so good."

They kept a steady pace as she worked herself along. He was getting so hard again that the pressure inside made a fluttery sensation in her stomach.

"Slow down," he warned.

She looked down into his face with a wicked grin. "No. I can always finish later. I want to feel you again if you can."

They stared at each other with mouths twitching and lips biting, waiting to see who would finish first. She was teetering on the edge when his mouth opened and his pulses tickled her on the inside.

"Damn. Sorry," he groaned and covered his face with his hands.

She let out a delighted laugh that matched exactly how she felt about it. "I love that you can't control yourself with me," she said as he finished and stilled.

Now it was her turn to lay on top of him while he traced patterns on her back with his fingertips. She had a rush of overwhelming emotion as she lay there, a deep connection that tied her heart to his like nothing she'd ever felt before. As her heart raced and her eyes filled with tears, she realized Christopher was slowly drawing letters on her back.

"What are you writing?" she whispered as she dried her eyes.

"A secret," he said and finished with the letter *E*.

"That's not fair, I didn't notice until the end." Finally getting herself under control, she raised up to kiss his nose. She intended to say something funny, but was thrown off entirely by his handsome features.

A wicked grin suddenly appeared on his face. "Move up. Straddle my chest then scoot forward so I can have you in my mouth."

"But I'm full of you. Isn't that gross?" she asked as she slid forward like he asked.

"Haven't you kissed me after I've had a mouth full of you? It's no big deal, I want to. Hold on to the headboard to steady yourself if you need to."

As she moved, he pulled the pillow out from under his head and scooted down the last few inches. With his hands gripping her ass, he pulled her body to his mouth and began to feast. She had to shut her eyes when his tongue opened her.

"Oh God, it's like riding a pillow with a tongue," she gasped as her fingers gripped the headboard. "That feels so... wait, what are you doing?"

He'd pressed his tongue against her nub so she could rub against it, but then he squeezed his fingers in from behind. One slipped in to press the wonderful spot on the inside that was like her magic cum button, but the other was slowly pushing in between her cheeks.

When the tip of his finger penetrated her ass, she froze for a moment. It was shocking, but it somehow raised her pleasure to a level she'd never known. At the same time he did that, he flicked his tongue against her nub making her thrum like a string on a guitar.

Riding the cusp for what felt like minutes, she finally cried out as she came. Violent spasms rocked her as she convulsed and pressed hard against his face. With her eyes screwed tight she had no idea what she was doing to him, but Christopher sounded like he was in heaven, moaning loudly against her mons and frantically licking everywhere his tongue could reach.

Then, suddenly, it was too intense, and she raised away from his face. "Stop, I can't take it anymore." Moving to lie down on top of him, she began to kiss his face with a heat she felt to her core. "That was so fucking good." His lips tasted like a crazy blending of them both.

He wrapped his legs around hers and held her tight. "Yes," he whispered. "I wish I could stay all night. I don't want Noah to wake up and find me gone."

"Thank you so much for coming by." She kissed him once more, then rolled off to let him get up. "Let me get a robe on and I'll walk you out."

He dressed quickly while Charlotte hung her dress up and put her underwear in the dirty clothes basket. Tying her robe, she opened the door and walked him to the front door.

"Can I see you tomorrow?" he asked in the open doorway. His hair was sticking up in all directions and his face had a warm, happy glow. "You could come over for breakfast if you want."

"I'd like that." They kissed once more before he walked away looking back to grin at her with every other step.

As soon as she shut the door, Polly came walking barefoot down the hallway, wearing a long t-shirt and carrying an empty glass to the kitchen. "Okay, spill."

"We worked it out," she sighed happily.

"Yeah, that was pretty obvious. I had to put on my headphones and turn my tablet all the way up."

"Stop it," she said as heat rose to her cheeks. Fanning herself with her hand, she said, "He wants to keep trying. God, he's so amazing."

"Good," Polly said. "Now I can text the girls back and go to sleep."

"What?" she laughed.

"Well I was giving them all a play by play from the window, so when he came in, they went nuts. You're lucky I didn't live blog the noises you guys were making!"

"Shut up! After you made me listen to you and Kurt that last time for *hours* you have no right to complain."

"It's not my fault he wouldn't untie me. I couldn't remember our safe word and he thought I was playing." She bit on her pinky as she walked back to her room. "I think I'll forget it again. That was fun."

"Stop! He's my brother for God's sake." Charlotte laughed and went back into her own room. The scent of Christopher was everywhere now. She turned off her light and climbed into the bed, avoiding the enormous wet spot in the middle.

When her phone buzzed, she grabbed it off the charger. Christopher had texted that he was home safe. She texted back sweet dreams, then put her phone down to have a few herself.

Chapter 22: Christopher

Christopher woke to the scent of frying bacon and the sound of cartoons playing at a ridiculous volume. He rolled over, yawning and scratching his head, then pulled on a pair of shorts laying on the floor next to the bed. After checking his phone for messages, he stuffed it in his pocket and shuffled through the living room where Matt and Noah were watching some cartoon show.

"Mornin'," he muttered as he passed by, lured by the barely detectable scent of coffee under the overpowering aroma of bacon. "How's your arm?" he asked Noah who was reclining against the end of the couch.

"Fine," he answered without looking up from the television, wiggling the fingers that protruded from the end of his cast.

"Good morning," Roger said from the stove when Christopher reached the coffee pot. "Did you straighten things out with Charlotte last night?"

He bounced his eyebrows a couple of times and gave his father a sly grin. "Sure did."

"Good." He finished flipping the bacon. "I didn't hear you get in last night."

"It was after midnight."

Grinning back at his son, Roger asked, "So is she comin' around for breakfast this morning?"

"I asked. We'll see what she says when she gets up." He poured himself a steaming cup of the strong coffee his father preferred and held it under his nose. "Man, I missed your old percolator."

"Yeah, those new machines may be faster, but nothing makes sludge like this old pot here."

As he sat the battered aluminum percolator back on the stove, Christopher's phone beeped. The text was from Charlotte asking if it was time for breakfast yet with a smiley face. "She's coming now," he told his father as he texted a reply.

By the time the doorbell rang, Christopher had quickly showered and shaved. Charlotte looked as lovely as ever standing in the doorway with her long hair pulled back in a ponytail wearing khaki shorts and pale blue t-shirt.

"Good morning! Come on in," he said, unable to take his eyes off of her smiling face.

As soon as he shut the door, she stepped into his arms and kissed him. He could feel her intake of breath like she was drawing in his scent. Her perfume and natural chemistry made him feel light-headed as they stood with their arms around each other.

"Good morning," she whispered into his neck giving him chills. "I'm starved."

"Who is... Oh." Noah stopped in the entryway and blushed, looking down at his feet.

"Do you have something you'd like to say?" Christopher prompted gently as he stepped out of her arms. Charlotte knelt on one knee to be closer to his eye level.

"Sorry," Noah muttered, but it didn't sound convincing.

"Can you give us a second?" Charlotte asked, looking up at Christopher with a nod at Noah.

"I'll be in the kitchen." Christopher left them alone and returned to help Matt and his father finish setting out breakfast. Charlotte and Noah stayed in the entryway for a while. At one point Christopher heard Noah sobbing, but Roger grabbed his arm when he headed that direction and shook his head.

"Don't worry, she's got this," he said with more confidence than Christopher felt.

When Charlotte came in holding Noah's hand, he seemed much less tense than he had been. Noah sat between Charlotte and Christopher and gave Christopher a thin smile.

"So what's everyone doing today?" Roger asked.

"A bunch of us are headin' over to swim at Katelyn's house," Matt said between bites. "Her Dad is throwin' her a graduation party."

"That sounds like fun," Roger said. "She still going to University of Texas with you next year?"

"Yup," he said with a wicked grin. "She's even in the same dorm as me."

Roger turned his attention to Christopher and raised his eyebrows.

Christopher roughed Noah's hair and said, "I've got to find a place to live before you sell the house out from under us."

"I ain't kickin' you out," Roger said with a dismissive laugh.

"No, but you've been plannin' on selling this place and buildin' a house on our land since we were kids. Besides, with Matt and Tyler both in Austin you'll only be an hour away from them up there."

"Can we come see you when you move up there? It was so much fun," Noah said.

"I hope you do," Roger said with a wink. "I'd love to teach you all the things I taught my boys."

"So where are you gonna look?" Charlotte asked.

"I want to find a small house near Maria's assisted living center. Noah, would you mind if we brought Charlotte along to look with us today?"

He glanced at her with a half-smile. "I guess not. Would you like to come?" he asked Charlotte.

"I couldn't imagine a better way to spend my day." Her smile for Noah warmed Christopher's heart, but when she glanced up at him, she melted it through. "What kind of place are you looking for?"

"Nothing specific. I was thinking about driving around to get a feel for the neighborhoods in the area and using that house hunting app on my phone." He grinned at Noah and said, "Maybe find out if their playgrounds are any good."

Noah grinned. "Yes!"

"Are you looking to buy or lease?" Charlotte asked. Her expression turned serious as she obviously switched to her analytical, problem-solving mode.

"Buy. I qualify for a VA loan and still have the money I'd saved for the move to Atlanta. Dad said he'd help get me over the hump on a down payment, but I may not need the help." He smiled toward his father. "You know all that work I did the last few weeks writing out the treatment plans for Maggie? She paid me for the whole thing even though I didn't take the job."

"Seriously?" he said. "Why'd she do that?"

"She kept going on and on about the program and documentation I came up with for her and said it was worth more than just the time I'd spent doing it."

Charlotte's eyes widened. "That's wonderful! I'd love to read them sometime."

"Thanks," Christopher said, a little red-faced by her praise. "I'll shoot you a link to the docs when I get online."

* * *

After breakfast, Christopher helped Noah take a bath without getting his cast wet while Charlotte helped Roger and Matt clean up. Once Noah's bath was over, Christopher helped get his shirt on around the bulky cast.

"Are you sure you're okay with Charlotte coming with us?" he asked.

Noah sat still while Christopher buttoned up the short-sleeved shirt for him. "Yeah."

"She really likes you, you know," Christopher finished with the buttons and adjusted the sleeve around his cast.

"I know," he said and looked up thoughtfully. "She liked Mom, too."

"Your Mom was one of her best friends."

Noah nodded and thought about that for a while. "I'd like to go see Mom today," he said in a small voice. "Nanna said it was pretty there, where they put her."

"It is," Christopher said. "We can pick up your Nanna, too, if you want."

"Good," he said and nodded. After a moment he asked in a rush, "Are you and Charlotte gonna get married?"

The question coming out of left field made Christopher gasp and then laugh. "Where'd that come from?"

"I just wondered is all."

"Are you worried what'll happen to you if we do?"

"Maybe," he said, but the suppressed grin on his face showed his embarrassment admitting it.

"You and me are gonna be together no matter what," Christopher said with his hand out. "Deal?"

Noah put his small hand in Christopher's and shook. "But it'll be different now. You're gonna tell me what to do and stuff, the way Mom did."

"Yeah, but I'll try to listen and be fair. Sometimes, though, I'm gonna know better and you're just gonna have to trust me and do what I say."

He sighed and asked, "Is it okay if I'm a little scared?"

The admission amplified Christopher's own fears. "I'm scared, too, buddy. I've never had to take care of anyone before other than my brothers. I want to do a good job for you."

"Then I'll take care of you and you'll take care of me. All right?" His confidence was infectious.

"You got it," Christopher said and hugged the boy close. "Let's go find a place to live."

* * *

That afternoon they drove around looking at houses together and dreaming. The Spring Branch neighborhoods they explored were older, with tall trees spreading across the yards and streets. Christopher noted nice houses on the house hunter app he'd installed on his phone. The three of them got out occasionally to peek into windows or over fences at the more likely ones.

Noah insisted they stop at a few of the parks they found so he could get out and try them out. Even with his arm in a cast, the boy's energy and exuberance was undaunted. They laughed together, taking turns swinging or going down the slides while Charlotte took pictures with her phone to send to Maria.

They arranged to pick Maria up in the late afternoon for dinner and then to visit the memorial garden. After debating what to eat, they settled on a burger and slushy at Noah's favorite drive in place before they went to see Emily's memorial.

When they got to the memorial gardens, Noah walked through staring at the walls covered in plaques, urns, and flowers. "Are all these dead people?" he whispered.

"Yeah," Christopher answered, sobered by Noah's observation.

"How'd they all die?" he asked, shaking his head at the sight.

"She's right down here, Noah," Charlotte said, changing the subject while giving Christopher and Maria a significant look over Noah's head.

Emily's urn had been sealed behind a marble plug with a small shelf holding an empty vase. Seeing her name engraved there brought the pain of her death back to Christopher, calling to mind the horrible night in the hospital and Maria's helplessness. Blinking back tears, he stepped backwards to sit on the bench opposite her niche.

"Do you want to put the flowers in, Noah?" Maria prompted, handing the boy the lilies she'd brought with her.

Charlotte left the two of them alone and sat down next to Christopher. He put his arm around her shoulder and pulled her close.

"You okay?" she whispered.

"Not really," he said, feeling overwhelmed by loss and the magnitude of the responsibility he'd taken on. Noah had climbed up in his grandmother's lap and was weeping quietly in her arms. "Sometimes I wish I could do that."

"What, cry?" Charlotte said looking around at his face. "Oh, baby."

The wall he'd kept up all week broke under the pressure. He let it go in a torrent, sharing all his fear and pain as she held him. When it passed he felt wrung out, but as he pulled her tight and kissed her wet cheeks, he felt their bond growing stronger.

"Thanks," he said, letting her go to look at her face. She had cried as well and quickly wiped her eyes.

"Sorry," she chuckled. "I guess we had a moment."

"Yeah," he brushed her hair out of her face. "How are you holdin' up?"

"Well, I miss my friend and hate my job. They keep moving me around so I never know what I'm gonna be doing when I go in. On the plus side, I made up with an old friend which makes me feel like I won the lottery." She touched his cheek and smiled.

"I know the feeling," he said as he searched her face. "Thanks for coming out with us today."

She looked like she wanted to say something serious, but just then Noah came up to squeeze in between them for a snuggle. "I'm hungry."

"You just ate two hamburgers, fries, and a slushy," Christopher stated in disbelief.

"I warned you," Maria said to Christopher as she rolled herself over. "You're gonna go broke tryin' to keep that boy fed."

"Dad has some leftover brisket you can eat, I guess."

"Let's go!" Noah jumped up, but before they walked too far he looked back at Emily's niche and whispered, "Bye, Mom. I'll see ya later."

* * *

Going back to work was like stepping into a pair of comfortable shoes. The rumor mill had been in full swing and everyone knew that he'd come back to care for his friend's little boy. Women came out of the woodwork to introduce themselves and give him flirtatious words of encouragement along with sincere offers to help. He thanked them all, careful to mention he was seeing someone to avoid any misunderstandings with Charlotte.

Back on the kid's floor, Deborah welcomed his return with a laugh and a hug. There weren't many patients still around from his last day, but the stories of him becoming Noah's guardian created a mystique with those kids who knew him. It didn't keep him from doing his job, so he just acknowledged it when it came up and carried on as he'd always done.

Some days he and Charlotte worked the same shifts and they would meet for their meals and breaks. He listened to her complain about the kinds of work they had her doing and shared his own stories of his first few weeks to encourage her.

On Tuesday and Thursday, Christopher invited Charlotte along with them to go looking at houses in the afternoons. With her help, they began refining what kind of house made sense. Noah was more concerned with it having a tree house and being close to a park. Christopher wanted to find one with a nice back yard and garage big enough for a workshop. Charlotte drove where they directed, seemingly content to listen to their lively discussions of what life would be like.

By the end of that first week, he'd established a daily routine of work and spending time with Noah. His father, Roger, kept Noah busy during his shifts by taking him around with him wherever he went. Then when Christopher got off work, he'd take Noah out for a slow jog or to the library for books. He'd finished the *Harry Potter* series and was slowly working his way through *The Lord of the Rings*.

When he returned from lunch on Friday, he found Doctor Osborne talking to Deborah at the nurses station on his floor. Deborah had an uncomfortable expression on her face when she saw him approach.

"Christopher," Doctor Osborne called with a jovial tone as he turned. "Just the man I was looking for."

Deborah caught his gaze and rolled her eyes as she walked away. He couldn't decide what the look meant before Doctor Osborne clasped his hand.

The doctor's expression turned serious when he said, "I heard about your friend's accident and what you've done to help her son. I'm sorry for your loss."

"Thanks," Christopher said and let go of his cool, dry hand. "I'm sorry I left Maggie in the lurch, but I couldn't walk out on Noah."

"Yes, Maggie was sorry as well. She told me you did a great job on the program plan and documentation. Any chance of you moving out there with your boy and seeing it through?"

"No." Christopher blinked at the question as he recalled Becca's odd reaction to his job offer. "Emily's mother is being treated for Parkinson's here in Houston. I couldn't take her grandson away after she's lost her only child."

"That's a shame." Doctor Osborne took a deep breath as he examined Christopher closely. He leaned in and whispered, "If I could offer you a word of career advice, don't get mixed up with Doctor Jenks again now that you're back."

The words and his irritated expression put a chill up Christopher's back. "What're you talkin' about?"

"Look, introducing you to Maggie proves how concerned I am about your career. Just take my word for it and keep your distance. I would hate for you to have problems here if you didn't." The subtle threat yielded to an overly large grin as he patted Christopher's arm just a little too hard. "Good to have you back, Christopher! I expect to continue hearing good things about you."

When he walked away, Deborah came up with a perplexed look on her face. "What was all that about?"

"I don't have a clue, but I'm gonna find out."

* * *

Christopher was walking out to the parking garage when he heard a voice calling his name. Turning back to look, he saw Becca hurrying to catch up with a beaming smile on her face.

"I'm so glad I ran into you today," she said as she fell in step beside him.

"How've you been? I haven't seen you since the funeral last week."

"I'm hangin' in there. Hey, did Charlotte tell you she's invited me to their girls night out tonight?" she asked as she dug her keys out of her purse.

"Yeah, she told me last night when she drove Noah and me around to look at houses. She was excited you said yes."

"I have to go to temple first, but the girls don't go out until eight or so anyway. I have to admit, I'm excited, too. My husband is the Cantor and plays music for our services, so I can't always let my hair down with my friends there."

"I thought your husband was a rock star?" Christopher said with a chuckle at her reaction.

"Only sometimes. Mostly we just work and raise our family, although the nest is pretty empty these days."

He held the door to the parking garage open and let her through. "You never mentioned you had kids."

"Harry, my oldest, is twenty-two. He's just graduated and moved home with no idea what to do with his music degree. My daughter Zevvy, who's nineteen, is studying abroad and I miss her so much. Anyway, how're you and Noah doing? Any issues with his arm?"

"It's been a big adjustment for me, but we're doing okay so far. The break itches him like crazy. I caught him pushing a Popsicle stick down from the top of the cast trying to scratch it."

She chuckled and said, "He'll get it off in a couple of weeks. Don't let him scratch too much or it could get infected." She stopped by a silver Mercedes she said, "Well, this is me."

"Listen," Christopher said as he looked around to see if anyone was close enough to hear. "Doctor Osborne came by to see me today. I know this sounds strange, but I think he threatened me."

Becca searched his face for a moment, then nodded to herself. "Do you have some time? I'd like you to follow me so I can show you something."

"Sure," he said, keeping his questions to himself. "Let me go get my truck."

"I'll be waiting by the exit."

Christopher turned the puzzle of the dueling doctors over in his mind. He knew there had to be politics in a big hospital just like there had been in the service, but it still seemed weird they would involve someone at his low level.

He pulled out of the parking garage behind Becca's silver car and followed it toward Old Spanish Trail. They passed through a sketchy area with older office buildings on poorly maintained streets. She pulled into a deserted parking lot next to a four-story building and parked, letting Christopher get out of his truck while she stood by her car.

"I didn't want to discuss anything at the hospital." She clutched at her purse and glanced around the deserted lot. "I've got a bit of a reputation there as a troublemaker and some people would like to see me gone. Their problem is that my practice is too big to risk me going to another hospital. And because I'm not interested in being a hospital employee, they can't force me to do things their way."

"Ok, I get that. So what does Doctor Osborne have against you and why the silly game of tug-of-war over me?"

"I go to bat for my kids. I don't let their insurance status stand in the way of their treatment. Since I bring in enough business to cover the occasional pro bono case, no one complains too much. Doctor Osborne got wind that I'm going to start a not-for-profit surgery and rehabilitation center and is trying to score points by outing me to the board. I've been grooming certain staff members to bring over when I throw the switch and he's been very *helpful* when he finds one, like getting them jobs out of state." She gestured to the building behind her. "This is where it's gonna be."

"Wait, you wanted me to come work for you out here?"

"I never got the chance to tell you about this. I need someone like you who understands that getting well is more than a physical process sometimes, like with Noah. He was depressed, which made him avoid exercise, which lowered his heart functions and put him at risk. You get it, Christopher. It's all tied together. There are so many kids like Noah out there who need help. You could be a part of this with me."

Christopher found himself leaning against his truck and running his fingers through his hair as he processed what she was saying. "Holy shit, Becca."

"I know it's a lot to take in at once, but things are starting to come together and I may be making a move soon. Think about it, but *please* don't say anything to anyone."

Looking at her, he realized his decision was already made. "You should talk to Charlotte. She wants to be a surgical nurse and they are wasting her talent by running her all over the hospital doing clerical work."

Becca raised an eyebrow. "Gee, Christopher, I wonder why *your* girlfriend has been getting a ton of shit jobs?"

Chapter 23: Charlotte

Becca walked into the steak house wearing a slim blue dress and low heels. Charlotte waved until she smiled and headed towards the group sitting at a large round table in the corner of the dining area.

"Everyone, this is Becca Jenks. She's Noah's pediatric surgeon," Charlotte said as Becca took the empty seat at the table between herself and Bonnie.

"Hi! Sorry I'm late. The service at temple went long and I'd forgotten there was a reception I couldn't skip." Becca put her purse strap over the back of her chair and turned to face the others with a smile.

Bonnie extended her hand and said, "I'm Bonnie. This is Julie, Cathy, Polly and of course, you know Charlotte." Her warm welcome brought smiles as they all got acquainted, asking the common questions of family and career.

Charlotte watched with an amused grin as Becca's outgoing personality won her friends over easily. It had been obvious to her that Becca would fit in their group and her connection to Emily and Noah sealed it.

After their talk the morning after Emily's accident, Charlotte kept running into Becca around the hospital. Finally they laughed, declared it was fate, and ended up eating dinner together in the cafeteria one evening. They spent that meal talking about Christopher and Noah, Becca's family, and Charlotte's career plans. It had felt like shameless begging to bring up the pointless jobs she'd been given and then mention wanting to work as a surgical nurse. After describing the classes she took and her work in the surgery at Lafayette General, Becca admitted with a grin that she'd already read Charlotte's employee file and knew of her interest.

On impulse, Charlotte had brought up her girls night out group and invited Becca to come out with them. To her surprise and delight, Becca agreed with the understanding that she went to temple on Friday nights and would have to meet them wherever they ended up.

Charlotte's steak was wonderful and the conversation was lively, but she kept looking at her phone to check the time. Polly noticed and elbowed Julie to whisper in her ear, making both of them smile at her. Cathy must have noticed as well because she chimed in with a teasing grin.

"So what happened with Christopher after last week?" Cathy asked Charlotte as she finished off the last bite of her dessert.

Feeling the heat rise in her face, she smiled and said, "You should already know since Polly texted you all a blow-by-blow."

They all laughed, then Becca asked, "I meant to ask that as well. I ran into him on the way to the parking garage this afternoon. He seemed positively smitten when your name came up."

Charlotte looked up with an excited thrill. "What did he say?"

"Nothing in particular, but when your name came up he smiled just like you are right now."

That made Charlotte chuckle. "We're taking things a day at a time. I'm just focusing on being his friend, like y'all said last week, and it's helped."

"Christopher brought Noah over for a sleepover with the kids tonight," Julie said with a sly look. "Any chance he'll be waiting for you in your parking lot again this week?"

Unable to meet their eyes, she tore up her drink napkin into pieces while everyone laughed at her reaction. "Maybe."

Polly smacked the table. "So that's why you said you didn't want to come with us to Ovations!"

"I really do have to work in the morning," she said to Polly with a sassy grin.

"Good for you, sugar," Bonnie said and raised her wine glass. "To Charlotte and Christopher!"

They all cheered and took a drink while Charlotte shook her head, unable to stop smiling at her friends. "You guys are crazy."

"So, how's he doing after his first full week at home with Noah?" Julie asked.

"Okay so far," Charlotte said. "I went by a couple of times to take them house hunting when I was off. They're looking for a small house in the Spring Branch area so they can stay close to Maria."

"Why can't they just stay with his father?" Cathy asked. "His house is just over in Katy. It isn't that far away."

"Roger wants to move to be closer to Matt and Tyler in Austin. He's planning to build a house on their family land which is about an hour away from there," Charlotte said and took a sip of her wine.

Bonnie perked up and offered, "You know, Frank is a real estate agent. I bet he'd want to do something nice for Noah because of Emily."

Charlotte watched the group pounce on Bonnie's idea and run with it. In moments, Julie had agreed to paint and decorate whatever house they bought, Bonnie offered to let them pick over some of the furniture from their warehouse, Cathy stepped up to help them move, and Polly volunteered Kurt to help move as well, which made everyone laugh.

Clapping her hands and laughing, Charlotte exclaimed, "Y'all are the best friends *ever*! Noah is so excited about finding a place with Christopher. Y'all have no idea how much this would mean to them both."

"I'll give Frank a call in the morning and see what he thinks." Bonnie pushed back her chair and said. "Well, the band goes on in less than an hour. We'd best be on our way."

"Who are you going to see tonight?" Becca asked as she stood and picked up her purse.

"It's a jazz quartet called Ophelia's Dive," Bonnie replied. "I'm friends with their sometimes-singer, Josephine."

"I know Josie!" Becca exclaimed. "Small world. Their keyboard player also plays in my husband's band."

Bonnie stopped dead. "Wait, your husband is Robert Jenks?"

Charlotte laughed at Bonnie's jaw-dropping reaction. "I never told them," she whispered to Becca.

"Oh my God, *now* I know where I've met you. It's been driving me crazy all night!" Bonnie looped her arm through Becca's and began to walk towards the front door, chatting happily.

"What's all that about?" Julie asked Charlotte as Polly and Cathy both came up with puzzled expressions.

"It's not a secret, but I didn't want to say anything without her bringing it up first. Her husband sings and plays guitar for *Hijinks*. You know, 'I Wanna Be Your Man.'" She sang a bit of the popular chorus as her friend's mouths dropped open.

"Are you kidding me?" Julie said. "Holy crap, I remember loving them when I was growing up."

"Jeez, I bet she's richer than God," Cathy muttered, then laughed. "Does she have a son?"

Charlotte nodded and smiled, "Harry. He's twenty-two and just graduated with a music degree."

"What a coincidence! I *love* musicians." Cathy said as they followed Bonnie and Becca, who were still chatting happily.

* * *

They all stopped around Julie's van before going their separate ways. Charlotte was excited by the prospect of spending the night with Christopher, but hanging out at a jazz club for a few hours with her friends sounded like fun as well. If she didn't have to work in the morning she'd have done both. Bonnie and Becca hugged goodbye, then Becca stepped closer to Charlotte with a smile.

"Can I give you a lift home? It'll save them from having to drop you off before the show."

"That would be great." She leaned through the open door. "I'm gonna get a ride home with Becca. Y'all have fun!"

"You too," Cathy called from the back seat. "Or three or four if you can keep him going!"

Polly winked as she shut the sliding door, then Julie turned up the music and pulled out of the parking spot.

"Thanks for the ride," Charlotte said as Becca led her towards a silver Mercedes parked nearby.

"I wanted a chance to talk to you about something anyway. Hop in!"

Wondering what the topic would be, Charlotte got into the passenger seat and immediately noticed the warm smell of leather. "I love your car," she said as she put on her seatbelt.

"Thanks," Becca said as she got in herself. "Robert got it for me after my old Volvo finally gave up the ghost. I had that thing for years."

"So what did you want to talk about?"

Becca waited until she was out of the parking lot before she spoke. "Tonight I shared something with Christopher that I'd like to keep private, but I don't want to force him to keep secrets from you." Charlotte didn't know what to say about that, so she sat quietly until Becca continued. "Being a doctor isn't just something I do for a living. My grandmother, Zahavah, instilled a sense of social responsibility in me. I want to do more."

"Like the extra work you asked Christopher to help you with?" Charlotte guessed. "Turn left here."

"That's only the start. I've been working on a plan to create a not-for-profit surgery and rehabilitation center for families who can't afford the kind of care Noah has received. A big chunk of the funding I've been waiting for has finally come through."

Charlotte looked at Becca's secretive smile as the implications of her revelation bounced around her head. Many poorer people utilized emergency rooms as their primary care providers, which only worked for certain kinds of problems. It was a constant struggle for parents with limited resources and time to get adequate care for kids with chronic problems that required multiple surgeries or long-term therapy. "I can see it. Oh my God, what can I do to help?"

Becca laughed as she stopped at a red light. "God, you and Christopher are so much alike."

"I'm serious! I want to help." Charlotte watched Becca's face go from amused to give her a penetrating look.

"Okay," she muttered as the car behind them honked to alert her the light had changed. "I'll pull you out of rotation and stick you under my head surgical nurse, Brenda. It won't be any fun for you and you'll probably end up hating her, but you'll learn everything you need to know. Then when the time comes to step out, you'll be ready to come with us."

Charlotte got chills up and down her arms. "You won't regret it. I'll work my ass off." She looked out the window and realized where they were. "Get in the right lane for the next light. What is Christopher going to do for you?"

"What he's doing now, mostly." Becca said as she looked behind to move over.

She thought for a moment before she spoke, but couldn't resist the temptation to brag. "You're wasting his talent. Did he ever show you the treatment plan and process documentation he wrote for that Atlanta job?"

"No, I figured he was going to do the same kind of thing as here but for more money." Becca wrinkled her forehead and frowned at the news. "I suppose I should have asked."

"He sent it to me to read and I was totally blown away." Charlotte pulled out her phone and poked around to her email. "Let me forward it to you so you can see what I mean."

"Is that your apartment complex?" she asked, nodding to the entrance.

"Yeah, pull in there, then keep to the right." She forwarded the email to Becca's personal address and put her phone away. "Thank you for trusting me with your plan. I won't breathe a word of it."

"I hope not. I don't want to have to jump until I'm ready and with Doctor Osborne gunning for me, that's gonna be hard enough to pull off as it is." She pulled up next to Christopher sitting on the tailgate of his truck. He was playing with his phone and only looked up when they stopped. "Here you go!"

"Thanks for the ride." Charlotte said as she opened the door and got out. Leaning back in she smiled and added, "And for taking a chance on me."

"I look forward to working with you," she said as she rolled her window down. "Have fun tonight," she said to both of them as Charlotte shut the door.

Christopher hopped down and leaned in the drivers side window while Charlotte came around. "You have fun with the girls?"

"They were wonderful and now I'm off to listen to some jazz with them. Ask Charlotte about our plan for you and Noah!" He stood up as she drove away with a laugh.

"What plan?" he asked as she came close and kissed him.

"We decided to help you find a house and move. Come inside and I'll tell you all about it."

He grabbed his overnight back and shut the tailgate, then took her hand on the way to the door. "Did you have fun tonight?"

"We always have a good time," she said as she bumped shoulders with him. "I'd like to go to that jazz club, Ovations, when I don't have to work in the morning."

"Then I'll take you," he said when they arrived at the door. As she fumbled with her keys, he took a deep breath and whispered, "Why am I so nervous?"

Charlotte felt butterflies herself as she unlocked the door. "I've been looking forward to this all week, but tonight does feel different for some reason." She led him inside and locked the door while he stood glancing around the room as if seeing it for the first time. Feeling embarrassed to admit it she whispered, "Honestly, I'm not used to being this horny, but I like it."

He chuckled and pulled her into his arms to press his growing erection against her stomach while kissing her deeply. When he pulled back, he said, "I think I can you help with that."

She looked into his eyes with a wicked grin. "I want to try some new things."

His answer was to pull her toward her bedroom. Charlotte had left the lamp covered with a sheer bit of fabric that provided a soft glow. The bed was already turned down and she had left the oil, lube, and her vibrating toy out on the nightstand.

After unzipping her dress so she could take it off, Christopher pulled off his jeans and folded them on the dresser. Watching him out of the corner of her eye, she felt a warmth in her center as his back muscles flexed and moved. He was already mostly erect when he slipped off his underwear and climbed into bed, she noticed with a shiver.

Christopher put his hands behind his head to watch her remove the lace bra and matching panties she'd worn for him. "You are so beautiful," he sighed.

She climbed up from the bottom of the bed, touching his feet and legs with her fingertips. She bent to kiss him as she went, enjoying his clean scent as her lips touched his thighs and stomach. "I love the way you smell," she said as she rubbed her face against his chest.

He rolled her over on her back to kiss her tenderly. "What can I do to make you happy?"

"I want your mouth all over me," she whispered between kisses. "I want it so bad I've even dreamed about it."

"Can I use your toy at the same time?" he asked as he sat up slowly.

"That sounds interesting," Charlotte said as she spread out to cover the bed.

"Shut your eyes," he said. "Relax and leave everything to me."

With her eyes shut she could only imagine what he was doing from the sounds. He turned on the vibrator momentarily as if he was checking to see how it worked. She heard him move the bottles and knew he got out some oil from the scent of rosemary that filled the room.

She could hear him rubbing his hands together to warm the oil, then he took her leg into his strong hands. His fingers worked into her calves and feet bringing a low moan to her lips. "Oh yes…"

The warm oil relaxed her, but the slick feeling between her legs began to demand equal attention. She moved her right hand down to run through her soft hair and into her hot center.

"What are you doing?" he purred.

"Helpin'," she said. Even with her eyes shut, she knew he was watching her touch herself because he'd stopped rubbing her foot. "I like knowing you're watching."

He chuckled and said, "You also got hot back at Uncle Jack's that time worrying about your family in the other room."

"That was so exciting," she whispered. "I can't believe we actually did it in the bathroom." Just remembering what happened added to her heat.

"I'll have to keep that in mind," he mused. "Maybe one day I'll get you off in public somewhere. Wanna go see a movie next week?"

The thrill of imagining him touching her in a public place made her hiss and move her hips. "I need you to touch me."

"You're doing a good job of it yourself," he said, but she could feel him lying down between her thighs. When she raised her knees to lift herself for him, he made a low hum like he was hungry. "Well, maybe I could help a little."

The moment his breath hit her wet skin, she froze with her mouth open. He kissed her along the crease of her thigh, then started the vibrator on its lowest setting. She gripped her sheets with both hands and whimpered as he made her wait.

He finally pushed her thighs back and kissed her swollen nub while slipping the vibrating shaft inside of her. Licking between her lips made her cry out and push herself towards his mouth. He kept trying different combinations of movements until he hit one that put her right on the edge.

"Keep doing that," she murmured. "Don't stop."

Instead of cresting, it kept growing to a level of pleasure she'd never experienced. She began to tremble from the tension, then to shake, but the pleasure continued to climb until it was almost unbearable. It went on and on, Christopher tirelessly circling her nub with his tongue while the vibrator buzzed inside of her.

At the moment of release, her hearing dimmed and she felt herself falling, losing all ability to think or control herself. The world exploded into bright sparks of color flying behind her closed eyes until all she could do was writhe in pleasure.

When she came to her senses, Christopher was spooning against her back and caressing her arm. "Are you okay?" he whispered, sounding a little worried.

"Oh yeah," she murmured as she snuggled against his chest. His erection was poking her comfortably between her cheeks so she flexed her muscles around it. "I owe you. How can I ever repay you?"

"I've got an idea," he said, but didn't elaborate.

Charlotte turned in his arms and opened her eyes at last. "Fill me up," she commanded.

"What a coincidence. That was my idea, too."

He rolled between her thighs and kissed her as he slipped inside. She realized that she wanted him with her whole heart at last. The fear was gone along with any misgivings or worry, and the pleasure on his face as she kissed him mirrored her own.

Running her hands up his back, she wrapped her legs around him to make the angle better. He kept kissing as he moved in and out, driving them both along while she encouraged him, begging him to let go, to fill her up.

"I want you to cum with me," he whispered.

"I don't think I can this way," she said. "But I love the way it feels when you do."

He slowed as he kissed her deeper, coming to a stop on top of her. "Let me try a different way then."

"No." She loved the full feeling he gave her and squeezed her muscles tight around him, flexing and releasing as his eyes widened. "I want to watch you first."

"I may not be able to go again," he gasped through his open mouth.

"I don't care." With every squeeze his eyes narrowed, but she held him so tight he could barely move. He struggled against her, sliding in and out as far as she let him. Holding him captive seemed to increase his arousal as his face flushed red.

He whispered, "I'm so close," as he pressed in all the way while she made herself as tight as she could for him. "Oh, baby…"

He buried his face next to hers as he spent himself deep inside. Knowing she could get him off this way gave her a thrilling sense of satisfaction. As she ran her hands across his back, he hummed deep in his chest. When he was still at last, she kissed his cheek and whispered, "Thank you."

He chuckled and shook his head in disbelief. "You do that to me and then thank me for it." She ran her fingers through his hair and held her lips against his. After a moment he pulled back with a sigh and smiled down at her. "So what's this about your plans for moving me and Noah?"

"Bonnie's gonna call Frank tomorrow to see if he'll act as your realtor. She and Julie also want to help you decorate and even have some furniture you can look at in their storage room. Cathy, Polly, and Kurt are gonna help you move in and set everything up."

"I'm not sure Kurt is gonna wanna help me do anything." Christopher rolled to the side but kept her close.

"I told him I was wrong," she said, but tried not to let the memory of the misunderstanding sour the moment. "He said he wants to hang out again when he gets back."

Christopher seemed to sense her change of mood and kissed her again to bring her back. "Well, you told me what everyone else was gonna do, so what are *you* gonna do?"

She suddenly wanted to tell him what she hoped in her heart. Looking into his happy face she felt the words on her tongue, but she didn't want to jinx what they had going. "You'll see. I've got a few surprises up my sleeve."

"I love mysteries." He shut his eyes and relaxed against her. "That was one of the things that attracted me to you most."

She traced his features with her fingertips. There was a strength in his face and when he loved, it was with his whole heart. Little Noah was the prime example of that, setting aside his own plans to care for the boy. Her own situation showed it as well in his patience as she struggled to overcome her fear. The words slipped out before she considered them.

"Mom told me that Dad always treated her like a precious gift. You made me feel special like that from the very beginning." Her emotions soared, making her chin tremble.

He opened his eyes as hers filled with tears. "Don't be sad now."

"Oh, I'm not sad. I've never been this happy. And the best part is, I'm not scared anymore." She kissed him then, wetting his cheeks with her tears.

"Oh, Charlotte," he murmured and kissed her back with a growing passion.

When she pushed him back he rolled over and let her caress him. He began to respond, growing in her hand until he was hard. "I want you again," she said. "I want to try again."

He knew that she meant more with her last words than she said. He helped guide her as she climbed on top and pushed against her until he was deep inside. Using her hand again, she ground against him as he pulled her hips down with each stroke. She shut her eyes and gave herself over the the feeling of being full of him.

"You feel so good," he strained to say.

She found a rhythm that felt the best, riding her hand as much as him. Touching his slick shaft underneath her as she slid back and forth made her shiver. *He's inside me,* she kept thinking, the thought driving her closer than she'd ever been with him.

"Slow down," he whispered.

"I can't," she said, focused entirely on the growing sensation of her approaching climax. "I'm so close. Oh baby…"

"Damn it," he muttered as she felt him let go.

The tickle she felt inside won out over her frustration and she began to laugh. It started off a chuckle, then he started laughing, too. The feeling of him moving as he laughed made her giggle, which made him laugh even harder. Soon the two of them collapsed on the bed in a quivering pile, kissing when they began to settle.

"I swear I've never had this problem before," he confessed with a deep flush.

"It's not a problem." She put her chin on his chest and beamed. "It's fun, and wet, and wonderful. I never imagined it could be like this. I always thought sex would be serious and passionate. I was so scared I'd be bad at it for some reason."

"Trust me, you're not bad at all." He laughed sadly and shook his head. "Me, on the other hand…"

"Stop it. You've set me free! I feel so relieved and relaxed now. I used to be embarrassed to even talk about sex, but now I get horny every time I think of you. You made this happen for me and I'll always be grateful."

"You're serious." He seemed genuinely puzzled.

"Don't jinx it! I'll stop being serious now," she said as she pulled up the sheets to cover him. "Get the bed warm. I gotta go pee."

She dashed to the bathroom naked and then came back to find him laying on his side waiting for her as she shut the door again. He fanned the sheets open for her to slide in, then made himself big spoon for her as he covered her up again.

"I could get used to this," he murmured in her hair.

She snuggled back against him and echoed the sentiment in her thoughts. *I want to get used to this. I want this every day.*

Chapter 24: Christopher

"Noah, you almost ready?" Christopher asked as he stepped to the open door of the boy's bedroom. The new furniture was a golden oak and the walls of the room were covered with happy pictures of Noah with his mother and father. While the boy sat on the bed putting on his shoes, Christopher took in the powerful mural of Bilbo taunting the dragon Smaug sitting on a mountain of treasure. Julie had done a masterful job of capturing the moment from the movie.

Noah's obsession with the world of Middle Earth hadn't ended with the books he'd read as his arm healed. Despite being a bit young to watch them, Noah nagged Christopher daily to see all the movies as a reward for doing his physical therapy. His broken left arm had required some rather intense work to get back his strength and range of motion, so it seemed a fair trade to watch them. As Christopher feared, Noah had bad dreams of being eaten by a dragon, but still insisted *The Hobbit* would be the theme for his birthday party.

After three attempts to tie his shoes he said, "I wish you'd gotten me the Velcro ones. I still can't tie these." He raised his feet and made the laces wiggle. "Can you do it for me?"

Christopher knelt down in front of the boy to pull the laces tight and double knot the bows. Noah was capable of tying his own shoes, but often just wanted the attention more than the help. "How's that?"

"Thanks," Noah said and stood up. "Let's go! I can't wait to see my presents!"

He followed the boy down the hallway into the perfectly decorated living room. It hadn't been an easy few weeks, but with the help of his friends and family, they'd made it into their own home. Bonnie had gotten carried away decorating, but he had to admit it he loved what she'd done.

She and Julie had photographed the whole process from the time he closed on the house until they were moved in. The decor was masculine, with clean lines and a modern feel that suited both Noah and him. When Bonnie discovered there was a Clan Dunlap tartan pattern, they'd accented the room with its familiar blues, black, and red. They'd even published a long photo journal of their work on Bonnie's website and it had gotten rave reviews.

Noah blew through the front door, leaving Christopher to shut and lock it behind them. The three bedroom, one-story house had large oak trees growing near the street that provided shade for the front yard. He pushed the button on his keys to unlock the Suburban parked in the driveway for Noah to climb inside.

Roger had traded the family Suburban for the truck Christopher had bought when he got out of the service. Having a back seat to keep Noah safe in his booster was a requirement for a few more years. His father was happy to have the truck for the move to their family woodlands he'd planned in the fall and was already driving up every week or two to supervise the construction of the sprawling home he'd commissioned.

Christopher pulled out of the driveway and turned towards Jack and Julie's house. His friends had insisted they have Noah's birthday party there because their house was large enough for all the guests. He'd originally planned a small party just for the kids, but once the girls started helping, it took on a life of its own.

That seemed to be the pattern since he and Charlotte had gotten closer. Just as his thoughts turned to her, his phone started ringing with her face on the screen.

"Y'all on the way?" she asked in her usual cheery tone.

"Just left the house and should be there in a few minutes. Need me to pick up anything?"

"Nope, we've got it covered. Noah is gonna love it! Julie has the back yard decorated like Bilbo's eleventy-first birthday with a pavilion and everything."

Her excitement was infectious. "I can't wait to see it."

"I gotta go help Polly finish the pigs-in-a-blanket. See ya!"

"Bye," he said and ended the call.

"Was that Charlotte?" Noah asked from the back seat.

"Yup, she was just checking if we were on the way."

He was silent for a moment, then said, "I like her a lot." Noah's voice had an odd tension like he was working up to say something.

"She likes you, too." Christopher wondered what he was dancing around. "Are you okay with her hangin' around so much?"

"Yeah," he said then went quiet again.

When they'd moved in, Christopher and Noah set up the third bedroom like an office for them to share. He'd picked up a student desk and computer for Noah to use along with high-speed Internet for work and for playing games together. There was some space left in the room, so when Charlotte complained that she didn't have room for a sewing machine in her apartment, Christopher suggested she could put one in their office.

At first Noah hadn't seemed very keen on the idea, but was never rude to her like he had been at first. After she got the secondhand sewing machine and serger moved in, her first project was a green felt cloak for Noah that looked just like the one Frodo wore in *The Lord of the Rings*. Noah announced she was welcome to join them then, grinning out from under the hood of the cloak.

After that, the three of them spent their evenings together most nights. They'd eat dinner, then either watch television or work together in their office and sewing room. Noah would sit with Charlotte while she sewed custom scrubs for work, dresses for Julie's girls, or patched the knee holes in his jeans. Although she never stayed overnight, it didn't take long for them all to get used to the arrangement. Noah clearly missed her when she had to work and couldn't come by.

"Is Doctor Jenks gonna be there?" Noah asked as they pulled into the community where Jack and Julie lived.

"Yup, and her husband, Robert, as well. Did you know he's a rock star?"

"Yeah, Charlotte told me. I've heard his songs before on the radio and never knew it was Doctor Jenks' husband."

Turning onto the street where Jack and Julie lived, Christopher heard Noah lean over to look ahead.

"Wow! Look at all the cars! Are they all here for me?" Noah asked.

"They are." Christopher looked up in the rear view mirror to see Noah's excited grin. "I guess we'll have to park here and walk in since there isn't room in the driveway."

* * *

After they got out of the Suburban, Noah ran ahead as Christopher put his hands in his pockets to follow at a more sedate pace. By the time he caught up, Julie was just opening the front door.

"Happy Birthday!" she exclaimed with a brilliant smile. "Come in, you two."

Noah tore past her with a quick, "Thanks!"

Christopher stopped to give her a hug at the door. "Thanks again for doing this for him." He noted her swelling middle with a smile. Some pregnant women seemed to glow, but Julie shone like the sun.

"You're welcome, but you don't need to thank me. At this point you're practically family," she said as she let him go. "Come on in and grab a beer. Your father and Jack are sitting by the smoker out back."

There were kids everywhere. Some were from Noah's class at school, but Christopher didn't know them by name. There were adults he assumed were parents of Noah's friends standing around in groups talking as Christopher wove his way through the sliding glass door into the patio and backyard. The pavilion was as grand as Charlotte had said, with tables full of food and brightly wrapped presents. Even more kids were out running around as the sounds of music and laughter filled the air.

"There he is!" Roger called and waved him over near Jack's smoker. "I got a cooler here for the cooks." He reached in and pulled out a cold Shiner Bock. "Here ya go, son."

"Thanks," he said as he took it and stepped into their circle. Kurt and Jack were standing across from him with welcoming smiles. Kurt had apologized for jumping to conclusions and the matter had been forgotten. Their friendship picked up again as if nothing had happened and Christopher had been grateful for the chance to repair his reputation.

"So how's family life?" Kurt asked with a grin.

"Fulfilling," Christopher admitted. "It's like surfing, in a way. As long as I keep moving forward and don't think about it, I can almost relax. Noah's doing okay, considering, and things like today are good motivation to keep him gettin' better."

"Polly says she hasn't seen Charlotte much lately." Kurt's mouth twitched and he glanced at Roger.

"Well, Charlotte only hangs out with us in the evenings. Maybe Polly has been distracted by something when Charlotte gets home late." He raised his eyebrows and laughed. "Besides, I've heard you hired some more shipmasters and have been home for almost a month straight, so where've *you* been?"

Both Jack and Roger chuckled at the subtle cock fight, but didn't get involved.

"Here and there." He smiled and took a sip of his beer. "Listen, I wanted to ask you something privately if you have a second."

The two of them moved away while Christopher scanned the kids to check on Noah. His paternal instinct had been tuned by a growing love for the boy and weeks of practice. Spying him having a sword fight with another boy, Christopher resisted the impulse to yell for him to be careful and turned back to Kurt. "What's up?"

Instead of answering, Kurt pulled out a small green box from his pocket and handed it to Christopher. When he opened the lid, there was a bright diamond set on a yellow gold band. Glancing back up, Kurt had a sheepish grin on his face.

"So, it's finally time?" Christopher asked with an answering grin. "Congratulations."

"Thanks, man," he said and shuffled nervously. "I don't want to mess up the day for Noah, but both my parents and Polly's are coming in for the party. This may be the only time we can pull it off before her parents head back to Botswana in the fall. Maybe after the kids wind down, I was thinkin' I might pop the question tonight."

"That's perfect," Christopher nodded. "I doubt Noah will care you stealing some of the limelight after playing all day and eating himself into a cake coma. Anything I can do to help?"

"Be my best man?" Kurt asked as his eyes got a little glassy.

"Done," Christopher said and pulled him into a back-slapping hug. "Damn, I'm so happy for you, brother."

"Yeah?" he asked as he pulled back. "Brother, huh? I always wanted a brother."

"Probably, yeah." Admitting his feelings to Kurt, even obliquely, made the hair stand up on his arms. "Someday."

"You got my blessing if you can stand her," he said and laughed. "Thanks for letting me get this over with. I've been a nervous wreck ever since we picked out the ring."

"We? You mean she knows already?"

"She doesn't know when," he said and winked. "I'm still nervous, I can't help it. Oh, and don't tell Charlotte. I want everyone to be surprised."

"Fine, just give me a heads up so I can take some pics of the moment for you guys."

* * *

Christopher left Kurt grinning and went inside to look for Charlotte. When he found her she was busy taking a tray out of the oven covered with little hotdogs wrapped up in golden brown crescent rolls.

"Can I help?" he offered as he approached.

"Yay!" she squealed and put the tray down on the stove to wrap her arms around his neck and kiss him. "I missed you all day."

"Me too." Her face was flushed from the heat of the kitchen and her hair had started to fall out of the ponytail she wore, framing her face with soft brown waves. When he gazed at her, all coherent thoughts fled as her beauty left him breathless.

"What?" she asked, looking embarrassed.

Knowing Kurt was going to propose to Polly, Christopher suddenly wanted to share how he'd been feeling towards her. It wasn't the right time, so he sighed and laughed it off. "Nothing. Let me help you."

She tucked the stray hair behind her ear, then slid the crescent rolls off the tray and into a large bowl lined with a kitchen towel. After covering them with the corners of the towel, she presented him the bowl. "Can you take this to the pavilion for me? Cathy or Polly will know where it goes."

"Sure thing," he said then laughed when she pinched his butt as he turned to go.

Polly was busy setting the tables around the pavilion. Julie had captured the rough hewn feel of the movie set with thick supporting ropes and unfinished wood poles holding up the canvas canopy. There were colorful paper lanterns and pennant flags hanging around the pavilion and large oak tree. They must have rented furniture, because there were six large tables with folding chairs set up around the fire pit which usually sat on the patio.

"Thanks, Christopher, those go over there." She waved in the general area of a table with cut fruit, cheese, and other finger food. The secret Kurt had shared made Christopher smile at her, but she was too busy to notice.

While Christopher helped get things ready, the party got into full swing as the remaining guests arrived. It seemed everyone who had ever heard of Noah wanted to come and wish him a happy birthday. Christopher sat with Maria most of the afternoon as she was sometimes overwhelmed by the number of people she didn't know who cared about her Noah.

When Charlotte's parents arrived, Christopher hugged Noëlle and shook Gerome's hand, then introduced them to both Maria and Noah.

"These are Charlotte's parents, Misses Noëlle and Mister Gerome." Christopher didn't mind Noah calling him by his first name, but for other people he insisted on honorifics. The adults smiled at each other, then Noëlle knelt down closer to Noah's eye level.

"Would it be okay if he called me Meemee Noëlle?" she asked Maria and Christopher. "It's less formal."

Christopher shrugged and Maria nodded her approval at the familial name.

"I thought Meemee meant grandmother?" Noah asked with a puzzled expression.

"I hope so, oh yes I do," she whispered to herself making Christopher's temperature rise at the implication. "Don't you worry, Lots of kids call me Meemee. Happy Birthday, *p'tit-garçon*."

"And you can call me PawPaw Gerome if you want." Charlotte's father extended his hand to the boy as he gave his wife an amused glance. He was stout and balding, but had a strong face and warm smile.

Noah shook his hand solemnly and said, "Thank you for coming to my birthday party."

"Papa!" Charlotte called from across the room. "I didn't know you were coming, too!" She squeezed between Christopher and Noah to embrace her father in a tight hug. "It's so good to see you."

"Well, your brother told me I'd regret it forever if I missed Noah's party. I had some vacation coming anyway and wanted to visit you two."

"Hi, Mom," Charlotte said with a laugh as she released her grip on Gerome. "How was your drive in?" She hugged Noëlle then kissed both cheeks.

"Fine, sha. You're lookin' so good." She smiled at her daughter's happy face. "How's the new position working out?"

"I love it! Everyone acted so scared of Brenda that I was worried at first, but she's got nothing on Nurse Lafonda back at Lafayette General. That woman could break you with a look. Brenda is strict, but all her rules make sense if you just listen to what she says."

"That's wonderful," she said. "Could I get a drink? It was a long trip."

Charlotte and her parents went toward the kitchen chatting happily while Christopher sat down next to Maria. Noah had a thoughtful frown on his face that his grandmother inspected by lifting his chin with a quaking finger.

"Is that a birthday face?" she asked in her gentle chiding way.

"No," Noah said, but his glance at Christopher seemed to say more.

Guessing at the problem, Christopher offered, "You don't have to call them Meemee and Pawpaw if you don't want to."

"It's not that." He looked down again. "Could I call your dad 'Pawpaw Roger' if I wanted to?"

Christopher laughed. "He'd probably prefer Papa instead because that's what my brothers and I called *his* daddy when we were little."

Maria nodded with a knowing smile. "Your Papi Manny would be so happy to see how loved you are. And I'll always be your Nanna, sweetheart."

"I still miss him, and Mom and Dad." Noah got a lip quiver for just a moment.

"And no one can ever replace them, but that's no reason to stop loving people and letting them love you, is it?" Maria patted her lap and Noah climbed up to hug her for a moment. She looked up at Christopher and tilted her head to indicate she would take care of Noah for a bit.

* * *

Christopher found Charlotte in the kitchen with Julie and her mother, Lily. Lily was good looking for a larger woman, but according to rumor, she'd lost a ton of weight after her grandson Jackson was born. Noëlle and Gerome were standing there as well drinking out of red plastic cups.

After grabbing another beer from the fridge, he heard Julie greeting Becca and her husband, Robert. When he shut the door, he noticed Lily had grown pale with her fingers over her open mouth.

"Hello Robert, Becca," she said. "You probably don't recognize me."

"Lily?" Becca exclaimed. "Holy crap, it's been years since we've seen you! How've you been?"

The two women gave each other a quick hug while Robert stood back. He was thin and tall, with long brown hair pulled back in a ponytail. Christopher felt a faint sense of dislocation. Seeing a famous person in the flesh wasn't an everyday occurrence. It brought a shock of recognition without the same sense of connection as seeing a friend.

Julie was staring between Becca and her mother with a wrinkled brow. "I thought you didn't know anyone famous," she whispered to her mother.

"I lied," she whispered back. Looking back at Becca she said, "Yeah, after Timmy and I broke up, I didn't want to hang out with his crowd. God, that was what, back in '86 I guess. I had Julie in '89 and it's been the two of us ever since."

"I can't get over that Julie Brousard is your daughter! We've known each other for months now without putting it together. What a small world. I ran in to Timmy a couple of months ago playing at Ovations with his jazz band. I think he was single," Becca teased.

"Oh, God no," Lily said with a laugh. "I'm too old and fat for that nonsense again."

"Are you still singing?" Robert asked, involving himself at last.

"Just karaoke at this bar I go to sometimes."

"You were good," he said, giving her a strange, piercing look. "I always respected your talent."

"Sure," she said with a bit of heat. "So, I hear you've got an autobiography coming out."

"It's more of a novel," he said with a shrug. "It's about the summer and fall of '82, just before the first *Hijinks* tour. I've, uh, taken some liberties with it."

"All I ask is that you make me skinny and hot," she said with a laugh.

"You were," he laughed with her. At this, Becca raised an eyebrow at him and scowled. "Give me your address and I'll send you an advance copy."

Charlotte had crept around the outside of the group as they continued to talk. "Holy shit, did you hear that?" she whispered in his ear. "I think they had a thing. Look at Becca."

She was pissed, that was clear. Meeting Lily had stirred something up that looked like an old fight from the tightness in her face and the distance she put between herself and her husband. Julie seemed to sense the tension as well and whispered something to her mother just as Polly came into the kitchen.

While she washed her hands in the sink she said, "Okay, everything's ready outside. Where's the birthday boy?"

"I'll get him," Christopher said as he went back to the living room. "Cake time! Let's head out to the back yard, Noah."

* * *

The swarm of kids and parents headed towards the sliding glass door. Noah tried to push Maria but couldn't move her very far on the carpet. Christopher stepped around behind them both and helped get her rolling then let Noah push her the rest of the way himself.

Christopher and Maria flanked Noah at the main table under the pavilion. His face glowed as he gazed out at the assembled friends and adults who were settling down for the festivities. Charlotte and Polly came out of the sliding glass door with a monstrous cake shaped like the lonely mountain. As they got closer Christopher saw sparklers sticking out of the top.

They all sang "Happy Birthday" while Christopher fumbled with the long lighter as he set off the sparklers. He lit each of the eight candles leading up the river into the mountain and just as the song finished he lit the last one, then leaned back for Noah to blow out the candles.

His eyes were screwed up tight like he was concentrating with all his might while his lips twitched and moved. The whole crowd was silent in that moment. It didn't last long, but to Christopher it felt like forever until Noah's eyes sprang open and he blew all the candles out.

The cheers came then as Polly, Cathy, and Julie moved in to cut and distribute the cake to the guests. Noah ate his first piece with gusto and ended up with blue icing from the river on his face. Maria patiently wiped it off with a napkin.

"We're not opening presents here, are we?" Julie whispered to Christopher.

Shaking his head, Christopher said, "No, I'll put them in the Suburban and we'll do it at home tomorrow. I need to keep track of them for the thank you notes."

"Good," she said. "Because Jack went a little crazy and picked up a bunch of bows and arrows, swords, and shields made out of that foam stuff. He wants to have a war in the back yard with the kids after this."

"Oh, man, Noah's gonna love that."

* * *

After the war came a dinner of Jack's barbecue brisket, then the guests began to leave with sleepy kids until only family and close friends were left. The women cleaned up while the men broke down the rented tables and chairs to stack them under the pavilion until the rental company came to get them. The kids that were left took over the living room to watch the animated version of *The Hobbit*, but none of them lasted past Mirkwood.

"Come see," Charlotte called to Christopher. He followed her into the living room to find Noah sleeping on the couch with Jack's daughter, Jen, snuggled into his chest. Julie was standing there with her hand over her mouth holding back laughter.

"Oh my God, that's adorable," Julie whispered.

Charlotte pulled her phone out and tweaked the settings, then took a few snaps of it. "If they end up married, this will be the picture at the reception." She showed the low light picture of the cuddling kids to Christopher and Julie.

"Let them sleep 'til we leave," Christopher said. "I'll just carry him to the car."

Julie touched his back. "No, let him stay tonight. I'll just cover them with a sheet and you can come get him in the morning."

Charlotte took that moment to sneak her hand over and squeeze his ass gently as she said, "Good idea, Julie."

They left the kids sleeping and went out into the back yard to join the family and friends who remained. Christopher knew what was coming and looked for Kurt only to find him in a serious conversation with Polly's father. He got a beer for himself and Charlotte from the cooler then sat next to her with Maria, Noëlle, and Gerome.

"How are the kids?" Noëlle asked.

"Sleeping so cute, Mama. Little Jen is cuddled up to Noah." She passed her phone over to show them.

Noëlle laughed and covered her mouth. "That is the cutest thing I've ever seen."

While the phone went around to show the picture, Christopher kept his eye on Kurt. Just as he got the phone, Kurt looked over and gave him a happy nod. Christopher brought up the camera app and switched to video, then started recording as Kurt walked over to kneel next to Polly.

"I thought you might do it tonight," she whispered as he smiled up at her. "I hoped you might."

"Polly, we both know we've got something special. I want to do this right, but I'll never find the words to tell you how much you mean to me. The only thing that matters is being with you, so I just talked to your father about it."

Everyone figured out what was going on as soon as he knelt down, but now their attention went to her father. "You have my blessing if you need it."

"Polly, will you make me the happiest man in the world and be my wife?"

"You already know the answer," she said as she touched his face with her fingertips. "I've been yours since Mardi Gras and would be proud to be your wife." Then Kurt slipped the ring on her finger.

The whole group sighed at the same time, then laughed and clapped as the couple stood to embrace. Christopher let the video record for a moment longer, then stopped it and tossed the phone to Charlotte. She fumbled the catch, but managed to grab it before it hit the ground.

"We're gonna have to work on your catch before next spring," he said to her.

She clutched the phone to her chest with a look of surprise that told him she understood his comment, but there was still a questioning expression on her face. His answer was to sit next to her and take her hand, watching as Polly showed off her engagement ring to the family.

Chapter 25: Charlotte

Charlotte sat on the trunk of her car in Christopher's driveway watching the video of her twin brother propose to her roommate. Each time the video ended, she heard Christopher's voice in her head say, *We're gonna have to work on your catch before next spring.* Then she would play it again with a silly grin affixed to her face.

She recalled that at one time she'd felt jealous of Polly and Kurt's happiness, but couldn't imagine feeling that way now. She had found her own happiness, both in herself and in her relationship with Christopher. It wasn't a trivial happiness. Rather it seemed to be a kind of peace anchored deep inside that she'd never known before. And while Christopher might have helped her find it, the peace was hers alone and that made all the difference.

When she'd left the party earlier to take Maria back to her assisted living center, she stopped at Christopher's house to wait for him to come home. With Noah sleeping over at Jack and Julie's, she hoped he would excuse himself and come find her. The warm feeling in her stomach needed his special attention.

Headlights coming up the road drew her eyes as Christopher's Suburban slowed and pulled up next to her car in the driveway. He got out with a bright sparkling eyes and came around to sit down next to her on the trunk.

"I hoped you'd be here," he said as he leaned into her shoulder. "Wanna come inside?"

"Yeah," she said as the video finished playing again. "I posted this and tagged a bunch of relatives. It's going crazy online."

"I bet," he said and they hopped off the car and walked to the front door.

"You knew he was gonna ask her, didn't you?"

"Yup, he told me not to tell you." When they got to the door, he unlocked it to let her inside. "He asked me to be his best man."

The giggle escaped her lips before she could stop it. "Oh my God, my brother is getting married." He'd changed so much over the last few months that she hardly recognized him. Polly had made a huge difference in his life.

After Christopher locked the door, he asked, "Do you want anything? I was gonna get a glass of water."

"Would you get me one? Take it to your room and I'll meet you there."

She went through his room and into his bathroom. Julie had done a wonderful job decorating the home, but Charlotte had managed to add her own touches as well. She'd spent a week helping Maria go through the things from Emily's apartment and found items that would comfort Noah. They'd hung pictures of Noah with his parents, a quilt that had been passed from Maria's mother, and little mementos from family trips and Emily's wedding that she put into shadow boxes for him to see and remember.

She also added some practical things, like covered trash cans in the bathrooms, a more complete set of kitchen gadgets and cookware, and her sewing machine in their office. And as the weeks went by, Christopher had offered her some room for a few things in his bathroom. She opened her drawer and pulled out her toothbrush with a grin.

They usually spent time at her apartment when Noah would stay with Maria or over at Julie's house. She hadn't wanted to get entangled in Noah's life until she was sure where her relationship with Christopher was going. After his comment about her inability to catch things, she realized how serious he considered it.

"Are you okay in there?" Christopher asked through the door.

"Yeah. Can I borrow a shirt to sleep in?"

"Of course," he said with amusement in his tone. "*Me casa es su casa*"

"*Ma maison, c'est ta maison*," she replied.

His closet was inside the bathroom and she loved the way it smelled. He had a natural scent, like rich leather and lavender, that permeated his clothes. She gathered his shirts in a bunch and pressed her face into them, taking deep breaths. It intensified that feeling of warmth in her center and made her panties grow damp.

Picking a soft button-down shirt, she quickly took off her clothes and put it on, leaving the front open and only buttoning from her navel down. After folding her clothes and leaving them on the bathroom counter, she stepped out to find him wearing nothing but his boxer-briefs while reclining on the bed.

His face flushed while his eyes traveled up and down her body. "Wow. Wear that more often."

She climbed into bed with him and let him pull her close, kissing her deeply.

"I need to go brush my teeth, too," he said. "Be right back."

The tight underwear highlighted his ass as he dashed to the bathroom, but the muscles in his back and arms were still her favorite parts. She sighed happily and closed her eyes for a moment. She loved every inch of him, from his slightly hairy toes to the top of his head. His mouth had given her more pleasure than anything in the world, and his cock filled her to satisfaction. The desire to have him was becoming unbearable.

"Hurry," she whispered more to herself than him.

When he came back into the bedroom, he was naked and his shaft was jutting up and away like it was seeking her out.

He climbed up from the bottom of the bed and said, "I want to try something."

"As long as you are inside me in less than a minute, you can do anything you want."

Opening her eyes, she found him folding a pillow in half and placing it next to her on the bed. "Put your butt up here."

The angle was odd, but she did as he asked while he unbuttoned the shirt to expose her naked body. She moaned with frustration while he ran his hands over her stomach and maneuvered closer. "Hurry," she whispered again.

He lifted her knees, moving them apart while he slipped himself inside her in one smooth motion. Being filled quickly like that made her flesh prickle as she gasped in surprise. While she gripped the sheets in her fists, he began to move faster until he had established a good rhythm for them both.

"Tell me if I hurt you," he whispered, then began to press his palm down against her mons, using this thumb to rub just at the top of her slit. The increasing pressure gave her something to push against as his thrusts rubbed against that magic spot inside.

"Oh fuck," she muttered, shutting her eyes as the chills started rolling over her body. It was like nothing he'd done before and she could tell instantly that it was definitely going to work this time. "Don't stop. Oh God, please don't stop."

Lost in the sensation of being fucked, he drove her quickly towards her first orgasm with him inside. It was unstoppable. When she cried out her pleasure, he was still seeking his release. Although incredibly sensitive after her climax, she held on to give him time and found her body still responsive to his touch. In moments, he had her back at the edge.

"Oh fuck, I'm coming again," she said as the sensation of release crested a second time, taking her voice away as she strained against him. He laughed between panting breaths, still driving her on while he continued to chase his own pleasure.

"Yes!" he gasped at last, then held his breath as he continued to press her down. His moment had arrived, but she was still in the midst of her own release, clawing the sheets as sweat poured off of her body. Her hair was in her face, a wet tangle that she ignored to focus on their connection.

It was so different this time; the deep pulsing intensity took away all of her thoughts. She laid panting on the bed as Christopher collapsed on top of her, his hot breath tickling her neck. As the two of them recovered, the giggles started bubbling out. She'd cum with him inside of her!

He giggled every time she did until her laughter pushed his softening shaft out and he rolled off of her to crow, "That was incredible!"

"We did it, oh my God!" Her body still shivered from the aftershocks.

"It was the pressure. Every time you cum you either have to have something pushing against you like that pillow you used to use or some kind of overwhelming stimulation like a vibrator."

"What did you do? Research it on the Internet?" She laughed at the idea, but she noticed the look on his face was serious.

"Yes, actually. I've been wanting to cum with you, and it's been driving me crazy. I found an article that said some women need different things to get off and mentioned your pillow trick specifically. For you, apparently it's pressure on your mons."

"You did that for me?" she asked, feeling a hitch in her throat.

"Of course," he said with an easy dismissal that said more about how he felt for her than all the words in the world.

She hid her face against his chest so he wouldn't see the tears and misunderstand. In the midst of taking on Noah, working at the hospital, moving into his house, and helping Becca bootstrap her secret surgical facility, he'd done a hundred little things to make room for her in his life. *Of course* he'd researched her sexual issues and made it his mission to help her cum during sex.

"I don't want to jinx anything," Christopher whispered in the quiet darkness. "Or make you feel pressured." He paused then.

She wiped her eyes and looked up at him. He was stuck trying not to say too much, so she rescued him. "Maybe I can get Noah to play catch with me sometime. For practice."

He chuckled and pulled her close. She meant to say something else, but sleep claimed them both.

* * *

In the morning, Christopher got up and showered while Charlotte dozed in his bed. There was a pleasant soreness inside that kept her smiling. In her dreams, she'd caught Polly's bouquet a hundred times and never once worried about dropping it. Her heart was telling her something in her dreams, she knew. *Don't jinx it!*

She slipped out of bed and padded into the bathroom to relieve her aching bladder.

"Scrub your back?" Christopher offered through the curtain.

"Yeah," she said and flushed, making Christopher yell in surprise at the suddenly hot blast. "Sorry!"

"I need to get a bigger hot water heater," he muttered.

She took off his shirt and stepped into the tub with him. He looked wonderful with the water slicking his hair back and running down his muscular chest. She reached over for the soap and lathered his washcloth, then began to scrub his chest.

"I got that spot already," he said as he wiped the water off his face to see.

"What about here?" She took his shaft in her soapy hands and washed him gently. He opened his thighs and rested his hands on her shoulders as she moved down to soap his balls.

"That's going to need some more work to get clean," he said in a tense whisper.

"You need to go get Noah. I'll cook breakfast while you're gone if you want." She still stroked his slippery shaft and balls.

"You're a cruel woman."

"You're the one who fell asleep last night instead of hitting me up for a second round while we had the chance!"

"Maybe you could stay over sometimes." He offered it lightly, but it stopped Charlotte's hands.

"You've got to be sure," she said. "I never want to hurt Noah."

"I kinda told your brother how I felt last night." Christopher said as he stared into her eyes. "And besides, your Mom told Noah to call her *Meemee Noëlle*."

She searched his face for doubt or fear. "Are you okay with all that?"

His smile broke open when he nodded. "I am."

She pulled him into a wet embrace, squeezing against his chest and kissing him hard. He answered her passion with his own, kissing her and whispering her name. When they paused she said, "I'm still worried about Noah. I don't want him to think I'm coming between you guys."

"Then let's play it by ear for now. We'll figure something out."

They played and washed until the water ran cool, then got out to dress for the day. She had a spare pair of panties in the back of her drawer and put the clothes she wore for Noah's party back on. Christopher dressed quickly and left her with a kiss to go get Noah.

She'd liked his kitchen from the beginning and he'd allowed her to arrange things the way she wanted. In no time, she had the bacon sizzling, toast browning, and coffee brewing. After setting the table for three, she got out the orange juice and poured them each a glass. The domestic task of cooking breakfast for her men gave her a happy sense of satisfaction.

Noah tore through the front door with a grin and yelled, "Hey Charlotte!"

"Hey, want me to make pancakes?"

"Do we have chocolate chips?"

"Sure do. I'll make a smiley face on yours like last time, okay?"

Christopher came in carrying an armful of bags and wrapped gifts. "I thought I asked you to help me carry all this stuff in?"

"Sorry," Noah said and dashed back out the door.

"He got side-tracked when I mentioned you were here cooking breakfast." He gave her an amused look and went back for the rest of the gifts.

She finished cooking while they sorted through the packages and bags, writing down the list of people Noah owed thank you notes to. The smile didn't leave her face the whole time the two of them opened gifts because she couldn't tell who was more excited about the video games, toys, and books. By the time Charlotte brought the food to the table, all of Noah's presents were unwrapped.

After getting Christopher and Noah to the dining table, she offered a prayer to give thanks for their food and watched as the two of them raced to consume the most bacon, eggs, and pancakes. By the end of the meal, Christopher was leaning back in his chair sipping coffee and smiling at the ceiling, lost in thought.

"C-Christopher?" Noah asked with an uncharacteristic hesitation.

"Yeah?" he responded, leaning forward to look the boy in the eyes.

"If I tell a birthday wish, it won't come true, right?"

"That's what I was always told."

He chewed on that a moment while Charlotte watched the two of them. Christopher was giving Noah time to think without rushing him as he always did. Noah glanced at Charlotte for a second, then looked down.

"Well, how about if I ask for a special birthday present? It won't matter if I wished for it, too, would it?"

"You can always ask," Christopher said, pitching his voice lower and inviting Noah to open up by leaning closer.

"I miss Mom. And Dad. And I know it won't be the same, but Nanna said I should still love people who love me anyway."

"I don't understand," Christopher said.

"We can't really be a family, like it used to be with Mom and Dad, but that doesn't mean we can't have something just as nice. Just something different."

Watching him struggle to get those big ideas out in words was killing her. She wanted to prompt him or help him say what he was clearly asking for, but she made herself wait to let him figure it out himself.

"I was thinkin' that maybe you and me and Charlotte could be like a family." He looked up between them, his face red from the effort of holding back his tears. "And then we would have Nanna, and Papa Roger, and Meemee Noëlle and Pawpaw Gerome, and Aunt Julie and Uncle Jack. We could almost be a family, right?"

Charlotte covered her mouth as her tears fought their way out. She glanced at Christopher who sat there stunned to silence, his own eyes getting glassy. Noah looked up at her then, a questioning expression in his face.

"I would love to be in your family," Charlotte said at last, pushing the words past the tightness in her throat. "Thank you so much for inviting me."

Noah got out of his chair and climbed into her lap. He clung to her as happy laughter broke through her tears and she kissed him on his hair and face. He responded with a huge hug, whispering something she couldn't hear into her neck.

Christopher got up and came around to kneel beside her chair, his face glowing at the two of them as he embraced them together. "I think that's a great idea."

Charlotte kissed her two men and laughed. "Did I see you had a baseball and mitt in your birthday haul?"

"Yeah," Noah said as he snuggled between them.

"How about you help me clean up breakfast? Then, we'll go in the back yard so you can teach me how to catch."

###

Did you love **Something Different: A New Adult Erotic Romance**? Then you should read **Inseparable: A New Adult Erotic Romance** and **The Perfect Match: A New Adult Erotic Romance** by Bella Chal!

Inseparable
"I've loved you since that first day when you saved my life..."

Life has never been easy for Julie. Between working her minimum wage job and living with a mother who never seemed to grow up, she couldn't ever find time to have a relationship of her own. After she meets Jack, a man who seems to have it all, she's surprised to find how miserable a wealthy family man's life can be.

When Jack's wife Sophie chafes at her dull marriage, she files for divorce. Worse, she files for sole custody of their kids, seizes half their assets, and continues to try and make Jack's life miserable. It's only through a new relationship with Julie that he's able to keep it together.

However, when it rains, it pours. Julie has a secret that could tear the budding relationship apart. Jack's great job and standing in the community evaporates underneath him. Will their relationship wither under the combined force of fate and a vengeful ex-wife?

Or can they listen to their hearts and stay the way they truly feel... *inseparable?*

The Perfect Match
"If Trey doesn't feel right, maybe your heart's trying to tell you something."

Polly had always been the good girl. Between her college program and her job as a pharmacist, she never did have time for men in her life. So when she takes a family trip with her friends Julie and Jack down to the Bayou, she's surprised to find two men that pursue her with equal fervor. Trey is a suave marketer, just graduated from college, a man with a future. His cousin, Kurt, works for a shipping company after dropping out of high school.

It seems like Trey has everything that Polly wants. He's going places, he's a fantastic lover, and he seems to be falling for Polly just as hard as she is falling for him. He's her perfect match.

So why does she keep thinking of Kurt...

Read more at Bella Chal's site.

About the Author

Bella Chal writes new adult erotic romance from a comfortable couch in the southern United States. Outside of writing, Bella spends time with family and friends, drinking wine, and plotting to take over the world.

To connect with Bella online visit http://bellachal.com/ or email at bella@bellachal.com.

Printed in Great Britain
by Amazon